A
MESSAGE
FOR
NASTY

T0307618

For Blossom
1932–2021

RODERICK FRY

A MESSAGE FOR NASTY

Hong Kong, 1943.
A family divided.
Two desperate journeys.

AWA PRESS

First edition published in 2022 by Awa Press, Level 3,
27 Dixon Street, Wellington 6011, Aotearoa New Zealand.

ISBN 978-1-927249-84-0
Ebook formats
Epub 978-1-927249-85-7
Mobi 978-1-927249-86-4

A catalogue record for this book is available from
the National Library of New Zealand.

Editing by Mary Varnham
Typesetting by Katrina Duncan
Cover design by Megan van Staden
Maps by James Bowman
Author photo by Laurence Varga
This book is typeset in Bembo and Nord
Printed and bound in Australia by Griffin Press

Awa Press is an independent, wholly Aotearoa New Zealand-owned company.
Find more of our award-winning and notable books at awapress.com.

Roderick Fry is a prize-winning New Zealand designer and essayist, who has worked in Taiwan, Hong Kong and Shanghai and now lives in Paris. From 1999, he retraced the route taken by his maternal grandfather across China during the Second World War to rescue his wife and children in Japanese-occupied Hong Kong, beginning a project to write a historically accurate novel based on their incredible story. He is founder and creative director of sustainable design company Moaroom.

Sham Shui Po Camp

Argyle Street Camp ●

KOWLOON

The Peninsula,
Salisbury Road

Kowloon wharves
Star Ferry wharf ●

The power station
at North Point

Office of Williamson & Company,
366 Des Voeux Road, Victoria

VICTORIA HARBOUR

VICTORIA

Star Ferry wharf

Offices of Hong Kong & Shanghai Bank,
One Queens Road, Victoria

VICTORIA
PEAK

● British Military
(Bowen Road) Hospital,
10–12 Borrett Road

Queen Mary Hospital,
102 Pokfulam Road

HONG

LAMMA
ISLAND

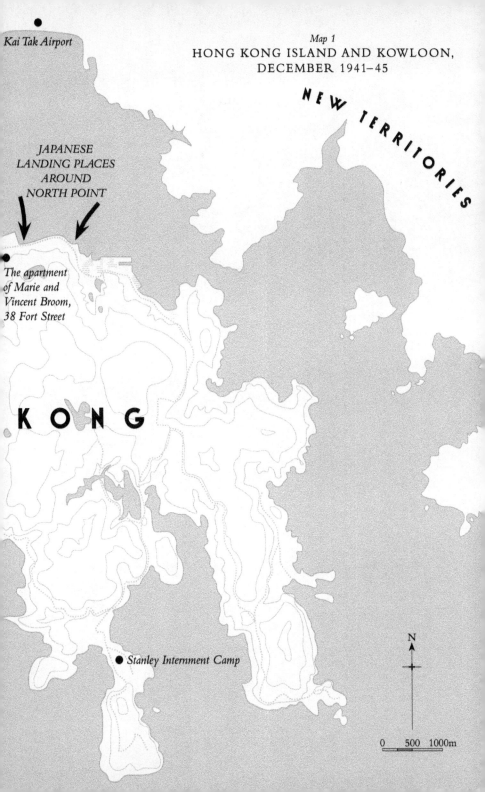

Kai Tak Airport

Map 1
HONG KONG ISLAND AND KOWLOON,
DECEMBER 1941–45

NEW TERRITORIES

*JAPANESE
LANDING PLACES
AROUND
NORTH POINT*

*The apartment
of Marie and
Vincent Broom,
38 Fort Street*

KONG

● *Stanley Internment Camp*

N

0   500   1000m

INTRODUCTION

My grandfather was tall and slim. When I knew him, his hair was white, and his sinewy arms and legs deeply tanned from a life lived largely in the tropics. I was fascinated by an old Swiss watch he wore attached to a wristband. He told me he'd made the wristband himself from stainless steel he'd recovered from the magazine of an American machine gun in a crashed plane.

When we arrived at our grandparents' house on one of our regular visits, one of us children would be sent out to the garden to tell Grandad he should come inside and wash, that the other guests would be there soon. Most often we'd find him in shorts and a threadbare polo shirt.

In those days I had no idea that the large brick house, with its shiny hardwood floors, delicately finished plaster ceilings and views over the harbour, was a sign of my grandfather's successful career. In my eyes he was notable for many other things. He could play the cello, which he usually did after dinner. He grew orchids, and his hibiscus and roses were the nicest in the street. He ensured his lawn was the most evenly cropped.

He could fix a bicycle faster than anyone. In a room with a small yellow door, which he had to bend double to pass through, he had every tool imaginable, laid out on a poorly lit bench next to the house's oil-fired central heating boiler. He made beautiful things in that room, as he had done when he was an apprentice in the oil-smelling below-deck workshops of his youth. There were miniature steam engines for the boats he wrought out of scrap metal, and a shoehorn with a finely etched handle in the shape of a woman's stockinged legs and French knickers. Years later, when my grandmother gave me the shoehorn, she said he had modelled it on her.

The house itself seemed to belong more to my grandmother. The silks, the porcelain and the polished furniture were always attributed to her fine taste. Witty and extravagant, she drove about Auckland in her V8 car imported from the States, with its tail fins and chrome dashboard. We would often find her hairdresser at the house, preparing her for a special evening. Style and fashion were important to her, just as they were of no interest at all to my grandfather.

As well as being elegant and exotic, born in Macau to Chinese-Portuguese parents, my grandmother was a star in the kitchen. *The New Zealand Herald* ran articles about her cooking, and notable locals and international visitors were invited to eat at her table. She even found ways to satisfy the spoilt taste buds of her grandchildren. The surprising thing was that she had learnt to cook only late in life when she settled in New Zealand and found herself for the first time without a cook.

To supply my grandmother with fish, my father, grandfather and I would head out on the Hauraki Gulf in my father's tiny boat. On these early mornings, as we sat and fished off one of the islands near Rangitoto, I got to hear stories of Grandad's adventures in Asia and the Pacific. Alongside Motuihe Island and the ruins of its naval base and quarantine station, which had been converted into an internment camp in the First World War, he'd talk about seeing the camp's most famous occupant, German naval officer turned pirate Count Felix von Luckner, who had been captured on Fiji's Wakaya Island by an armed policeman in September 1917.

He also talked of sea snakes as long as the Asian coastal trading ships he had worked on during the Depression, of Buddhist monks who were raised with chains around their legs so that when the chains were removed the monks could leap over a man, and of his run-ins with pirates in the South China Sea. These stories have led me to spend many years in China and on the Silk Road. They have kept me away from my homeland for almost thirty years.

As an adult I learned there was one story my grandfather almost never mentioned. During the Second World War he had walked and begged rides across China in a desperate attempt to rescue his wife and four children, who were trapped in Japanese-occupied Hong Kong. My grandmother had taken the children on an equally dangerous journey from Hong Kong to southern China to meet him. Fortunately, family members and close friends had helped my grandfather document his extraordinary journey before his death. And in the last three years of my grandmother's life she told me her story.

Born Maria Angelina do Rosário da Luz in 1912, she was her father's only child, the daughter of one of his Chinese mistresses. She grew up knowing little about the radical social and political changes taking place in nearby China, other than stories from servants arriving from the mainland. Her

father's family had links with the Catholic community; Marie
was educated first in Cantonese and later in Portuguese,
French, Latin and English at an Italian convent in Hong
Kong. Her social life revolved around dancing, gambling,
going to see the latest American films, and outings in the
American cars of her cousins and friends.

At the age of eighteen she met Vincent Broom. She
was not long out of convent school. Her father had already
chosen a husband for her – a young Macanese man – but
she had refused to marry him.

One of her friends from the convent was engaged to a
New Zealander, and introduced Marie to one of his friends.
Vincent was twenty-six. He had recently begun working
as a merchant marine chief engineer for Williamson and
Company, a shipping firm in Hong Kong owned by a fellow
New Zealander. He was the youngest chief engineer on the
China coast.

Within a short time he and Marie were married. Ten years
later, when war broke out in the Pacific, the couple had four
children. Margaret was nine, Marie junior eight and Cynthia
five. Vincent junior, the baby, had turned just turned one.
Where his sisters closely resembled their mother, Vincent
junior was strikingly blond.

The family lived in a third-floor flat beside Fortress Hill in
North Point, a district in the northeast of Hong Kong Island
overlooking one of the colony's two electric power stations.
They had four amahs – Lizzie, the senior amah, Ah Sup and
Ah So, and Ah Ng, the cook.

When Japanese forces began their invasion of Hong Kong
on December 8, 1941, Vincent was out of the country.

MARIE

I.

As she woke up Marie heard explosions in the distance. Nothing to worry about, she decided. The local defence forces must have just started their exercises earlier than usual. She lingered in bed, thinking fondly of the fun the family had had the day before. Her oldest daughter Margaret had turned nine. They had celebrated with a picnic in the New Territories with Arthur, an old friend of the family.

The explosions seemed to be getting louder. She got out of bed, walked to the window, pulled back the thick curtains and peered over the electricity plant and across the harbour. She would never forget what she saw. Small planes were flying over the short stretch of water, sending bright flashes of flame down on the peninsula. Moments after each flash there would be a loud bang and dust shooting into the sky.

It had been a year since Japanese activities in China had begun to be talked of as potentially endangering British outposts in Asia. The threat to Hong Kong had been serious enough for the administration to put resources into helping what it called 'unessential' expatriates to leave the colony.

But, like many people, Marie and her husband Vincent had stayed on. Just a few months earlier they had visited New Zealand with their youngest daughter and stayed with Vincent's parents in the small town of Te Puke. The quietness of the rural life had turned Marie resolutely against waiting out the war in New Zealand. She had insisted the family stay in Hong Kong, gambling that the Japanese would not want to invade the colony and incur the wrath of Britain. It seemed she had been mistaken.

Lizzie, the family's senior amah, had been with them a long time; before coming to Hong Kong she had worked for Marie's father in Macau. When the planes began flying over she had hesitated about disturbing Marie. When she finally knocked on the bedroom door Marie was scrambling to get dressed. 'Lizzie,' she shouted, 'how long has this been going on? Are they definitely Japanese planes?'

Without waiting for an answer, she ran out of the bedroom and paced around the living-room windows, anxiously scanning the sky. Suddenly, she looked at Lizzie. 'Where are the girls?'

'They left for school a few minutes ago,' Lizzie said.

Marie flew out the door and down the stairs. Catching up with Margaret and Marie junior at the bus stop, she hurried them back up the hill. As they climbed the stairs of their building she noticed the doors of most of the flats were open: their occupants were talking to their neighbours, trying to work out what the planes were up to. What a disastrous time for this to happen, Marie thought, with Vincent working on a salvage job 1500 miles away in Singapore.

She thought about the last few days. Things she had attributed to local army exercises had taken on a different complexion. If the attack was coming from the Chinese mainland, the Japanese forces would have had to come down the peninsula through the New Territories. The place had seemed calm and peaceful when they were picnicking there, but on the way back they had seen young Canadian soldiers driving north in a convoy of old army trucks. She had recently met some of these soldiers at a fundraising dance on the island. They were new recruits, sent to Hong Kong with hardly any training.

At one of the army checkpoints, an officer had instructed Arthur to come back after he'd dropped Marie and the children at the ferry. He was to pick up some army men and take them to the docks. As an officer in the Hong Kong Volunteer Defence Corps, Arthur hadn't been in a position to refuse. He'd brushed off the order as just 'a bit of a nuisance': he'd hoped to finish the day enjoying a quiet drink and meal with Marie at her flat.

It dawned on Marie she had been hopelessly naïve not questioning why Commonwealth soldiers such as the Canadians had been sent to Asia, rather than to Europe where the war was raging. It seemed the British government had been keeping the people of Hong Kong in the dark. For the first time she worried that the island might not be able to resist a Japanese invasion. And what of Vincent – would he be able to get back to Hong Kong before it was too late?

She isolated herself in her bedroom to think. How could the family get enough money and food to get by if Japanese forces took over the island? How long would the invasion last? What could they do to protect themselves? It was overwhelming. She needed to go to the centre of town immediately. While there she would visit the bank and Vincent's office, talk to his boss Mr Williamson.

Before leaving, she checked with Lizzie about the where-abouts of Lizzie's nineteen-year-old daughter. Mary had gone to the same elementary school as Marie's daughters; Vincent covered the cost. As a result she was one of the rare children of an amah to be completely bilingual. Mary was in the rooftop add-on. 'Bring her down to the flat,' Marie said. 'She will be safer here.'

Marie hurried down to the main road. It was clear the threat to the island was being taken extremely seriously. Army trucks like the ones she'd seen the day before in the New Territories were rumbling past, dodging cars packed with worried-looking locals and expatriates. Most taxis were full. The drivers of the few empty ones drove past her, waving their hands to apologise for not stopping.

As she walked towards Causeway Bay she felt oddly self-concious. She was wearing her usual clothes: high-heeled shoes and a light floral dress and cardigan. Almost all the women were in white volunteer nurses' uniforms and flat soft-soled shoes. Volunteering as a nurse had been a condition for the expatriate wives who wanted to stay on in Hong Kong with their husbands. She'd vaguely noticed their uniforms before. Now they looked ominous.

An army truck stopped at an intersection ahead of her. She approached the young British soldier at the wheel. She could get in, he said, but she would have to get out again if someone in uniform needed a ride. He passed on some news. Japanese planes had staged a surprise attack on the American naval base at Pearl Harbour in Hawai'i. There had been a massive loss of personnel and ships. Then, as if it were just a minor detail, he added that Singapore had also been hit.

Marie felt as though she'd been struck in the chest. This was terrible news. Noticing her taking a handkerchief out of her purse, the soldier offered to drive her all the way to the bank. She thanked him, but for once she preferred to walk. She wove her way around the maze of small lanes and buildings where Chinese merchants lived and worked. Whenever she had to leave the shaded streets she sprinted across the palm-filled gardens in front of the vast colonnaded colonial administrative buildings. Not one of the usual legion of gardeners was to be seen. At the town centre dozens of people were laden with food and lining up to get rides out of town. The place had never been so busy, especially on a Monday morning.

Mr Williamson was not in his office. According to his secretary, he'd been and gone earlier that morning. They'd heard nothing from Vincent since the previous Wednesday, she said. They knew of the rumours about Singapore but had been warned by the office of the local governor, Sir Mark Young, to take everything they heard with a large pinch of salt.

Marie asked if she could get Vincent's December pay cheque in advance. January's too, if that could be arranged. It seemed her request had been anticipated. Williamson had authorised his secretary to give Marie an advance, but only for half a month of Vincent's salary. It would, he'd told the secretary, be 'imprudent' to hand over any more. It was a word Marie would long remember.

She walked quickly across the road to the office of The Hongkong and Shanghai Banking Corporation and asked to speak to the manager, a man she and Vincent knew socially. She was informed he was engaged in a very important meeting with a colonel. 'Blow the colonel,' she said and stormed into the manager's office. Two men rose startled from their chairs. 'Mrs Broom,' the manager stammered out. As he ushered her out the door, he assured her he would see her immediately after the meeting.

During the half-hour she waited, Marie's hands and legs began to shake and she was overcome by a strong sensation of nausea and dread. By the time the manager invited her back into his office, she had decided to cash up all of her and Vincent's accounts, as well as the advance pay cheque. Normally the manager would have tried to dissuade her from such a drastic action. This time he simply nodded.

While the money was being prepared in the large denominations Marie insisted on, a stream of agitated employees and clients rushed in and out of offices. She heard women crying at their desks behind the flimsy partitions.

Marie had been prescient: at noon the governor would order the bank to stop all withdrawals.

Out on the street there was mayhem. People were darting in all directions, looking flustered and confused. On one corner Marie passed a tall English woman standing frozen and crying. People were racing around her, barely acknowledging her presence.

In the stores, stockboys were replenishing shelves that had already been emptied several times that morning. The owner of Marie's favourite Chinese grocery store shook her hand and smiled awkwardly. Her credit would still be good, he assured her, but he had no one to make deliveries. Three of his four staff hadn't shown up for work.

Struggling with her crate of provisions, Marie stopped at the corner of Des Voeux Road, opened her cardigan to cool down, and looked up at the clear blue December sky.

Her mind zigzagged around what to buy next. What fresh produce would keep the longest? If there was a battle, how long would it last? Even if the Japanese couldn't take control, would they be able to cut off food supplies? What could she carry?

There was a long wait for a taxi. Marie recognised a number of familiar faces, businessmen and bankers, bustling past in ill-fitting military uniforms. They exchanged a few pleasantries but offered little or no help.

A taxi with three passengers stopped in front of her. As the man in the front seat got out, Marie quickly slid in. The driver yelled and gestured frantically but she refused to budge. As he drove off, he muttered that he had to first drop off the English couple in the back halfway up the Peak.

She and the couple struck up a conversation. They had heard the Japanese were entrenched in the New Territories, but they believed talk of a fullscale attack on the island was probably just 'Jap propaganda'. As they went to get out of the taxi, the woman paused, looked at her husband and turned to Marie.'If the Japanese do make it here, what do you think the Chinese will do?' she said. 'Whose side will they be on?'

'Who can tell?'Marie blurted out. She regretted the words as soon as they left her mouth. From the way the woman looked at her, it was obvious that whatever she said would be passed around as the opinion of a knowledgeable local. 'I'm sure, no…' She hesitated. 'I know most of the Chinese police would die for the British if they had to.'

The woman looked at her intently. A small frightened smile formed on her face as she touched Marie's hand. They wished each other the best of luck. As he drove away, the driver turned to Marie. 'What did they mean about the Chinese?' he said.

2.

As soon as Marie got back to the flat, she and Lizzie divided the bank notes into six tightly rolled-up bundles and secured them with rubber bands. They placed the bundles inside the piano, in the springs of the sofa, and in the picture rail that ran around the top of the living-room walls.

From early next morning there were more explosions. Some sounded far away; others felt as though they were right on top of them. Bombs shrieked and whistled downwards. Others exploded without warning. The atmosphere in the flat was tense. Marie and the amahs and children sat hunched over, their shoulders aching with fear.

Later in the day, when the bombing seemed to have stopped, Marie decided to hitch a ride downtown to get more supplies. There were now many gaps on the shelves. Unlike the day before, she had to pay the grocer in cash and he asked her to start paying off her account.

There were also many fewer European faces. A man on the street told her the British women still on the island had been called into the hospitals to care for the stream of wounded people arriving from the New Territories. As she walked back up the hill she saw that many of her neighbours had already taped strips of paper across their windows to protect themselves from flying glass.

Margaret asked if there was a telegram from Daddy. 'Not yet.' Marie smiled. 'But I didn't expect one today. We should get one tomorrow though.' It was a lie. She had no idea when or even if Vincent would be able to contact them.

She asked Ah Ng to prepare lunch for everyone, making only one meat dish and keeping the rest of the meat for later.

She took Vincent junior from Ah Sup and fed him, then retired to her bedroom, closing the door and lying down on the bed. She stared for a long time at the photo of herself and her husband on the bedside table.

Meanwhile Lizzie and the other amahs took down all paintings and photographs from the walls and stored them under the bed of the guest bedroom. They then prepared bowls of paste by mixing together flour and water, tore a stack of old newspapers into long strips, and pasted the strips across the panes of every window in the flat.

Marie was startled out of a wakeful nap by Ah Ng banging on her door. There was no gas to cook with. She slipped on her shoes and rushed downstairs to her neighbours to see if the entire building was cut off.

Mr Wong had two wives. The first Mrs Wong answered the door and invited Marie inside. She would go into the kitchen to check the gas. 'No. Nothing,' she said when she returned. 'The electricity will be next.' Marie should send her amahs to collect firewood and buy charcoal.

Mr Wong had not been back to the flat since the previous morning's air attacks, she said. He was head of the Commercial Press, a stressful and dangerous role: if Japanese soldiers made it to the island he could targeted by their propaganda corps.

The second Mrs Wong emerged from the sitting room, where she had been reading to her disabled daughter. The Wongs were escapees from the 1937 battle for Shanghai. They seemed pragmatic, calm, prepared. If the bombing came any closer, they said, Marie should bring the children down to their flat. It would be safer than being on the top floor. But they believed the building would be relatively secure: the Japanese wouldn't want to risk hitting the power station.

Had Marie had any news from Vincent? No, she told them, not since the telegram he'd sent for Margaret's birthday five days earlier. She didn't know how long she was going to be able to cope without him.

The women exchanged glances. 'It could be a blessing for you that he is not here,' the second Mrs Wong said. 'This way you and your children may be able to pass for full-blooded Chinese.'

Marie tried not to cry as she made her way to their front door. As the first Mrs Wong moved past her to open it, she slowed Marie gently with a hand on her arm. The last thing she wanted to do was cause her even more sadness, she said, but she felt obliged to tell her that, from what they had heard, Singapore was facing as much danger as Hong Kong, and in both places the situation was likely to get much worse. Marie should not count on any help from Vincent. It would be up to her to fend for herself and her children. They would give her whatever assistance they could.

3.

The shelves of the store were now largely bare and the floor was filthy. Marie took a sack of rice and a slab of gorgonzola cheese. There was little else left.

Directly in front of the store she hailed a taxi and caught herself smiling: at least something was going right. At the intersection with Connaught Road the taxi stopped. A convoy of Volunteer Defence Corps trucks was crossing. Marie looked around at the empty offices and shops. Some were already boarded up. It was as quiet as Chinese New Year.

The taxi started moving again, past the docks towards North Point. Suddenly, as Marie stared absentmindedly at the car in front, the glass in the car's windows shattered and flames shot into the air. Her driver screamed and swerved, trying to keep control as the taxi jolted over debris from the car's engine. Marie and the driver turned back to look. Two motionless bodies were sprawled inside the wreck. Both were burning.

At Mass that afternoon the church was full. Marie took communion and prayed, gripping her rosary so tightly the beads dented her fingers and made the joints ache. She prayed that the Japanese wouldn't come any closer; that her family would remain in good health; that Vincent was on a boat out of Singapore and would soon be home to take them to Australia or New Zealand. She prayed that the men she knew in the army would be able to gun down any Japanese soldiers who tried to come too close.

More than anything she prayed that Hong Kong Island would stay beyond the reach of the Japanese, that it wouldn't be another Shanghai or Nanking. She knew about the Nanking massacre. Rich people, poor people, the slaughter had been random. No one had been able to negotiate, charm or reason their way out of deadly confrontations. Finally she prayed that Chiang Kai-shek's army in China would be given the strength and support to defeat the Japanese from behind.

On the way home she stopped at the flat of a neighbour-hood friend. Jane and her husband Tony were Chinese but they'd grown up and gone to school in the expatriate area of Shanghai known as the Concessions. Tony worked for an international British food company.

As Marie and Jane talked, the couple's four children played noisily in the next room and Tony walked quickly to and from his study. Jane took a long drag on her cigarette. Tony was convinced there was no hope, she said. The Japanese army had rendered the airstrip on the island useless and had taken up a position on the peninsula, so the battle was essentially lost. Soon they would be all over the island. They would go from flat to flat looking for anyone with a connection to the British. Most people in the territory, including the British, had been stupid to think Japanese expansion into Asia would not include Hong Kong. How could they have been so arrogant?

Since sunrise Tony had been trying to destroy every incriminating document: visas to visit the US and the UK; postcards and letters he'd sent his family from these places; every piece of paper that linked him to his job. He'd started on the terrace, burning things in a Buddhist urn he'd bought especially. After this had smoked out the flat and shot flames above the balustrade, he had started flushing documents down the toilet.

Jane giggled as she told the story.

'You're laughing,' Marie said disapprovingly.

'No, darling, of course not. I'm just on edge. There's nothing to laugh about at all.'

In July 1940, when authorities in Hong Kong had begun to consider evacuation plans, officials had separated British passport holders into those of 'British origins' and those of 'other blood'. Marie knew that Chinese who managed European businesses had been furious at the racist distinction. Now things had reversed: people with links to Britain were rushing to hide the evidence.

Marie turned to Tony. 'Surely there wouldn't be enough soldiers for them to check every home in Hong Kong?'

'Marie, when they come there will be twenty thousand of them,' Tony said sharply. Taking her silence for doubt, he repeated, 'Twenty thousand. And who's going to stop them? Our two thousand British schoolboys and two thousand fat pencil-pushers?'

As Marie left, Jane suggested she come back the next day and bring the children. It would give her an excuse to get something reasonable prepared for lunch.

Walking back to her building Marie could clearly see the peninsula on the other side of the harbour. Frequent clouds of dirt and smoke in the hills were followed by the now familiar sound of explosions. As she watched, a plane flew across the water and began strafing targets on the island. It was obviously Japanese – according to Tony all British planes had been destroyed on the first day of the bombing.

On the way upstairs to her flat, she knocked on the Wongs' door. Mr Wong had still not returned, the first Mrs Wong said, but if Marie wanted she could bring her children down to sleep with them that night.

4.

Next morning Marie had to search hard for food. Almost every shop in the city centre was closed and boarded up. The empty streets were full of soldiers who had fled the peninsula, shouldering their battered weapons.

After walking up and down side streets she found a place that was open and dragged a sack of rice to the counter. The note she handed over was twenty times the normal price of the rice but the shopkeeper refused to give her change. She hesitated and looked out the door for another open store but couldn't see one. She thought about taking an additional sack of rice to make up some of the value but realised it would be pointless: she couldn't carry two sacks. Reluctantly she paid the man, telling him he was a crook and she would never shop with him again. He shrugged.

Back at the flat, she waited anxiously for Margaret and Marie junior. She had stopped them attending school, but let them go with Lizzie to their usual private English class in a house a short distance away. Perhaps this had been the wrong decision.

Planes were now flying straight over their building. The amahs stood at the windows, screaming in fright whenever they saw a bomb drop. Marie avoided talking to them. She would soon have to let them know she couldn't keep paying them, or even providing them with food. Together with Lizzie's daughter Mary, they consumed a saucepan of rice a day. Marie had never given a thought to such things before.

Eventually there was a break in the bombing. Soon afterwards Marie heard a clattering up the stairs. Margaret and Marie junior appeared. They were laughing, panting and out of breath.

'What's going on?' Marie demanded. 'Stop your laughing and go into the kitchen.'

'But Mummy, it was so funny.' Marie junior was determined to speak. 'When the bombing started, the teacher told us to get under the table with her and say, "Hail Mary." Each time a bomb fell, she'd say "Hail Mary", rise up and hit her head on the bottom of the table. Then she'd bow down again.'

Later, Lizzie told Marie that the usually prim, self-controlled teacher had been terribly distressed. Marie began to laugh uncontrollably. When she was alone again, her laughter turned into wrenching sobs.

5.

Music and propaganda were being blared across the harbour from speakers on the end of Kowloon Wharf – nostalgic British songs and messages to the army. The air superiority of Japan meant Hong Kong Island would inevitably fall, the speakers boomed. To spare the lives of the men under their command, the British officers should surrender.

Everyone knew this was part of the game, but it was hard not to worry about the effect on the morale of exhausted, scared young soldiers. The Japanese had now driven all British, Indian, Canadian and Hong Kong Volunteer troops off the peninsula and on to the island. With them had come most of the British women and children who lived in Kowloon and the New Territories, the parts of Hong Kong joined by an isthmus to the swathe of the Chinese mainland now occupied by the Japanese.

If you had the courage to risk being shot at or have a mortar bomb land on you, there was a lot to be seen from the docks. From the end of the Star Ferry pier, Japanese soldiers could be seen scurrying around the sandbagging on Kowloon Wharf. Nearby, ships that had been scuttled by the Hong Kong Royal Naval Volunteer Reserve lay tilting dangerously or sunk down to their masts. Giant guns and mortars had been set up in front of the Peninsula Hotel, pointing at buildings on the island.

People who came from the peninsula talked about confused and bloody battles, with huge casualties on both sides. Clothing on the bodies of dead Japanese officers had been found to carry detailed maps of Hong Kong's defences, both on the peninsula and the island. These had presumably been drawn up by Japanese residents. The barber who cut the governor's hair was Japanese. The bartender who mixed cocktails for military officers and businessmen was Japanese. A young Japanese soldier had recently been seconded to Hong Kong government offices.

There was talk of indiscriminate rape and murder, the same sorts of stories that had come out of Nanking and Shanghai. A rumour circulated that any Chinese person who helped the Japanese early on would be treated with certain privileges when the army won and took over. These worthy locals would be guaranteed food and would benefit greatly in the allocation of housing once the British had gone.

At night in the Wongs' flat, Marie held baby Vincent in her arms. She hadn't slept well for days. In the darkness she could hear trucks rumbling up and down the hill outside. She imagined how frightened the soldiers must be. At a fund-raiser she'd danced with a young Canadian. He had seemed innocent, unworldly. He and his fellow soldiers would now be down on the cold beaches, straining their eyes in the dark and flicking their searchlights in the direction of any suspicious noises.

Marie had never spent so much time at home with her children. The baby slept soundly. He'd be walking soon. Marie knew his father would be missing him. Vincent was in his late thirties. He shouldn't still be going to sea, working for long periods on ships around Asia and the Pacific, but the money was good.

Margaret was growing quickly. Soon she would need a completely new wardrobe. Cynthia had taken to following Marie junior around. The two girls seemed constantly agitated by a mixture of fear, excitement and curiosity. They stood at the windows of the flat or on the balcony, looking down the hill and over the harbour, or hovered in the amahs' rooms, watching soldiers moving around on the hill behind or among the rocks and ruins on Fortress Hill. They never stopped laughing. They might get themselves into real trouble if the Japanese arrived.

6.

A few nights later Marie heard rifle shots. She guessed they couldn't be more than half a mile away. She looked at the glowing clock dial: it was two a.m. The first Mrs Wong came and told her to wake the children and go back upstairs. It was clear the Japanese had landed. Marie should avoid being seen in their flat again: it would not be safe for her to have any known connection with her husband.

Both Mrs Wongs and their daughter were gone by the time the sun rose. Marie assumed they were attempting to get to Free China. She wished they'd shared their plans with her. She would miss their support and kindness.

Next morning a small car pulled up outside their building. Marie looked out the window to see Arthur disappearing into the front entrance. 'Hello. Are we glad to see you,' she called. Arthur didn't return her greeting. As he made his way up the stairs he was shouting at her to start getting some essential things together.

Inside the flat he took her hands in his and kissed her on both cheeks. Arthur was the most relaxed and least serious of their friends. He was not as physically imposing as Vincent, but he was sharp and always had a plan to beat the system. He was unfailingly polite and generous. Now his hands were shaking.

Marie was suddenly aware how she must look. The skin around her eyes was puffy and pink. She was bare of lipstick. Arthur might not have recognised her if he'd passed her in the street.

He repeated his message. She should quickly get money, papers and a few precious items together. He was going to take them to a flat further away from the harbour.

'Arthur, we can't leave.' Marie's eyes filled with tears. 'We have to stay here in case Vincent can get help for us.'

'You can't wait, Marie,' Arthur said. 'The Japanese have landed right here. They're already in the hills behind you. Don't you understand? There's nothing Vincent can do for you now. He's probably having enough problems fending for himself.'

She asked if he would like a cup of tea. He looked at her dumbfounded. 'Marie!' he yelled.

'We can't come with you, Arthur. Anyway, that car's too small for all of us.'

Arthur pleaded. He doubted he'd be able to get to them again. The Japanese were too close to the building. She'd be much safer further away from the harbour and not near the power plant.

'No,' she repeated.

He left, saying he'd do his best to get back. If he managed it, was there anything she needed? Going down the stairs, he turned around. 'You might not get any more chances like this, Marie. Try to understand. You have to be careful that each decision you make now is the right one. Your options are going to get fewer and fewer.'

She closed the door with a push and went to the window. The tiny car started up and turned into the road. Then she went to her room to pray.

There was no way of going back to sleep. She would hear a shot, then listen for the next one and gauge if it was closer or further away. Vincent would have moved the piano and all the heavy furniture against the door, she thought. He would have collected guns from their friends in the police force so the Japanese would see it was best to leave them in peace.

As the sun rose she heard shouting, and then screams from the amahs. She rushed out to the living room. Marie junior and Cynthia were standing by the window, staring up the hill. As she reached them, they started to wail. On a paved slab at the front entrance of a building a hundred feet away lay several bloodstained bodies. The girls had seen a group of Sikh soldiers hiding. Two Japanese soldiers had come silently up behind them. The girls had yelled a warning but they hadn't turned in time. As soon as they saw the enemy's guns pointed at them they'd raised their rifles in surrender, but rather than being marched off they had been forced to kneel and immediately beheaded.

Marie heard that a week earlier the Japanese had offered reasonable terms of surrender to the British governor but he had turned them down. Some people still believed that Chiang Kai-shek's army was on the way to help. Others thought Winston Churchill would send troops and ships from Europe.

Next night she heard men yelling and shots being fired no more than a hundred yards from their building, then the noise of smashing glass and crockery. There was silence for an hour, then a woman screamed. A few minutes later she heard her sobbing. It was now the only sound in the still, dark night.

7.

In the early morning, Ah Sup yelled. She had spotted the body of a British soldier between the buildings of the power plant below. The ground around him was stained black. The angle of the man's neck made it clear he was dead.

Marie junior, still in her pyjamas, made it halfway to the window.

'Go back to your room!' Marie shouted.

Looking wide-eyed at their mother, Cynthia and Vincent junior began to bawl.

Marie threw on her shoes and raced along the road to Jane and Tony's place. Jane agreed to have them to stay for a few nights. Marie ran back home and told Lizzie to pack everything the children would need. The other three amahs and Mary should also pack their belongings. Ah Sup and Ah So should help Ah Ng carry as many provisions as possible up the hill.

Marie packed a bag and put on her favourite fur coat. The coat looked ridiculous over her short skirt but she thought it might come in useful. With the bag over one arm and the baby cradled in the other, she stumbled down the stairs, calling to Lizzie and Mary to bring the girls and lock the flat. The other amahs had already left.

Half walking, half running along the road, she stopped in a panic. Out of the corner of her eye, she could see Japanese soldiers running between the buildings below. Further down the alley lay the bloodied body of an Indian soldier. She looked back just in time to see Lizzie and Mary emerge from their building, with Margaret, Cynthia and Marie junior behind them. Some hundred yards down the hill another four Japanese soldiers carrying fixed bayonets were walking in their direction. She froze. Suddenly, the soldiers veered right and strode into a building.

There were now two men in Jane's flat. Jane's brother Mark had left his home in Kowloon and moved in with them. Marie felt reassured by the men's presence. They seemed to understand what was going on. She told them about the Japanese soldiers she'd seen and they described their own sightings. It was clear Japanese soldiers were now everywhere. When Jane and Marie were alone, Jane told Marie that Tony had destroyed most of his suits, anything that looked too European.

Marie junior and Cynthia had taken up their usual place at a window. Marie took Lizzie aside and told her she must stay with the girls at all times and try to keep them calm. They should not disturb Jane and Tony. She intended to go back to their flat to retrieve the money from the hiding places.

Lizzie insisted that Mary go with her. As they hurried back down the hill, Marie told Mary that if anyone asked she should say they were both locals, didn't speak English, and had no connection with British people.

Four of the Japanese soldiers she'd seen earlier were standing at the entrance to their building. A lump formed in Marie's throat and she struggled to breathe.

'You – what number?' The Japanese interpreter spat out the Cantonese words. Marie tried desperately to think how best to respond. If she sounded weak they might do what they wanted to her without thought of repercussion. If she sounded strong she might be killed right there and then.

Mary remained half a step behind, looking down intently at the soldiers' rubber-soled boots.

'What number?' the interpreter repeated.

Marie gripped her purse. It contained the family's personal papers, which she had grabbed before going to Jane's. She wished the purse was at the bottom of the harbour.

One of the soldiers was holding a bunch of maps. Perhaps they had been targeted, knew Vincent's address and had come to find him and his family.

'Thirty-eight,' she said. 'Third floor.'

The soldier said something to the interpreter. The interpreter asked if the girl was her daughter. 'Yes,' she lied. The interpreter told them to stand next to the entrance and wait. The two armed guards spoke to each other and smirked. They studied Marie and Mary from their ankles up while the other two soldiers consulted their maps and notes.

Further up over the crest of the hill there was a burst of machine-gun fire. The two younger soldiers walked to where they might get a better view, then signalled to the others that they couldn't see anything. They laughed as they walked back. Marie noticed how tired they looked. Perhaps this would make them trigger-happy.

The older men talked together for a long time, repeatedly looking over their maps, and then sent the two younger soldiers into the building, rapping out a list of instructions.

After twenty minutes Marie was overcome with the need to urinate. She crossed her legs and tried to think of something else, anything else. She took deep breaths and clutched her purse to her waist. She didn't want to be escorted to a toilet by a soldier. She thought about the stories of rape that had come out of Shanghai and Nanking, the screams of the woman the previous night. If this happened to her she would make sure no one ever knew, even Vincent. She would wash herself until all the skin the men had touched had been rasped away. She was

sure she could eventually convince herself that such a thing
had never happened.

A grey-haired woman came up the hill lugging a sack
of rice. Marie knew the woman's family were successful
merchants and lived on the second floor. The soldiers asked
for the woman's flat number but didn't stop her. As she
walked into the building she cast a glance at Marie. Marie
detested what she saw in her eyes – the pity, the 'you poor
thing', the 'you should have known not to dress like that'.
She turned to Mary. The girl's face was a blank.

People from other flats came and went. The soldier with
the maps and notes approached Marie again. As she looked
down at the papers he was holding she saw there was a
cross over building number thirty-eight. If only she wasn't
carrying her identity documents, she thought. Apart from
baby Vincent with his blond curls, all the children could
pass for local Chinese, but what would become of them if
she was taken away and locked up in a Shanghai-style camp?

The two soldiers who'd been in the building returned and
talked to the older soldiers, who again studied the papers
and maps.

'What floor? You, what floor?' The interpreter's words
snapped Marie out of her trance.

'The third floor,' she repeated.

'All right, you are permitted to go in.'

Marie turned and took Mary by the hand. As they
climbed the steps she felt the eyes of the soldiers on their
bodies. As they passed the Wongs' flat, she noticed the door
had been forced open. She felt sick. What if her flat too had
been broken into and the money taken?

To her relief the door was still intact. She bolted it behind
her and looked around. It was clear no one had been inside.

She raced to the toilet with tears pouring down her face. When she returned, she put a chair against one of the living-room walls, climbed on it and ran her hand along the wooden beading. The money was still there. She checked the other hiding places, retrieving most of the bundles of notes. In her bedroom she thought about taking a small framed photograph of Vincent but decided against it. Better not to have evidence like that on her.

She went into the kitchen to see if anything was left. There were some wilted vegetables and an open sack of rice. She picked up the sack and called to Mary that it was time to go. As she followed the girl down the stairs she noticed for the first time that she was no longer the child she'd watched growing for the past eleven years, since she and Lizzie arrived from Macau. Her hair had become full and shiny, her hips had widened and her chest now pressed against her school blouse. It was all the more reason to worry.

They left the building. The soldiers were no longer there.

8.

That night Marie gave Jane and Tony a detailed account of what had happened. The soldiers' coldness had been frightening, she said. She described them as 'hungry'. Lizzie needed to be careful what Mary wore.

Next morning a Japanese flag had replaced the Union Jack on a building below. 'What does it mean?' Marie asked Tony.

'It doesn't mean a goddamned thing,' Tony snarled.

Jane remonstrated with him; the children were listening. More calmly, he explained that the flying of the flag didn't necessarily mean the governor had surrendered. If he had there would have been an official announcement. He was certain it was just part of a plan by the Japanese to put the wind up British soldiers hidden in the mountains.

Marie asked Ah Ng to go down to their flat and collect some cooking utensils. The cook was old and homely. Marie figured she would not be at risk from the soldiers.

'Christ!' Tony was standing on a chair to get a better look over the buildings below. He had spotted a pile of headless bodies. It seemed the Japanese had been attacking anyone in uniform, even workers of the bus company.

Soon afterwards there was a sharp metallic clack on the door of the flat. The noise vibrated and bounced off the plaster walls. The amahs and children looked anxiously at Marie, Jane and Tony.

Tony went to the door. It was blocked from view by a small foyer, but there was no mistaking the sounds: the click, the whine of the door opening, the shouted words in Japanese, the interpreter's Cantonese translation.

Four soldiers pushed past Tony into the living room. They summoned Jane and Marie and told them to sit on the couch. One of the soldiers, carrying a rifle and a bayonet, barged into each room in the flat, one by one. If a door was closed he turned the handle, kicked the door open and leapt back ready to shoot.

Cynthia ran to her mother and stood, enveloped by Marie's legs, staring at the soldiers. From time to time she seemed to be about to say something, but Marie squeezed her knees, signalling for her to stay quiet.

The interpreter received a barrage of instructions, then turned. 'Too many people,' he said loudly. 'Ten beds, twenty people. Who does not live here?'

Marie stood and placed her hands on Cynthia's small shoulders.

'Sit!' One of the armed soldiers moved towards Marie, who quickly sat back down. 'We are from the building along the road,' she said. She pointed to her children, Mary and the amahs.

'You go home,' the soldier barked. 'You stay home until soldiers come. The Imperial Japanese Army has taken control of Hong Kong.'

The soldiers checked the papers Tony had carefully set aside. All identified him as Chinese; there was nothing relating to his British citizenship or his memberships of upper-echelon associations and clubs.

The soldier who appeared to be the highest-ranked looked through half the bundle, then tossed the lot on the floor.

He looked around at them again.

'You – stand up!'

Margaret looked sideways at her mother and slowly stood up.

'How old are you?'

'Nine.' Marie answered for her.

'How old are you?' he repeated, staring at Margaret.

'Nine,' Margaret said. She continued to stand, shaking visibly. She was almost as tall as the soldier. He turned and laughed with the men behind him, saying a word that might have been 'nine' in Japanese.

'Your father – a soldier?'

Margaret turned to her mother, who remained expressionless.

She looked back at the translator. 'No.'

'Where is your father?'

'Singapore.'

The other soldiers turned to one another and laughed.

'Don't you worry about him,' the translator said. 'He is also being looked after by the Japanese Imperial Army.'

The man smiled at Margaret. To Marie's relief she smiled back.

The soldiers turned and walked out the door. Tony closed it gently behind them. Five minutes later he gingerly opened it again. The soldiers were still in the building.

Marie, the amahs and children walked down the stairs. The soldiers were standing just inside the open door of the flat below. One was facing them. His eyes disclosed nothing as he watched them pass, their arms laden with the clothes and food they had carried up the day before.

9.

Marie checked the time. It was three a.m. A woman was screaming in the building across the road. She took her rosary beads from her handbag under Vincent's pillow and prayed.

She tried to recall the faces of women she had seen coming and going from the building. One of the amahs was quite beautiful, she remembered. There was also a married woman about the same age as her and a girl of thirteen.

Every so often the screams became muffled, but then they would start again. After a long period of silence Marie heard a faint drawn-out whimpering that barely made it through the night air. She pictured one soldier leaving and another replacing him as the cries and shouted words started again. Another woman began to scream for help further along the road.

In the terrible sleepless hours, Marie's mind churned. If Singapore had fallen, how could Vincent get back to help them? 'Please God, let him be all right,' she said out loud. She knew the sort of Japanese soldiers she'd met would despise Vincent. He looked so British and was so tall. He'd be beaten and shot without question, in or out of uniform. But he was too smart to play the hero when his family needed him. She was sure he'd have got out of Singapore on a friend's ship. He could get passage anywhere. He knew people in almost every port in Asia.

The screaming began again. Marie put a pillow over her head and lay in a tight ball in a corner of the bed. She pulled the blankets and sheets firmly against her but it was impossible to sleep. She got up and walked quietly through the flat. The morning light, still an hour from sunrise, was enough for her to see that the children were sleeping. Fourteen-month-old Vincent seemed to be frowning.

In the kitchen she went over what food they had left. There was perhaps enough for two more weeks if they couldn't go out and get more. But what if the Japanese started taking their provisions? Christmas was just a few days away.

She went back to bed, and woke again mid-morning. She opened her eyes but didn't move. A crook in her shoulders had seeded a migraine headache. It was climbing from the back of her neck to her eyes. She pressed her skull above the temples in the search of relief. It had been fifty-two days since she'd seen Vincent. If they couldn't leave the flat, how would they be able to find out if he'd sent them a telegram?

Through the morning calm she heard Japanese being spoken near the entrance of their building and gunshots and booms up the mountain. 'Why don't they just surrender?' She noticed she'd again spoken out loud. She wondered whether she would go mad.

Later she heard the amahs and children shuffling about. She decided to stay in bed. She had to think, had to be sure she'd have her wits about her the next time she was confronted by soldiers. As night fell the screams began again. Some of them seemed to be coming from one of the same women as the night before.

10.

The banging that filled the flat was accompanied by rapid-fire yelling. It was nine in the morning but Marie had already been up for three hours. She'd had breakfast with the children and run down to a small local store, where she'd managed to buy an armful of bread.

There were two soldiers at the door. One was armed. They walked straight past her and stood in the centre of the living room. 'Blankets and food!' the armed soldier demanded in heavily accented Cantonese.

'No. We can't. We have to keep everything we have for the children,' Marie said.

'Imperial Japanese Army has conquered Hong Kong.' The rote-learned English phrase seemed to be a defence against looking directly at the children or giving a real explanation.

Marie pleaded: she had to keep all the blankets.

'Get blankets now!'

'What are my children supposed to do?'

'You, kowtow! And you, you, you, you and you.' Marie and the amahs were pushed into a line and then down on their knees in the centre of the room. 'Imperial Japanese Army has conquered Hong Kong!'

Vincent junior started to wail.

The armed soldier screamed. 'You!' He grabbed Ah Sup by her hair and lifted her up off her knees. 'You – you get blankets now!'

Ah Sup looked at Marie.

'Now!' the soldier repeated.

Marie didn't look up. 'Ah Sup,' she said quietly, 'get him some, but only five.' She tensed, ready for the swipe of a rifle butt, but nothing happened.

'Now bung!' the unarmed officer shouted.

'Bung?' Marie said.

'Bung! Bung!'

Marie looked up at him. 'Bung?' She was desperate to understand.

Ah Sup returned with the blankets and put them on a chair by the door. Then she knelt back down in the line.

The soldier made a gesture of bringing something to his mouth. 'Bung!' he repeated.

Marie shook her head. She couldn't think of anything that could be called 'bung'. She looked at Lizzie but the amah was as lost as she was.

The soldier seemed upset and agitated. He ran to the kitchen, leaving his partner standing over the prisoners. The first cupboard he opened was the one Marie had just filled with bread. He turned and stared furiously at her as the loaves fell to the floor around him. 'Bung! Bung! Bung!' He had been trying to pronounce bao, the Cantonese word for bread.

Marie realised with horror that she might be punished. The soldier guarding the line brought his bayonet swiftly down beside her cheek. The sharp point touched her throat. No one made a sound. Marie sensed it would mean nothing to the soldier if the bayonet were to pierce her skin, jugular vein and larynx. She gave an involuntary gasp. Tears streamed down her cheeks.

The older soldier muttered angrily at his colleague. Marie clenched her eyes shut and breathed a silent succession of Hail Marys. There was a pause, the blade was lifted, the men moved swiftly to the door and disappeared.

Next day three different soldiers burst into the flat. They went through each room and seemed to be making a list of the furniture. Marie stood with her arms tightly crossed. She heard solid objects falling on to the hard floors, and porcelain and glass breaking. What was happening? She looked down the hallway. One of the soldiers waved his rifle to warn her not to come any closer. The smashing continued. Each plate, bowl or saucer being destroyed seemed to make their situation more real. Would Vincent's and her life ever return to the way it was before?

The soldiers came into the living room and started to examine the tables and chairs, walking around them and lifting them up. Marie assumed they must be taking over some buildings to use as barracks and needed to furnish them. Thank God they're not searching for money, she thought, but at that moment one of the soldiers lifted the lid of the piano and started to test every key. The eighth note made a dull thud. Margaret turned to see what her mother would do. Marie stared fixedly ahead.

'Tomorrow we come for the piano,' the soldier said. 'Make it polished.'

At five o'clock that evening Marie was in her bedroom when there was another banging at the door. She heard Lizzie

scream, 'No, no, no, stop,' and ran out to find a soldier with
a rifle across his back opening the doors of the sideboard
and ornamental Chinese boxes.

'No bung. No blankets. No more. We gave already to a
senior officer.' Marie's instinct was to scream the words, but
she managed to sound like she was pleading.

'Tummy bunds.'

'Tummy bunds?'

'Tummy bunds.'

The soldier gestured around his midriff, crossed the room
and held out a piece of curtain. He looked at Marie for a
reaction. Then he noticed Mary. His eyes moved from the
girl's face, down to her legs and back to her chest.

'Cummerbund?' Marie tried to distract him.

He nodded.

'No cummerbunds,' she said.

Suddenly everything was silent. The soldier fixed his gaze
back on Marie. He crossed the room and headed for the
bedroom. As he passed, he shoved her sideways so the butt
of his rifle hit her hip. She bent over in pain, then turned
and limped after him. He went directly to a trunk in which
Marie had packed many essential clothes and personal effects.
A wave of panic came over her: she had carefully folded
and placed one of Vincent's merchant navy uniforms at the
bottom of the trunk.

'No,' she said. 'Nothing inside.'

The soldier pushed aside the carefully folded dresses and
rummaged down to the bottom, pulling out the epauletted
jacket and trousers and scattering the other contents on to
the floor. He looked intently at the buttons on the jacket
and then held up the trousers, seeming to notice their length
and the roman lettering.

Marie had a sudden thought. 'Wait!' She rushed to the bureau in the living room and searched for a letter from an officer in the Japanese navy, whom Vincent had met when he was an engineering apprentice. She found it immediately. Never had she been more glad of Vincent's habit of filing things in order.

The soldier was still examining the contents of the trunk. She handed him the letter. He scanned the letterhead. She made eye contact with him, slowly opened the wardrobe on the far side of the bedroom, took out one of her prized pale green silk cheongsams and handed it to him. The soldier looked at her and laid the uniform back in the box. He spread the cheongsam across the bed, folded it carefully and placed it in his satchel. Then he turned and walked out of the bedroom, across the living room and out the door.

II.

Despite the Japanese soldiers' assertions that they had conquered Hong Kong, there had still been no formal surrender. Marie found it hard to make decisions when information was restricted to what the family and amahs could see from their windows and news from friends who'd had the courage to go into the town. There had been no official notification that the curfew had been lifted but that morning Marie had seen many neighbours moving about outside.

For five days no one had seen a Hong Kong soldier in the area. Whatever was happening elsewhere, it appeared their district was under the complete control of the Japanese. Senior officers had been installed in blocks of flats on their street. Soldiers had taken over the buildings below them as barracks and seemed to have control of the power station.

They spent Christmas Day at Jane's, along with some other families who lived nearby. Each child was given a small bundle of sweets that Jane had been guarding in her cupboard for a month. Despite the gift, the children had cried and complained. It was the worst Christmas they had ever had, with their parents anxious and short-tempered.

None of the adults had slept for more than two hours a night. They'd all heard the screams of women in nearby buildings. Margaret had twice been accosted by soldiers. Mary had narrowly escaped being raped. As she'd walked past a building that housed a group of soldiers, two had come out and grabbed her by her arms. They had dragged her inside and halfway into a side room before an officer had arrived and ordered them to release her.

Jane's brother Mark explained that if the Hong Kong defence troops surrendered, the soldiers would not be able to flee to Free China. They would be under orders to formally cede their rights and authority to the Japanese.

Nerves were frayed. Jane demanded Marie stop her knitting and its incessant click, click, clicking. Marie responded angrily. Perhaps her friend should calm down and try knitting herself.

'I don't want to bloody knit,' Jane retorted.

The children turned to look at their mothers.

'Get back to your playing!' Marie cast a steely look at the frozen young faces, then slowly pulled more wool from the ball.

As tears welled in Jane's eyes, Tony spoke up. Marie should take a break from knitting.

'Look, Tony,' Marie said, 'this is the only thing keeping me relaxed. If I stop doing this I'll end up as uptight as Jane.'

She stood up, pushed her knitting into her bag, and went into the bedroom where the baby was sleeping. Although she wanted to slam the door, she closed it gently and sat down beside him on the small bed. She watched him breathing and studied again the frown, the strong brow, the unmistakable shape of his mouth. It was so like his father's. She lay down on a rug on the floor, pulled two blankets over her and closed her eyes. Before the air between her skin and the blankets had warmed up she was asleep.

12.

On Boxing Day, news of the surrender brought a strange overwhelming sense of relief. Marie let the amahs take the girls outside. They had been crotchety, constantly pestering her with questions. Why, they wanted to know, was Margaret no longer given Vincent to look after? It was true: Marie wouldn't let the baby out of her sight, even when she was in the bathroom. What if Japanese soldiers arrived at that moment?

When the girls came back, Cynthia raced across the living room with news. The English and Indian soldiers were having a parade. Marie had already learned from a neighbour that this would happen. The soldiers had been given instructions to report to sites around the island; from there they would have to march to the confinement camps allocated to them by the Japanese. They were to take only what they could carry on their backs by way of money, medicine, blankets and clothing.

'Did any of them appear to be hurt?' Marie said.

'Yes, many. Some had blood all over their jackets. But at least they hadn't had their heads cut off.'

'You shouldn't say things like that, Cynthia.'

The small girl stood looking at her mother. 'It's true though,' she said.

Ah So had taken Cynthia on a visit to a Chinese herbalist. A neighbour's amah had told her that the herbalist's husband, a postman, had had his head cut off and put on display. She and Ah So had seen three heads on display, Cynthia reported, but the postman's was not among them. There were also heads on the spiked railing they'd passed on their way back. They thought they recognised some of the faces.

VINCENT

13.

As projects went, the one in Singapore was about the most original and interesting Vincent Broom had ever been given. He was the sort of engineer whose passion for building and fixing machines had its roots in his boyhood fascination with mechanical toys, and later with motorbikes. Working out how to raise a sunken ship was a dream assignment – or would have been if a Japanese invasion wasn't looking increasingly likely.

At the end of each workday Vincent took a swim. With his mask on and his arms outstretched he would float face down and motionless in the water for as long as his lungs allowed, contemplating the work that had been done that day by his men on the sunken hull far below.

The water was clear. From where he was, directly above the ship's bridge, he could see no evidence of the holes that had landed the vessel, perfectly upright and intact, on the bottom of the channel. The big Russian diver walking around on the deck with his lead boots and brass helmet looked just like any sailor in wet-weather gear collecting his tools. Through the watery silence Vincent heard only the clicking of the diver's air hose from the barge.

Gazing into the deep water helped him stop thinking for a few moments about the fate of his family. It was two weeks since Hong Kong had fallen. What was happening to Marie and the children? His inability to contact them was anguishing. One day he'd hear some snippet of news from the papers or from sailors arriving from the north that made him confident that, as Asian-looking civilians, they would be safe. Another day he'd hear reports that made him think they might be suffering unimaginable horrors.

He rolled over and floated on his back. Marie's name formed on his lips between deep breaths. He'd feel happy for a second and then a tightening in his brow would spread quickly to his neck and through his whole body. It was a month since he'd had any word from her, two months since he'd last seen her and the children.

He turned over for a final look as the last diver was hoisted back up. He thought about the hundreds of sailors who had perished four weeks earlier on the *Repulse* and the *Prince of Wales*, barely a day's sail north. He remembered watching in awe as the magnificent ships had set off from Singapore. He imagined the men now stranded, dead, in flooded engine-rooms and passageways below deck.

Vincent and most of the men he worked with were familiar with the massive uncertainties that came with war and civil unrest. The head of the Russian divers came to Vincent daily to talk about the evolving odds of Singapore being invaded. How long would they be able to keep working on the salvage if it became clear they wouldn't have the time and resources to see the ship refloated? And when would he and his men next be paid?

These White Russians, refugees from the 1917 Bolshevik revolution who had escaped to Manchuria and Shanghai, knew more than anyone that clarity was important. If there was a risk of the work stopping suddenly, or funds they were owed being blocked, they had to find other work now: their families had learnt first-hand that having enough money put aside could mean the difference between surviving or not. Vincent, for his part, wanted to keep the men employed and motivated, but he needed to be realistic, and fair to them and their families. How long could this last? The Allied troops were just managing to hold back the Japanese army in Malaya but Japanese reinforcements were advancing fast.

Intuition told him the situation was likely to get worse. Intimidation had been going on for weeks. There was a high chance of an attack by Japanese planes flying low across the water. Out on the barge he and his men would be an easy target.

He made a decision. That afternoon, as the men packed up, he told them they should take all the tools they could back on the boat. Next morning he sent a telegram to Hong Kong advising his boss Stewart Williamson what he was doing. He did not expect an answer.

Later the next day, over morning tea in the workshop, he found himself sitting on a low stack of wood with his Russian head diver, Jean. Both had been in Shanghai in 1937 when the Japanese invasion began. Jean had been living there; Vincent had been working on one of the last trading ships to leave before the city fell.

'Your wife is half Chinese and half Portuguese?' Jean said.

'Yes. Well, that's what she tells people. In reality the Portuguese blood has been watered down. She looks more Chinese than anything.'

Jean nodded. 'That detail will be useful to her and the children.'

Both men knew that the Chinese wives of expatriates in Shanghai and their children had fared better under the Japanese than the wives and children who looked too obviously European. The European-looking women and children had been interned immediately.

The morning had already been difficult and Vincent's emotions were close to the surface. As he'd made his way to work he'd noticed that the watchmen who usually stood on every corner were nowhere to be seen. There was no sign of anyone bothering to sweep up glass from the pavements in front of bombed buildings. The streets were eerily empty.

At the telegraph office there was no news from Hong Kong. He'd have to tell his Tamil and Malay workers they would be picking up their final pay envelopes that afternoon. They would not be needed until further notice.

Next morning there was still no news from Williamson or Marie. The newspapers could shed no light on what state Hong Kong was in after the British surrendered on Christmas Day. Were the Japanese working towards stabilising administration of the colony, or just raping and pillaging?

14.

Around ten that night there was a knock on Vincent's door in the guest house. He was in bed and hadn't bothered locking. He was raising himself up on one elbow when the door opened. As his eyes adjusted to the darkness he identified the shape of a woman. She was slim, Asian. For a moment he thought it was Marie.

'Who are you?' The girl seemed as shocked as he was.

'I'm Vincent Broom. This is my room.'

'Where's Pete?'

'I don't know Pete.'

'Pete the American.'

'Oh, the pilot?' He remembered what he'd heard about the previous occupant of his room. 'He left two months ago.'

The woman paused again. 'I'm sorry.' She closed the door behind her and was gone.

The only confirmation he'd not been dreaming was the laughter that rose from the bar moments later. He pictured the young woman rushing down the stairs and out the main doors, followed by the stares and smirks of the regular crowd of European men who hung out there in the evenings.

He turned over to face the wall but couldn't get back to sleep. There were so many desperate unanswered questions. Was Marie still in the flat? Were her Portuguese papers keeping her and the children safe? Was Lizzie with her? Had they gone to Macau?

Or had the family's English and New Zealand papers been discovered? Were they interned? What did the baby have to eat? Was there even food? Had Williamson been able to do anything for them?

For the next five hours his mind went over and over these questions and the worst imaginable scenarios. He rolled from one position to another. He heard the sounds of the last drunken patrons spilling out on to the street, the rumble of chairs and tables being dragged across the floor to be set up for breakfast, the high heels of a woman coming up the stairs, an army truck rumbling along the road towards the docks.

Soon after he arrived in Singapore he'd bought his daughters silver bangles for Christmas. They were sitting

on his desk, a reminder of how cut off he was from Hong
Kong. He should have mailed the bangles. A letter he'd sent
from Shanghai just before that city fell had taken three years
but it had arrived in the end.

He tried to distract himself by searching for warm
thoughts of Marie. There was her fire, the spark that made
everyone look at her as soon as she entered a room. She was
original, different, but that strength was also her weakness:
she expected a lot from life, sometimes more than people
found reasonable. He knew she would have antagonised
people in Singapore.

Thoughts and opinions on what was happening up north
and what might soon happen to Singapore were varied
and changeable, but they could suddenly congeal with
solid news. Instantly everybody would change their minds.
Hope and determination one day turned to pessimism the
next. The Japanese would be turned around in the jungles.
The Japanese would be here within weeks and it would be
Shanghai all over again.

15.

Returning home from work next day, Vincent turned into
his street to be greeted with smoke, steam and ash billowing
around the guest house. A bomb had gone through the
southern wing, taking out half of the end wall. Manual-
pump fire engines and men in tin hats were on the scene.

Vincent walked past the cordoned-off area and was
waved through to the front door by the Hungarian building
manager. Neither of them spoke. Climbing the stairs to his
room in the undamaged wing of the building, he thought

that even if he hadn't seen the destruction from outside he would have noticed things were different. The light was wrong for that time of day. There was too much reflection coming off the matt green walls and brown floor tiles. There was a different smell too, and a thin layer of ash on everything.

At the top of the stairs he saw that a massive section of the wall at the far end of the long hallway had gone. There was now an open view along the street: A cleaner was sweeping furiously as ash continued to fall from the murky air.

He unlocked the door to his room and stopped just long enough to toss his jacket and satchel on the bed. As he walked back down the hallway the smell of explosives increased but little else was different. The building was more solid than he'd given it credit for.

A line of tiles demarcated the doorway to the damaged wing of the building. He had seen a young woman who rented a room just through the doorway a few nights earlier, fumbling with her keys to get in the door. Later he'd seen her talking to the staff at the entrance and deduced she'd lived there for a while.

The room was still the way it had been left by the explosion. There were shards of porcelain that had once been lamps and bowls. The wardrobe had been reduced to a pile of kindling. Strips and ribbons of beautiful floral cottons and silks that had once been blouses or dresses dangled from shrapnel pins imbedded in the wall. In the middle of the room there were pieces of mirror and a bed almost split in half. As he left he touched the plaster on the wall. It was still warm. But there was no sign of blood. He assumed the woman was all right.

Back in his room, he lay on the bed and stared at the ceiling. There were a few cracks he was sure hadn't been

there before. Somehow he managed to sleep. When he woke
two hours later, it was dark. The hum from the bar sounded
louder than usual, perhaps because of the hole in the building.
Or maybe there were more customers than usual.

He took down his suitcase from the top of the wardrobe
and pushed aside the neatly folded contents to unearth a
bottle of scotch. He poured himself a large nip, drank it and
refilled the glass. Then, before closing the case, he took out
a satchel that contained papers he'd accumulated over the
last few years on various merchant navy ships. He opened
the satchel, unsure what he was looking for, until he saw at
the back a small map of Asia.

He looked at the map carefully. From what he knew, every
port to the northeast of Hong Kong on the China coast was
now controlled by the Japanese. Macau was free, but it was
surrounded by a maze of Chinese islands and waterways.
Japanese boats were bound to be patrolling, destroying enemy
shipping and checking craft for what they were carrying.

All the seas around Taiwan, the Pescadores, the Philippines,
Vietnam and Burma would probably be the same. Malaya
and Thailand would also be impossible to get to. He took
another gulp of whisky.

After his long time working in the East, Vincent had
excellent contacts: a network of seamen; owners of boats
large and small; people who might smuggle him in the
hold of a ship. After ten years of working every river and
channel between Singapore and Hong Kong his knowledge
was thorough. But he knew none of this would get him
anywhere without a high risk of detention or death for him
and anyone who helped him.

He looked at the map again to remind himself of the
inland roads and borders. He took a newspaper from his desk

and compared the names of places in an article about the Japanese army's movements with those on the map. There were no functioning Allied warships or military bases left between Singapore and Hong Kong. In fact, it looked as though the Japanese had already established an impenetrable barrier across land and sea stretching from India to Hawai'i. As things stood, you'd have to get across the Taklamakan Desert or over the Himalayas from Calcutta to get from Singapore to Hong Kong.

He tore out the newspaper articles, folded them together with the map and put the bundle in the inside pocket of his jacket. He knew his Russian friend had been trying to calm his nerves by pointing out the benefits of Marie's Chinese looks, but he had seen for himself the desperation on the faces of Chinese escaping the Japanese in Shanghai. He especially remembered the children being unable to keep up with their parents because they had eaten almost nothing for months.

He thought of Marie. She had become just a haze, a blur of happiness and beauty, her soft skin draped in silk, her lips shimmering, her fire and laughter. He felt his head spin and his body ache. She was most likely going through hell.

16.

The Japanese had not so far managed to destroy many of the substantial buildings in the centre of Singapore. Some people thought the bombing had not been a genuine attempt to take the country but rather a way to dissuade any forces based there from messing in affairs in Malaya. Perhaps Singapore would remain beyond the reach of the Japanese forces, with their resources overstretched elsewhere? Their supply lines could break, or they could be too slow to make it all the way to the island.

Vincent thought otherwise. Things in Singapore could get much worse. The island might fall completely and become a Japanese colony, like the port of Kaohsiung that he knew so well, and the rest of Taiwan.

Again there were no telegrams for him at the office. The clerk said there had been little communication of any kind from Hong Kong. When Jean arrived for work, Vincent told him about the direct hit on the guest house. He was, he said, pessimistic about Singapore's future.

Jean had a favour to ask. He had bought a dhow. 'The hull is in pretty good shape,' he said, 'and I've managed to get a whole set of charts, but I need to do some work on the engine and shaft. I was wondering if I could borrow some tools to work on her after hours.'

Where could the Russian hope to get to in such a small coastal boat, Vincent wondered. 'If need be,' Jean said as if reading his mind. 'My mother and I will aim for Australia.' He knew it was unlikely they would make it all the way. They might be captured by a Japanese patrol boat, for example. But he thought the voyage could be made without them ever being too far from land. If they thought there were Japanese patrols about, they could hide in a bay or on the far side of an island.

'Why not leave on a ship?' Vincent said. 'If things get that bad there'll be evacuation ships.'

'I doubt many of them will make it through,' Jean said. 'And anyway we Russians would be the last to be allowed on. I know for a fact that our old papers won't get us far.'

That evening Vincent pulled shut the giant doors of the workshop and chained and padlocked them. All things considered, the day had been productive. The team had finished the first few heavy wooden hatches that, with rubber seals attached, they hoped to bolt to a selection of openings in the hull of the sunken ship before filling parts with air. They had had to do all the welding outside on the concrete dock because much of the space inside had been taken up by the barrels of oil already salvaged from the ship's tanks. It had been hot thirsty work.

As he walked towards the city centre, air-raid sirens sounded. By now all the Brewster Buffalo planes that had been sent by the British to protect Singapore from airborne attacks had been destroyed; the Japanese could do whatever they wanted if they could avoid the big guns on the ground.

Vincent, like many in the city, was less worried now about finding an official shelter area than he had been when the air raids began. He jumped into a monsoon drain in a garden. Drains like this were a good five feet deep and there were so many they were never full.

After twenty minutes the all-clear sounded without a single bomber having gone over. Back at the guest house Vincent ate supper alone in the dining room. The men he usually dined with were out at their volunteer defence posts. It had been a week since he had last had company.

Late that night there was another air-raid warning. Vincent put on his slippers and went down to the designated shelter in the basement of the building next door. Even through the thick walls and floors he could hear planes flying over and deafening explosions. When he emerged, the Singapore sky was aglow with orange reflected flames.

17.

The workshop was gone. All the completed hatches and most of the engineering equipment had been transformed into tangled piles of metal, charcoal and burnt rubber.

A volunteer fire brigade officer told Vincent the fire had been one of the hottest they'd ever had to deal with. It had taken a lot of creativity and effort to stop the entirety of the stored oil bursting into flames.

When the rest of the salvage team arrived, Vincent arranged to meet them at his guest house the following day: he would pay final wages and sign them off. He told Jean to keep whatever tools he had already taken. He would pass by in the next few days to see if he could help with work on the dhow.

Still unsure if anyone was in the office in Hong Kong, he sent a message asking for permission to leave Singapore. He added a plea for information about Marie and the children. He hoped someone would be sent to check on them.

He took his lunch alone and washed it down with his usual cup of milky English tea. He felt as though he were in a trance. Real life was being lived elsewhere and he was blocked from being part of it.

The hot afternoon stretched on. He went to his room to take a nap. When he couldn't sleep he went down to the bar and started reading a book someone had left there. Time had suddenly slowed. Every extra hour in Singapore seemed a waste. At one point he took out a piece of paper and made a list of places he'd like to take the family on holiday after everything had died down. But when would it be safe to travel to Europe again, even to London? The New Zealand countryside had always been enough for him, but Marie liked cities, cinemas, shopping, good restaurants. He promised himself he'd take her wherever she wanted to go.

A young waiter came in to set up for the dinner shift. He looked shattered. He had just seen a horrible mess of limbs and body parts. A group of people taking shelter in a monsoon drain had suffered a direct hit.

All this murder, lives disrupted, families torn apart. Vincent thought back to when he was in Shanghai. He had been on a ship tied up on Huangpu River near the mouth of the Yangtze, well away from the heart of the city. As the ship was pulling out from the dock, a Japanese destroyer had come up beside them and begun firing at buildings on the waterfront. Some dockworkers and starving refugees had scattered, but others had been gunned down where they stood, paralysed with fear and unable to decide which way to run. Some of the shells had passed overhead, but fortunately his ship had been allowed to leave the port.

Back then he'd felt pity for the Chinese but no over-whelming animosity towards the Japanese. It was just war, he'd thought. He had met a good number of Japanese over the ten years he had been working along the Asian coastline and had got on well with them. Now, to his surprise, he was feeling real hatred.

18.

The man standing in front of Vincent in the telegram line was in his late fifties and almost certainly a veteran: a long scar ran up the side of his neck and into his hair. Ahead of him another twelve people were also waiting for news from the outside.

The man was finding the long wait annoying. Every
minute or so he sighed deeply. At any other time he would
have been been treated with respect, allowed to walk to the
front of the queue, but no one stirred.

'Letting your family know you're all right?' he said to
Vincent, who was gazing absentmindedly at the teak panel-
ling on the ceiling.

'Yes. And seeing if there's any news from my employer in
Hong Kong.'

'They're in bad shape up there.'

'Seems like it.'

'I'm just trying to get to Sydney.'

'Is that where you live?'

'Yes. This was my first visit here. Would you believe it?
Bad luck, eh.'

'Yes.'

'Could have been worse, I suppose. I could be in Hong
Kong like your boss.'

The line moved forward a few steps. 'I heard that terrible
things happened there before the surrender. They've been
torturing our boys. Bloody Japs. Bloody animals. At least
the Krauts play by certain rules.'

'Yes.'

'Your employer been locked up?'

'I don't know.'

'Those camps sound dreadful, like the ones in Shanghai.
Worse for the women though.'

'Yes!' Vincent snapped. 'I'm hoping they won't put
everyone in Hong Kong in camps.'

The man seemed affronted by Vincent's sudden change
of tone. 'Anyway,' he said, 'I hope you'll get some good
news.'

Later that day Vincent found himself in another office. Every now and then the young Australian soldier behind the desk paused from taking his details and glanced towards the waiting area. There was an ever-increasing accumulation of people.

'On what grounds did your wife stay in Hong Kong when the evacuation was organised?'

'She's Macanese. Portuguese papers. Third-nation status. She wouldn't budge from there.'

By 'Macanese' did Vincent mean his wife had some Chinese blood as well as Portuguese? Yes, Vincent said. In the right clothes Marie could pass for a full-blooded Chinese woman.

'She is very lucky then,' the soldier said. He added that with luck she'd have been able to stay outside of the internment camps, where all the British, Australians, Kiwis, Indians and Canadians had been placed. Those in the armed forces who'd survived the fighting had been in camps since the surrender.

Vincent followed the newpaper reports, but hearing this news directly from a soldier who was in daily contact with affairs beyond Singapore reassured him.

Was there any way, he asked, to get a telegram to his house, or even a letter via official or unofficial channels? The young man shrugged. It was clear he thought the army's time and resources were better spent on more important matters.

Vincent stood and shook his hand. As he turned to walk away, the soldier leaned over his desk. 'Sir,' he said, 'normally these things, civilian communications, are handled by the Red Cross. They're just not up and running yet.'

'Thank you,' Vincent said. 'With the information you

have, what advice can you give me? What should I be doing? Waiting in Singapore for things to be better organised?'

The man leaned in further to speak to him quietly. 'From what you've told us, you're in a category that my superior thinks should just get away from here. Civilian authorities will say the same thing. Of course, with your New Zealand national service training we could use you here, but you'd be of more use to the war effort on the Sydney docks as an engineer. I was going to confirm the details tomorrow, but I can tell you that we've put you on a priority list to get to Sydney on a Qantas flying boat. You'll have to go to the Qantas office to sort out the details. Just give me a day to finalise it.'

'I should wait to be released from my duties here by my employer,' Vincent said.

'Of course, but your employer may have no way to contact you. Don't wait to plan your voyage.' He looked at Vincent, who'd started to laugh quietly. 'What's so funny?'

'I'm sorry. It's just my nerves, the thought of getting away from here. I was thinking about my wife, your saying she'd be unlikely to be interned. I was picturing her in a camp with a hundred British tai-tais. She'd kill them, or they'd kill her.'

'Character, is she?'

'Oh yes.'

'Try and keep your spirits up. Come and see me tomorrow.'

That night in his room Vincent stripped down to his singlet, trousers and socks. He placed his shoes by the bed and his passport, papers and wallet in his coat pockets. An air-raid evacuation order might come at any time. He needed to be able to get out fast.

19.

Vincent read the cable for the fifth time. 'WILLIAMSON
INTERNED STOP.' This should not have been a surprise but
he was still shocked. 'MARIE CHILDREN GOOD HEALTH HOME
8TH DEC STOP ADVANCED SALARY DEC STOP.' No matter how
often he read the words he got the same rush of shivers
through his chest. December eighth. That was about seven
weeks ago, before the real fighting. Where was the family
now? Why didn't his office have more recent information?
'REQUEST APPROVED WILLIAMSON STOP TAKE RESPONSIBILITY
ALL SYDNEY STOP.'

The telegram was signed by Williamson's secretary. God
knows where she was now. What would she have done after
sending these final messages? Perhaps she was attending to
these last tasks before being interned herself?

Even at this early hour the Qantas office was besieged.
Despite having his ticket and papers, Vincent was told he
wouldn't make the list for that day. He sat for a while in
the waiting room anyway. The day before he'd seen the
clerks give passage to someone who wasn't on the list. If that
happened, he decided, he'd just get on the plane. He didn't
need all his clothes and could send money to the guest house
from Sydney to pay for his room and meals.

During the next hour it became clear there was no point
in staying. Even Qantas staff waiting for places were being
told to go home. All flights had been cancelled.

'You're still here.' Jean smiled broadly. He looked undaunted
by the dhow voyage ahead of him. He wiped the grease off
his hands and climbed up on to the dock.

'Everything working all right?' Vincent said.

'Should be. We're going to leave a few hours before dawn tomorrow.'

'How is your mother?'

'Extremely nervous, but doing a good job of hiding it and finding ways to distract herself,' Jean said. 'Right now she's out buying final provisions.'

Vincent told Jean he was beginning to worry about his own chances of getting away. Even though it was considered important for the war effort that he get to Sydney to take up his post, and all his papers were in order, there didn't seem to be enough planes and ships for the evacuation.

The Russian frowned. 'Any news from Hong Kong?'

Vincent told him about the telegram. He hoped to be able to find out more and make a plan to help Marie and the family when he got to Sydney.

'We'll see you there.' Jean seemed uncharacteristically subdued.

'Let's hope,' Vincent replied.

He wasn't sure if any more planes would take off from Singapore. Tomorrow he'd see if he could get on a ship. He knew of at least one old friend, an engineer, who was sailing in the next few days. Maybe he could share his cabin.

'You see, your luck is working.'

'It strikes me that in times like these there can be only so much good luck about. Let's hope it's with both of us and we'll meet again.'

'Sydney then.'

'Yes. See you in Sydney.'

20.

Over the cries of the hawkers, Vincent made out clanking sounds around one of the *Vyner Brooke's* newly installed pieces of armour-plating. He hadn't seen the ship since she'd been painted grey and had guns fitted.

Dropping the name of his friend Jim, an officer on the ship, he walked up the gangplank, trying to make the small suitcase in his hand as invisible as possible. He pushed up the narrow ladders and along the decks, past families and groups of nurses trying to organise their bunk allocations. None of the children he saw were playing or laughing. A steward watching over them was insisting their mothers keep them under control while final details were sorted out.

Vincent spotted Jim sitting on a hatch at the aft. Jim's expression went from happy surprise to a wary smile between old friends caught in an unbelievable situation. How were Marie and the children, Jim said. Vincent told him they were well, but trapped in Hong Kong.

Finally Jim noticed Vincent's suitcase. The news was bad. He had been advised that no one, not even the captain, was permitted to offer berths to family or friends. They were to take only those people on the list the authorities had provided.

While Jim was still talking, Vincent stood and picked up his case. Jim also rose to his feet. He looked embarrassed. As they shook hands Vincent told him not to worry. He had other options. Something would work out.

Vincent swore under his breath as he went back down the gangplank. He had started to believe he was lucky, that he was going to stay ahead of everything. With new urgency he looked at the other ships tied up alongside the docks or anchored further out. One, the *Madura*, looked as though she had taken a minor hit from a bomb while in the harbour. Many of the others were cargo ships. There were not nearly enough vessels should the word come for an evacuation of all expatriates. There seemed barely sufficient to take the groups of people even now huddled on their trunks in the long shadows of the warehouses that remained standing between areas strewn with flattened piles of metal and concrete.

At one of the ticketing offices he checked again to see if he could get on the *Vyner Brooke* officially. The young Chinese clerk went through the papers in his files, intermittently asking questions.

'Sorry, sir, no chance,' he said finally. 'But there is another ship going tomorrow morning, the *Madura*. According to our latest communications, we can give you a berth on that.'

'I just saw her. She's fit to sail?'

'Yes, sir.'

Vincent paid immediately. With this and his now obsolete Qantas ticket, he had already used up half his cash. He had woken that morning thinking the relative silence meant the Japanese were still a long way off. He now knew he had only a few hours to get away. Even the next day might be too late. He caught himself crossing his fingers.

21.

Never in all his years at sea had Vincent seen passengers take a lifeboat drill so seriously. At the end, the first officer announced that if planes were sighted everyone was to go to the dining room. It was ten on the morning of February 2, 1942, quiet and calm. The *Madura* had left Singapore just after sunrise and was now steaming slowly through the Riau Archipelago. While most of the passengers were European expatriates or members of well-off Chinese families, there were some other men on their own. One with his arm in a sling was also a Kiwi, Vincent thought, judging by his accent.

Vincent had been given a small cabin to himself. He took the map from his satchel and checked it against the newspaper articles he had cut out the day before, looking again at all possible shipping and overland routes into Hong Kong. The Japanese superiority in the air and the speed with which they had destroyed the capability of the British to defend themselves had allowed them to rapidly take complete control of the territory. Many of their soldiers were now so far down the Malay Peninsula that the date of the fall of Singapore must be a mere detail to be decided upon by their generals. They could probably walk into the town centre in a matter of hours if they chose to.

The soft breeze and the hum of the engines, combined with the gentle rocking and the shifting light through his porthole, lulled Vincent into a doze. Suddenly he heard the captain calling for the alarm to be sounded, then the rising and descending whine. As he raced to the dining room clutching his life jacket he heard the engines of far-off planes.

An elderly man with a walking stick was sitting beside one of the long tables. The rest of the passengers were silently leaning with their backs against the walls. Some children were huddling with their mothers; the rest were playing under tables.

There was the sound of a plane high above them, and after a long pause a loud dull bang against the side of the ship. 'Be stunned fish for dinner then.' The man with his arm in a sling shuffled into the space next to Vincent. 'I guess so,' Vincent answered with a wan smile.

A baby started to cry and scream, then another and another, until their combined wailing drowned out all other noise. Vincent thought of Marie as he watched four Chinese children push even closer under their mother's arms. By the time the ship's single gun began to fire, most people had their heads in their hands.

The next explosion was deafening. The ship had obviously taken a direct hit. There was a roar of tearing metal and voices yelling in the corridors. Then the lights went out.

'Are we listing?' the man next to Vincent said. 'Can you hear water coming in?' And then, 'Can you hear me?'

'I can't hear any water,' Vincent said. 'If we're holed it will take a few minutes before we list.'

'Do we wait for a signal to go to the boats?'

'We should just hold tight. How's your arm?'

'No worse than usual.'

Some passengers sprinted to the door but were prevented from leaving by a young Indian seaman standing guard.

'Listen. Is that the plane?'

Vincent shook his head.

The lights came on again.

'That's reassuring.'

'It certainly is. It means they're able to keep the engines running.'

Another young seaman came to the door. 'We need volunteers from the men.'

Vincent and six others got to their feet.

'Good on you,' the man said. 'Take a few of those young fellows with you. I'd just be in the way with this bloody arm. Good luck.'

The corridors were filled with dense smoke. Vincent stumbled to the aft of the ship and stood in the bucket-line. It was a relief to see that the bomb had hit above the waterline, even if it had destroyed a good part of the promenade deck.

'How is it?' Vincent shouted to the captain.

'Five dead. A lot injured. They were too high up for our gun.'

'How's the hull?'

'Looks like we'll be all right. Fire's out. Could you and one of the young blokes help us with the injured?'

As Vincent and another man stepped over and around twisted pieces of sheet metal, they saw that the bomb had exploded somewhere between the refrigerator and the sickbay.

'Bloody hell. We've been lucky, eh,' the man said.

'You feel up to this?' Vincent stepped out of the way of a running crew member as his companion got his first look at the mix of blood, oil and water coating the floor. As a breeze blew away some of the smoke they could see dismembered limbs, and gashed and bleeding sailors leaning against the wall.

'Just tell me what you need me to do,' the man said.

With help from some of the crew, and frequently tripping and falling as they went, Vincent and the man ferried the wounded sailors up to the music room.

The all-clear sounded. 'See what painkillers, splints and bandages you can salvage from the sickbay,' Vincent said.

'I assume the doctor was in there?'

'Blown to pieces, according to the captain. Same with the second steward.'

As Vincent tried to organise the men on the floor of the music room, he was astounded by the bravery of the Indian sailors. None was screaming or moaning. One had been just outside the refrigerator when the bomb hit. As Vincent took hold of his head to check the deep cuts around one ear, his hair disintegrated into ash.

The man had found some bandages. There were no splints, he said. All pills had been smashed; they were lying among splinters of glass at the bottom of the medicine cabinets.

Vincent asked around the crew. An officer offered to get a bottle of chlorodyne from his cabin. When he returned with it, Vincent read the instructions and decided to give the maximum dose to everyone who was in pain. He dispatched his assistant to search for whisky and any other spirits. Meanwhile, he asked a crew member to get a saw and sheets of thin metal or wood from the engine-room workshop. Using torn sheets and twine, he worked with two crewmen to make troughs in which to lay smashed legs.

One after another the men were treated. When Vincent judged that the large doses of alcohol or chlorodyne were having some effect, he would attempt to line up each shard of bone. Handling the men's limbs felt like trying to manipulate broken pieces of bottle in a wet sack. 'These will never heal,' a voice in his head said over and over again. The men bit silently on wooden offcuts.

The ship stopped early the next day. There had been no enemy sightings for a good twelve hours. The captain's assessment was that the closest islands and channels were unlikely to conceal Japanese planes or ships.

Having learned of Vincent's extensive experience at sea, and recognising his work helping the injured men, he had asked him to be part of the funeral ceremonies. Vincent dressed in his chief engineer's uniform, trying in vain to smooth out the creases. The morning was silent, with calm water in every direction. The sun was just rising. Benedictions, prayers and short eulogies were said before the bodies of the doctor and the second steward slid off a plank into the sea. The men would lie for eternity in the depths of the ocean.

The ceremony for the three Indian crewmen was then taken by a holy man, a senior member of the crew. The lilt and rhythm of his words moved Vincent deeply. With great sensitivity and gentleness the three bodies were lowered one by one into the water from a lifeboat tied to the ship. Throughout, the holy man cradled the men's necks, shoulders and heads as if they were babies being bathed.

Later that morning a northeasterly wind picked up. The propellers started again and the ship cruised comfortably. By late afternoon they were at a river mouth near Palembang in Sumatra in the Dutch East Indies. As they made their way upriver, thunder filled the air. The ship tied up at seven that night. Passengers were kept on board as injured crew members were carried to ambulances waiting on shore.

22.

Immigration officers came aboard. They agreed to let women and children wanting to disembark go onshore and take the train south to Batavia. Many had been shaking constantly since the bombing. What if the already damaged ship took another hit while at the port?

The women filed down the gangplank, clutching their children. The grey skin under their eyes showed their stress

and exhaustion. Word came that there were places left on
the trains if any men wanted to leave. After a few sideways
glances, a number of men rose wordlessly and went to
pack their bags. Only half returned to the top deck to say
goodbye.

As the ship steamed out of the river mouth, the remaining
passengers went to the starboard railing and took in the
sobering view of a ship's funnel protruding from the calm
twilight sea. They were still within the range of Japanese
bombers.

The engines rumbled at full speed through the night in
a drive to be clear of the channel when the sun rose. At six-
thirty Vincent woke and took a cup of tea up on deck.
The ship was following a zigzag course and there were no
islands or other ships in sight. At ten o'clock a Catalina
flying boat, the first friendly plane the passengers had seen,
flew overhead. It seemed to be keeping a watchful eye
on them.

At the wharf in Batavia, passports were quickly and
efficiently processed. As the men passed through the gates,
an official from the local colonial authority directed each
of them to a bus or car that would take them to the house
of a trader or civil servant. Vincent and his fellow Kiwi,
whom he now knew by his surname, Robb, were billeted
in the substantial house of a man whose wife and family
had left for safety a month earlier. They exchanged news
with their host and another man staying at the house. They
were lucky to have got out of Singapore, their host told
them. From what he'd heard, they would have been among
the last to leave.

The men retired well before midnight. Vincent left the
doors of his room open to the wide terrace. Through the

bed's mosquito netting he studied the room. The potted orchids, polished mahogany floors and jungle-like garden of flowers and ferns made him think of Marie. She would have loved this place. It was the sort of house she'd always said she wanted: a large living room and dining table for entertaining, an impeccable mirror-like floor.

He took out the photographs he'd transferred from his luggage into his wallet – one of Marie, one of Margaret, Marie junior and Cynthia, one of Marie with baby Vincent. He remembered how stunned he'd been when he was introduced to Marie by his friend Jack's Portuguese fiancée, Adelaide. He was usually shy and awkward with women, but to his surprise Marie had seemed to like him right away. She could have had any man and yet she chose him. She had even had to break off a relationship with another man to marry him.

His thoughts went back to the day he had taken that photograph of her on their balcony. Marie liked posing. Even after ten years, her beauty still took his breath away. She was warm, intelligent, a loving if not always present mother. She never stopped startling him. Most incredibly, she seemed to love him. When would he get to wake up next to her again?

23.

Batavia was full of dishevelled men from Singapore. How had they all got there, Vincent wondered. One day, rushing around a corner he came face to face with the Hungarian manager of his guest house in Singapore. He was flanked by some colleagues from the Singapore volunteer defence unit and had a small rifle strapped over his shoulder. Two days

before departing Singapore, Vincent had spotted him leaving
for his defence station. With similar disbelief he encountered
a group of men from one of Williamson's ships at a roadside
café. They told him their ship had been sunk but the crew
had survived.

Every day Vincent applied for travel papers, checked
for telegrams and helped Robb get medical attention.
He also developed a new obsession: reading lists on bulletin
boards. There were lists of the known dead; lists of people
who had reached Batavia from Singapore; lists of people
who were missing and those who were looking for them;
lists of ships that had been sunk. He also checked vessels
and planes that might be departing and put his name on
their lists.

He was now out of money. The local bank manager
informed him that since his accounts were officially in Hong
Kong and Hong Kong was occupied territory, they couldn't
help. After several anxious days he found a sympathetic
Qantas branch manager who agreed to refund his flying-boat
ticket for cash.

Air raids on the town became ever more frequent. One
day, as Vincent was having a cup of tea with a group of old
and new acquaintances and telling them he had to get to
Sydney, they saw black columns of smoke rising from the
direction of the airfield. The men laughed. 'You'd better
hurry,' one said, 'or the Japs will make it there before you.'

Each day the lists of the dead grew longer. After a week
Vincent began to worry. For every familiar face he saw in
the street, there should be many more. He started making
a mental list of the people who hadn't turned up. They
mightn't all pass through Batavia, but there were few other
routes out of Singapore.

The next day there was a new announcement pinned to the town's noticeboard. The *Vyner Brooke* had been sunk in the Bangka Strait, just off Sumatra.

24.

After two weeks, with the Japanese rapidly closing in, Vincent managed to get passage to Perth on a Blue Funnel Line ship, the *Charon*. He and Robb were put in a cabin with fourteen other men and told it was that or nothing. They sat out a twenty-hour delay on their bunks in heavy humid weather. People continued boarding the ship until the last possible moment, filling it to the brim.

Soon after the ship sailed, the two men were given their own cabins. The solitude became a burden. Vincent's thoughts raced from one scenario to another. If the British struck a deal with the Japanese to evacuate British women and children from Hong Kong, would his family, earnestly blending in with the local population, miss out?

Heading south, away from Hong Kong, didn't feel right. Perhaps he had been too hasty getting on this ship? If he'd waited in Batavia he might have been able to get first-hand news from people coming out of Hong Kong. Maybe he could have even got back to mainland China. Back in his early years working from Hong Kong, he had watched from the deck of his ship as an elderly chief engineer gave up an attempt to row back to the ship in a bad storm after carrying out a survey of a stranded vessel close to the Chinese coast. The man had left the lifeboat on the beach and signalled that he would make his way back to Hong Kong overland.

This had amazed Vincent. Although he'd spent fifteen years working along the coast of mainland China, the countryside outside the port cities was completely unknown to him. He'd only ever observed it from the safe vantage point of river channels. Three days later, only twenty hours after they arrived in Hong Kong, the old man had walked into the company's office. He had zigzagged through a series of villages and hitched rides down the peninsula.

MARIE

25.

Ah Sup was taking her turn as lookout. She called out to Lizzie that a strange amah, someone she'd never seen before, was entering the building. Lizzie opened the door slightly, just enough to watch and listen as the woman climbed the stairs. Clutching a broom as a weapon, she prepared to turn her away.

The stranger finally reached the top floor.

'Lizzie,' she said.

'Mrs Ma! Is it really you?' Lizzie flung open the door. Marie emerged in her dressing gown, rubbing her eyes. A woman in rough working clothes was standing in the living room. It was not until the woman grinned that she recognised her. Kay Ma was an old friend, a Chinese American from Montana.

'Come into my room and change out of those clothes, Kay,' she said. 'Lizzie, please make some tea.'

'No, no,' Kay said. 'I can't stay. I have a lot of things to do. How are you all?' She seemed nervous and alert, as though ready to turn and leave at any moment.

'We're all right,' Marie said, 'but you're crazy to come

here. There are Japanese everywhere. Are you still living in
your flat?'

'Yes, yes.' Kay spoke rapidly. 'I have a big favour to ask.'

'How did you get across the harbour?'

'On the ferry. I was okay though – the disguise works.
I need your help.'

'Of course. What for?'

'You're the only person I could think of who might come
with me.'

'Why, what do you want to do?'

'My boys. I haven't seen my boys for two weeks.' Her
voice quavered.

'Oh, Kay.'

'They're not in any of the camps. One of their friends is
though. He told me they've both been hurt but are still alive,
thank God. He didn't know where they'd been taken. I want
to go to all the hospitals today. Will you come with me?'

'Sit down,' Marie said. 'I'll get ready. Ah Sup, please get
me one of your work outfits and shoes.'

Lizzie followed Marie into the bedroom.

'Are you sure?' she said.

'Look, Kay needs my help. I have to help her.'

'But what if something happens to you? What about the
children and us?'

'Kay's boys are hurt.' Marie sounded determined.

Lizzie hesitated, took a few steps back and stood motionless in the corner, unsure what to say next.

'Lizzie, I'll be fine. Nothing happened to Kay coming
here.' Marie straightened up, looked in the mirror and ruffled
her hair. 'There are a lot of things we're missing out on here.
They could be giving away rice in Causeway Bay and we'd
never know.'

After she put the finishing touches to her disguise she joined Kay in the living room. 'Shall we go?' she said.

The two women headed in the direction of Bowen Road Hospital. It was an hour's walk away and the roads were hilly. It took some time for Marie to get used to wearing Ah Sup's flat shoes but she felt an overwhelming sense of freedom. This was tempered with fear when they passed groups of Japanese soldiers. It was strange to see the streets almost completely empty of Europeans. People who passed them made no eye contact and hurried past with their heads bowed. Many shops had reopened but they noticed the shelves were nearly empty. There were barely any cars on the roads.

At an intersection, a large group of Japanese soldiers marched past in formation, making clopping noises with their hard-soled boots. They had obviously requisitioned the boots from the British army: up until then Marie had seen soldiers wearing only light rubber-soled boots that allowed them to move with stealth.

At the next intersection, just before the rise to the hospital, the women were stopped by two soldiers. In heavily accented Cantonese the soldiers demanded to know where they were going.

'Wilson-san.' At first Marie didn't understand what Kay was attempting to say. It took a few seconds for her to detach the Japanese word 'san' from the name. Bill Wilson was a man they both knew well. He lived near the hospital. There had long been rumours that he was an enemy spy. These were based solely on the fact his mother was Japanese.

They were allowed to pass, but Marie felt her heart racing. 'Tell me when you're going to do things like that, Kay.'

'Don't worry,' Kay said. 'I've been planning this for days. Just let me do the talking and if they want to search us let me go first. They're stupid. You'll see. We are going to be fine.'

On entering the large open ward of the hospital they opened the tops of their tunics to reveal their Western-style blouses, suspecting the staff might ignore questions from people they thought were only poor servants. A young nurse spoke to them. When Kay explained she was looking for her sons and described them, the nurse led her to them at once. It seemed a miracle. Both young men had been shot but seemed to be healing well. It seemed they were being treated according to the conventions of war.

As Kay quietly spoke with them Marie walked through the wards. She thought she recognised a number of faces but didn't want to cause them or herself trouble by greeting them.

'Do you want to go home?' Kay had caught up with her.

'No, I want to see if I can find my friend Arthur. Also Lofty and Harris. They aren't here but perhaps they are in Queen Mary.'

Queen Mary Hospital was nearly two hours away. After about an hour's walking they reached a Japanese checkpoint. Older women, men and children appeared to be going through the checkpoint freely, but young women were being detained. Marie and Kay hesitated and looked at each other. They had passed the point of no return. To turn now could attract undue attention.

Kay went first. The soldier forced her to raise her arms and then pressed his hands down the sides of her torso and around her back. He crouched down and checked her shoes and ankles. He rubbed his hands up the insides of her legs and pressed hard at the top, forcing his fingers firmly against her crotch. He then pushed his hands up inside her top and on to her breasts, closing his thumbs and index fingers on her nipples.

'That's not searching!' Marie was sure the soldier didn't understand Kay's Cantonese but she sounded authoritative.

The soldier raised his arm and slapped Kay across the face.

Marie started silently praying, worried that Kay would retaliate, but her friend said nothing more. The soldier uttered a verbal barrage, complete with a shot of saliva, and shoved Kay through the passage between the barbed wire fences.

She didn't stop for Marie until she was fifty yards down the road. 'It's going to be like this,' she said. 'Every day. We just have to get used to it.'

'You have to control your anger though,' Marie said. 'You can't yell at them and expect to not get slapped. I was scared for you. It's just not worth it.'

'The slapping doesn't matter, Marie,' Kay said. 'Almost all the women I know around my house have been hit. We say it makes you a member of the Kiss Kiss Club. I'm a member now. I've joined the Kiss Kiss Club.' She laughed.

The women continued through back streets, avoiding checkpoints. In some narrow alleys the smell of rotting bodies shoved against the walls made them retch. In the worst places they pinched their noses and tried to hold their breath. Some corpses looked recent, others as though they'd been there since before the surrender. All were naked, their clothes stolen long ago. In some cases skin gaped open, revealing tendons, veins and bones.

When at last they made it to Queen Mary Hospital, Marie asked among the patients. Had anyone seen her friends? She was directed to lists in the corridors. There was no sign of

Arthur, Lofty or Harris. She asked a nurse where else they might be, explaining they weren't soldiers but worked in the office of the Hong Kong police. They might not have been imprisoned, the nurse said. They could be part of the group being forced by the Japanese to help with the handover of the colony's administration.

Kay checked the nearest list again. The name of a friend jumped out at her. When the women found Harry Long, their hearts sank. He had lost a leg. In its place there was a bulky bandaged stump.

'Kay, Marie, what a sight you two are.' Harry smiled. 'What's happened to you? Look what they've bloody done to me,' he said, gesturing at his leg.

'What did you do to the Japs to get that sort of treatment?' Kay said.

'Just minding my own business. Bomb landed right next to me. Didn't hurt particularly. Honestly. Bloody thing didn't come off properly though. I was a sitting duck in the middle of the street. Ears ringing like nobody's business, and more planes and bombs coming every few minutes. Dead weight, slowed me down like you can't imagine, having to drag around that lump of steak and bone.'

Seeing that his efforts to make light of the situation were not working, he fell silent.

'They haven't knocked the wind out of you,' Marie said.

'Never. How are you girls anyway? Where's Vincent?'

'He's in Singapore.'

'Oh, Marie.'

'I'm sure he's all right. We've just found Kay's boys in Bowen Road Hospital.'

'All right I hope?'

'They're fine,' Kay said and began to cry. Marie had been

expecting this all day. Even so she was surprised. Kay had seemed so stoic.

'You two need to look after yourselves,' Harry said. 'Don't go out any more. Don't come back here to see me. The nurses won't tell you, but there have been some horrible goings-on. They've sworn a pact of silence among themselves, but I know no young woman is safe. Go now, before it gets too late.'

26.

Marie walked quickly past Lizzie and closed the bedroom door. After she'd had a sleep she'd tell Lizzie about some of the terrible things she'd seen and why it had seemed safer to stay the night at Kay's flat.

The children followed her with their eyes. Lizzie had fretted when Marie hadn't come home. It had been a long night. The children had picked up on her anxiety.

Later that day, standing at her bedroom window, Marie saw something she had trouble believing. Two European men, one tall, one short, were walking up the hill carrying sacks of rice on their shoulders.

She ran down the stairs to meet them. Lofty and Harris dropped the sacks on the ground and took turns to wrap their arms tightly around her. 'Thank God you're all right, Marie,' Lofty said. 'And the girls?'

'We're fine. But you two, where have you been? I've been so worried. Yesterday Kay Ma and I searched for you at Queen Mary's.'

'It's a long story,' Harris said.

They had remained free longer than most British people on the island because, as the nurse had suggested, the

Japanese authorities had needed them to keep managing police affairs until they could take complete control. Neither man had been harmed but such luck had been rare among their friends.

They weren't sure how long they'd be free. They might soon be interned. They'd heard the Japanese were vicious captors and the conditions harsh. Because of their work in the police they knew the sites the Japanese were using as camps all too well. Sanitation would be poor, space limited and food in short supply. They feared there would be frequent beatings.

They passed on a smidgeon of good news. On January 9, Lindsay Ride, an Australian doctor who'd been head of the Field Ambulance in Hong Kong and a colonel in the volunteers regiment, had managed to escape from the camp at Sham Shui Po Barracks in Kowloon and flee to Free China. The camp would undoubtedly be made more secure, but further such escapes might be possible.

Before they left, the men apologised for not bringing sugar. They had been carrying a sack but a pair of Japanese soldiers had taken it from them on the final leg up to the flats. A lot of new food shipments had been let through since the surrender, they said. Some stores in the centre of town now had rice, vegetables and poultry. Despite a disapproving look from Lizzie, Marie announced she would go down to the town next day.

27.

Marie walked along the painted line in the middle of the road, determined not to look at the expressionless faces of people standing in the doorways. Sweat trickled inside her layers of winter clothing, down her neck and on to her shoulder, where she'd balanced the twenty-pound sack of rice. Whenever someone crossed the street she slowed down so they wouldn't come too close. There could be a frenzy if someone knocked the sack and its contents spilled on to the street.

When she got back to the flat, she sat down exhausted at the kitchen table. In a notebook she added to the list of food supplies that came into the flat and what was used each day. She had left three more sacks of rice downtown. As usual the shopkeeper had refused to give her change, but this time she had been able to take goods to at least two-thirds of the face value of the large bank note. What she couldn't carry back up the hill that day she had left in storage at a shop owned by Kay's uncle.

She went to the bathroom and took off her blouse. There were white wavy patterns on her skin where the salt from her sweat had dried. She removed her bra and silk underpants and examined herself in the mirror. The underpants were old. She had meant to throw them out before all this happened. She folded them and put them carefully on a shelf.

Using one of Vincent's rough facecloths to clean herself with soapy water, she took stock of the changes to her body. She had always been slim but a month with little food had caused bumps to protrude at the top of her hip bones. The once smooth flesh on her legs and ankles was now intersected with tendons and muscles. Her breasts had shrunk. She could count almost all her ribs.

She put on her dressing gown but couldn't bring herself to leave the sanctuary of the bathroom. She sat on the edge of the tub and continued to stare in the mirror.

The renewed hope that came from securing the sacks of rice quickly evaporated. Even if they kept to the restricted regime they had grown used to, the food would last them only three weeks. Five weeks after that, even if Marie were lucky enough to find provisions at the same price, their money would run out. If Vincent didn't send funds by the end of March, they would run the risk of starving.

One question had been haunting her. She wouldn't be able to keep paying the amahs, but how could she tell them? If they wanted to stay she could feed and house them for a short time, but that was all. She knew they sent most of their pay to their families on the mainland, whose situation must now be desperate. The money their daughters sent was not for luxuries but survival. Now it was a choice between these families and Marie's. When Hong Kong was thriving, the expatriates and Chinese businesspeople had barely noticed the small amount they paid their staff. Now everyone was in the same situation, struggling to have enough food and other basic necessities to stay alive.

Marie looked again into the mirror, noticing the redness of her eyes and the deep shadows under them. No, she thought, she had to tell the amahs right away. It would clear the air. She gathered herself together.

Lizzie understood immediately. She was prepared to stay, even without pay. Could Mary stay also? She could send her to stay with her brother for part of the time. 'Yes,' Marie said. 'That would be best.'

Marie and Lizzie explained the situation to the other three amahs. They would be paid in full for their work up until that day. After that they could stay but they could not be paid. None spoke directly to Marie but their anger and resentment was palpable: this was not the way honest servants should be treated in hard times.

Marie felt she had done all she could. She had treated the amahs equally and left them to decide for themselves who would go and who would stay. She would like the cook to remain but she knew this would be unfair: cooks had more chance than other amahs of finding paid work.

The next day Ah Sup told Marie she would stay. The cook, Ah Ng, left and quickly found work with the Japanese. Ah So returned to Macau, where she had lived before getting the job with Marie and Vincent. There were now eight in the flat, or seven when Mary was staying with her uncle.

28.

Across the small stacks of vegetables the two women acknowledged each other. Marie raised her eyebrows and nodded self-consciously. The woman looked back with an expression of abject sadness. Marie thought her husband was an English importer. She was certain Vincent knew him. They lived nearby and had seen each other at the usual parties but had never spoken directly.

Marie flashed a quick smile before moving into the covered part of the market to examine the overpriced fish on display.

'It's Marie isn't it?'

Marie swung around. 'Yes.' She turned back to face the fish stand so they would not draw attention to themselves. 'I'm sorry, I don't know your name.'

'Lily. You're still here. I was surprised to see you. Where is Vincent?'

'He was in Singapore last news we had. With God's will he'll be somewhere else now. And your husband?'

'He went to Sydney in November.'

'We were the unlucky ones, weren't we?' Marie said.

The woman looked on the verge of tears.

'I'm sure they're better off where they are,' Marie continued. She glanced around nervously. 'They'd stand out like sore thumbs here.'

Marie noticed the stallkeepers were looking at them intently. Luckily, a Japanese soldier standing in the corner was yet to notice them.

'Do you want to go to the teahouse?' she said softly.

'I'd like that very much,' the woman said, 'if it's not going to inconvenience you.'

They took a table near the front window. At first they made small talk about where they lived, whether they still had water, gas and electricity, and what the Japanese had been doing in their respective neighbourhoods. It struck Marie that they could have been talking about the weather, but Lily seemed increasingly agitated. Eventually she began to sob. 'I'm so sorry,' she murmured.

'Don't be silly. Things aren't easy.' Marie was polite but she was growing frustrated. She wanted to move on. She was worried at the lack of care this woman was taking in public.

'How many children do you and Vincent have?' Lily said. 'I don't remember. Are they all here?'

'Three girls and a baby boy. Look, I had better get back to them.'

'Be careful with the girls, Marie.'

'Yes, I know. We've heard the screaming. We make sure none of them are ever alone.'

'Good.'

'It was nice to see you,' Marie said. 'I'm sorry I can't help you more. You seem to be having a very hard time.'

'Yes. But I'll survive.'

Marie stood and offered to pay for the tea. Lily remained sitting. She gazed out the window, away from the other people in the teahouse. After paying, Marie tried to get her attention to wave goodbye, but she was frozen, her elbow on the table, her chin resting on her hand.

Marie walked back to her. 'Good luck,' she said.

The woman continued to gaze out the window. Then she said something in a low voice.

'Lily,' Marie said impatiently, 'I'm sorry I didn't hear you.'

Lily turned to face Marie and took her hand firmly in both of hers. She talked even more quietly, but this time she mouthed her words with exaggerated emphasis.

'We were raped, Marie,' she said.

Marie sat back down without letting go of her hand. 'I am so sorry.' She leaned in closer. The woman was staring back at her, as if she wanted Marie to read something in her eyes.

'Who is "we"?' Marie said.

'They raped me, and then they raped my daughter.' She spoke in a flat even tone as tears poured from her eyes. 'She's only thirteen, Marie. Damn them to hell.'

Marie squeezed her hand. She felt numb.

'What's my husband going to say?'

Marie couldn't help looking around to see if any Japanese soldiers were watching them. 'He'll understand,' she said.

'I tried my hardest to protect her.'

Marie gripped the woman's hand even harder. 'He'll understand.'

'I tried. They followed her upstairs from my mother's flat. She never even left the building. I thought she'd be safe. They were standing behind her, two of them, when I opened the door for her. She was crying and they'd already torn her dress.'

'You don't have to—'

'I tried, I really did. I pulled her in. They pushed past me and tried to grab at her when she ran to hide behind me.' Her breath made a whining noise as she filled her lungs. 'I told them to take me. When they didn't understand I took a hand of the one who was trying to grab at her and put it on me. And then he understood. And they took me.'

Marie forced herself not to shake. She glanced around. Everyone in the room was looking at them and then out the window anxiously.

Lily was now weeping uncontrollably. Marie moved around the table to sit next to her and placed her arm across her shoulder. They lowered their heads until they were nearly touching the table. 'But they took her anyway. They took her anyway. They held me down and I couldn't move or scream.'

Marie helped her up out of her seat, and taking their shopping bags in her other hand, guided her outside. At a quiet secluded bench on the other side of the market she kept hold of Lily's hand until she began breathing normally again. Then she explained she had to go home to see her children. She was so sorry. Her words sounded pathetic. She walked home silently. As soon as she'd passed her shopping on to Ah Sup, she left the flat and went straight to her church.

29.

The man who entered behind the two Japanese soldiers was dressed in a completely different style of uniform. Marie deduced that he must be an officer. She remained seated on the couch. The man bowed his head to her and placed his hand on baby Vincent's head, despite Lizzie's efforts to turn away.

'We have no food for you,' Marie said.

There was a pause as the translator, a local man Marie knew by sight, politely conveyed her words. The officer cast a look at Marie that gave nothing away. Lizzie and Ah Sup glanced at him, trying to gauge what he would do next. When he didn't speak immediately they bowed their heads to the ground.

Hands clasped behind his back, the man walked across the living room into the main bedroom, then into the study and the children's rooms and back through the kitchen.

When he next spoke the translator seemed even more courteous. 'He asks if you have any friends nearby.'

While he waited for an answer, the officer picked up one of Marie's favourite Ming bowls, the best in her collection. Marie looked at him and then down at the floor before replying.

'Yes.'

The officer and the translator spoke softly to each other.

'These are all your girls, he asks,' the translator said.

'Yes. The baby is a boy.'

The men spoke again.

'The colonel says you have a very beautiful family.'

'What does he want?' Marie's voice cracked.

The officer's eyebrows rose slightly as this was translated.

'The colonel needs to borrow your flat. The colonel is sorry for any inconvenience but it is unavoidable.'

'What about my children? Where are they supposed to sleep?'

'The colonel hopes you may stay at one of your friends' homes. You will be free to move about wherever you wish.'

'You can't take our food. We need that food.'

The two men conferred.

'The colonel says that he does not want to deprive your family of food.'

Marie was unsure what to say or do. In the silence that followed, the colonel took out a small book, looked at it carefully, and in a slow deliberate voice formed an English sentence.

'You should not be afraid, Madame. All officers of the Imperial Japanese Army are gentlemen.'

30.

Marie and Jane moved about distributing red hong bao envelopes to the children and the amahs. The New Year greeting 'Gung hay fat choy' rang out around the room. The children knew not to have high expectations. Jane joked to one of her boys that he should keep the money safe because she might have to borrow it back later. Meanwhile the men set up the mahjong table.

Back in the kitchen Marie sliced onions and peppers into thin strips under Jane's guidance. She was learning to cook and had helped prepare at least one meal a day during the two weeks they had lived with Jane and Tony. The women's friendly conversation filtered out into the other room. Occasionally, when the subject was delicate, their voices dropped to a whisper.

Marie had returned to her flat that morning to collect the hong bao envelopes she had saved. The colonel had let her walk about freely while he worked on papers and files

arranged in orderly piles on the dining table. Music filled
the room from a gramophone. She thought she recognised
it as Mozart.

She had expected to find her furniture rearranged or even
missing. She had prepared herself to reproach the colonel
if she found him at Vincent's desk, using his pens. Instead
she saw he had gone as far as to arrange a cloth underneath
his gramophone to protect the polished wood of the sideboard. Her bed had been made up with his linen, and her
belongings were carefully folded and stacked on one side of
the wardrobe.

She had quickly found the red envelopes and made her
way to the front door, planning to leave without saying a
word. Just as she reached the door the colonel had stood,
bowed and wished her a well-rehearsed 'Happy New Year'.

She stopped and looked at him. 'Happy New Year,' she said.

The mahjong session continued long into the night.
Afterwards, Marie found it difficult to get to sleep. Huddled
on a mattress in the corner of the room she shared with
Lizzie, Ah Sup and the children, she used a torch to read
a romance novel, one of the sort she had hidden from the
girls after they learned to read. She tried to picture where
Vincent might be. Safe and sound in a hotel, she hoped, his
feet sticking out over the end of the standard bed as usual,
his arms under his head, thinking about her and the children.

31.

The young man behind the counter of the telegraph office
seemed determined to talk to her. He spoke quietly, barely

moving his mouth. His English was faultless. 'It's not very good news I'm afraid,' he said. It was official: Singapore had fallen and the governor had surrendered.

Marie stumbled down the steps of the building and sat in the park to gather her thoughts. This explained why she hadn't heard anything. At least Singapore had managed to hold out for over two months. That would have left plenty of time for Vincent to escape. If he'd wrapped up the salvage job at the beginning of December, he might have reached Australia by now.

As she started to walk towards Happy Valley, Jane saw her from across the road.

'What's wrong?'

'Singapore has surrendered.'

'Oh, Marie. But you knew that had probably happened. Vincent will be fine. He'll be in Sydney trying to get money to you.'

'I want to go straight home. I don't have the energy to carry stupid sacks of rice today.'

'Marie, the rice could cost twice as much tomorrow.'

'I don't care.'

Jane had learnt that the Red Cross had started to negotiate with the Japanese, but there were still no systems in place to help the wounded, sick, hungry and imprisoned.

'How long is it going to take?' Marie said. 'We have barely enough money for another month.'

'Something will happen. We'll be all right,' Jane said.

'What about Chiang Kai-shek's army and the British forces in China – what are they doing?'

'The Red Cross lady said that there is no hope of anyone liberating us. She said we should be rationing for the long term. The Japanese are even going to change the currency. Imagine that – all our money will be worthless.'

'Just walk with me, will you?'

Jane agreed, on the condition they bought at least a few provisions before heading home.

As Marie and Jane walked up the final hill, a Japanese soldier came out of the front door of a building. He was wearing filthy dishevelled army pants and a tunic. Moving towards the two women he stood facing them, took out his penis and urinated into the gutter.

VINCENT

32.

After a long pause the train began to move again. The last person to get off to stretch his legs, Vincent had to run to catch up and leap back on board. The train was packed. Sleeping cars had been replaced with regular carriages to accommodate the massive numbers of men desperate to get from Perth to their homes in Melbourne, Sydney or beyond. The canvas blind covering the window of Vincent's carriage offered little respite from the searing heat of the Nullarbor Plain.

It was March 6, a week since Vincent had landed in Australia and over a month since he'd got out of Singapore. He'd managed to jump to the top of the long list for a place on the train thanks to Robb, who'd told the ticketing officer he needed Vincent to accompany him because of his damaged arm.

The excitement was palpable. The men on board had escaped extraordinary danger. They would soon see their families again. Each would probably receive a hero's welcome. Vincent felt like an outsider, with his family far away.

33.

Melbourne's diners and bars were under siege from the
thousands of men who'd escaped from Southeast Asia. As in
Batavia and Perth, Vincent was encountering the same
people. A few of them nodded in recognition.

The city's museum was the only place of sanctuary he
could find. For the last fifteen years, when his ship was in
port he'd usually forgo bars and seamen's clubs in favour of
touring a city and its museums with like-minded members
of the crew. He was not surprised, then, at coming across
men from MV *Forafric*, the last ship he'd served on before the
Singapore salvage job, in one of the museum's echoing halls.

During his hours alone in his cabin and on the train
Vincent had made a mental list of who might help him get
a message to Marie if the army and the Red Cross let him
down. The second engineer from the *Forafric* had seemed the
most obvious person. Now he was standing in front of him.

Alberto de Mello was Macanese and Vincent knew him
well: he had spent shore leave with Alberto's family whenever
he and Alberto visited Macau on the same ship. Alberto and
his companions greeted Vincent warmly, but they had bad
news. The *Forafric* had been sunk by the Japanese in the Sulu
Sea, south of the Philippines. Fortunately, the ship had been
close enough to shore for them and the rest of the crew to
make it to safety in lifeboats.

Alberto had sent a telegram to Macau and had received
one back saying his family were well. However, he'd
learned that despite Macau's neutrality its waters were being
thoroughly patrolled by the Japanese and its streets were
crawling with agents and spies. The Japanese were, he said,
unconcerned about the fine line they were walking between

merely keeping tabs on the activities of their British and American counterparts and potentially sparking an international incident with Portugal.

He suggested he and Vincent go to the telegram office and send a coded message that his family could pass on to Marie. As they stood in line with hundreds of others, they composed some words they hoped would not bring unwanted attention to Alberto's family, rendering Vincent's surname in the Portuguese 'Vassoura' and keeping the text free of details. It simply read: 'Mr Vassoura has safely made it to Australia.'

Over dinner Alberto and the other men from the *Forafric* described the horrors they'd faced in the days before the ship was hit. The Japanese patrol boats were ten times faster and more manoeuverable than any of the old merchant ships they were chasing. The men had known for days before the attack that if the Japanese arrived it would be the end. Each had been pushed to the limit by a sense of impotence.

'They can't cover all the seas,' Vincent said. 'Is there *no* way in or out of Hong Kong?'

'Not even if you're in a local vessel,' Alberto said. 'They're searching dhows, sampans, junks, everything.'

'What about overland?'

'From where to where!' Alberto's voice cracked. 'They're everywhere. They're positioned on every point along the coast. Even Chinese coming out are having their papers checked. Any gweilo will be shot on the spot. The best you can do is use the Red Cross to get a message to your wife. Try and get her to go to Macau. It doesn't sound like people have much to eat there, but at least she won't have to deal with Japanese soldiers at every turn.'

On his way back to his hotel room Vincent ran into
Robb. His friend was unusually quiet. Early that morning
he'd gone to the local army base to see if he could help
with intelligence work and had discovered he was far from
the only refugee from Singapore offering his expertise on
Japanese jungle tactics. In hindsight, he confessed to Vincent,
he was glad to have his arm in a sling or he might have
been tempted to get into a fight when a senior officer said
sarcastically, 'With so many experts, I'm surprised there's
a single living Jap soldier in the whole of Asia.' Numerous
able-bodied soldiers who'd fled Singapore were volunteering
to help. It seemed many in the army considered them not
much better than deserters.

34.

The train got into Sydney at seven-thirty in the morning.
Vincent dropped off his bag at the seamen's lodgings, washed
and went straight to the Williamson office. Everyone there
knew of his family's situation. Although they were worried
about burdening him with too much work, they didn't
hesitate to tell him about the problems they'd been encountering. Those of their ships that hadn't been destroyed had
been requisitioned by the Australian army. Their fleet had
been reduced to a single vessel, the *Kenilworth*, but it needed
a lot of rapid work done on it to fulfil contracts in the South
Pacific – largely aid for French Polynesia. Fortunately, there
was enough money to pay for salaries and provisions.

Vincent spent the afternoon making a round of offices
that might help him get more information on Hong Kong
and the chances of getting Marie and the children out. Most

had long queues. Instead of joining them he studied the lists and announcements on their noticeboards. Some lists included familiar names of Chinese friends or their wives who had walked out through Canton in the early days of the occupation. Seeing this gave him more hope than he'd had in weeks.

He finished the day with a whisky in the office with his second-in-command. The man handed him an envelope.

'What's this?'

'Just skip to the last line.'

'Broom dead.'

Vincent grinned. 'Why didn't you tell me earlier?'

'I hadn't told the others. I just got it yesterday. I was waiting for confirmation and then you turned up.'

'Damn,' Vincent said. 'Do you know if it went to Hong Kong too?'

'I don't see how it could have got to your wife, but who knows?'

Next day, Vincent saw Robb off on a hospital ship to New Zealand. Back in the office, between calls to every chandler in Sydney to find the spare parts he needed for the *Kenilworth*, he received a personal telegram. Jean and his mother had survived their voyage in the dhow. They had made it far enough out of Japanese-occupied territory to be wrecked on a reef in the Timor Sea, where they'd been quickly rescued.

Vincent smiled. Jean had had his share of luck after all. But his sense of joy quickly turned to frustration. He was going to be sitting idly in Sydney until the parts he needed arrived. There seemed little he could do for Marie from here. He might be better visiting his parents in New Zealand.

35.

The deep blue sky framed the unmistakable shape of Rangitoto, an extinct volcano, as the ship sailed into Auckland's Hauraki Gulf. The first sight of the island brought a simultaneous sigh from the New Zealanders on board.

Vincent scanned the waiting crowd as he disembarked. Seeing no one familiar, he pushed on through, stopping regularly to rest his suitcases on the dock as parents, wives and lovers hugged new arrivals with unrestrained elation. He was not the only person unable to enter into the high spirits: many others had been in tears during the voyage for those they'd lost in Singapore. They would now have to share and relive the horror with loved ones. As they stumbled off the ship, some needed to be held from falling.

Vincent and his father shook hands firmly, reluctant to let go but wary of coming closer. They said little on the way from the railway station. Did he know how Marie and the children were, his father finally asked. No, Vincent said. The last message had been a letter written a week before the invasion, telling him about the celebrations for Margaret's ninth birthday. Anything could have happened since then.

'They'll be all right,' his father said. 'They look Chinese. The Japs will leave them alone. Why would they bother with a Chinese woman and her children?'

'Perhaps. I just wish I could get closer so I could have better information.'

'Everything will work out.'

As they drove through his parents' town of Te Puke in the Bay of Plenty, Vincent noticed the lack of young men on the streets, and the large number of women in overalls and other work clothes.

'Can you believe we don't have enough food?' his father said. 'Here we are in God's own garden and we can't even get a decent cut of meat.'

'You're getting by though?'

'We're getting by. We're fine. It's all the folk around here who have lost a boy, or even boys in some cases, to this bloody mess in Europe.'

'There've been a lot?'

'Hundreds. Then the Japs come into the Pacific and we can't do a thing. At least the Yanks are finally getting off their bums.'

Vincent's mother Nettie pulled herself up awkwardly from her chair. She had only one leg, the result of a horse and carriage accident when the family lived in Fiji thirty years before. As she and Vincent hugged each other, Vincent sensed her unspoken question. 'No, Mum. Nothing new. I went to the telegraph office in Auckland on the way to the train.'

'Oh, Vincent.' She looked sad, tearful.

How was his sister Dot, he asked. Well, she said. She would visit them the next day. His brother Harry, an army captain, was working as a pharmacist on the *Maunganui*. This was the hospital ship Vincent had put Robb on. He hadn't seen his brother for two years and by a twist of fate he'd missed seeing him when they were probably 50 feet from each other on the dock in Sydney.

That night he didn't sleep as well as he'd hoped. In the years after his mother's leg was amputated, he had often gone to the hospital with her. There he had seen maimed, blinded

and burnt soldiers who had come back from the Great War.
The images were still vivid. Then in 1936, on board a ship,
he had seen headless bodies floating out of the mouth of the
Yangtze. He had seen children as thin as skeletons in the arms
of their exhausted mothers who were trying to get on any
boat or barge that would get them out of Shanghai. In the
silence of the night the memories haunted him. He couldn't
stay here long.

36.

It was well before the dinnertime peak. While most of the
men in town rushed to have an after-work beer in one of
Sydney's harbourside pubs, Vincent sat alone at the corner
table of a small Chinese restaurant. It was April 17, his thirty-
eighth birthday. It was not the first time he hadn't been with
Marie and the children for his birthday, but this time the
pain of separation was almost unbearable. As he watched the
waiter move back and forth among the few other diners he
tried for the thousandth time to imagine what life must be
like in Hong Kong.

In the weeks since Vincent had returned to Australia, his
days had been split in two. Half the time he had been getting
his hands dirty working directly on the *Kenilworth* with the
ship's engineer and the company's small number of remaining
staff. It was complicated work: the exact part required often
had to be improvised. And the pace at which the local men
worked was slower than he was used to in Asia.

The other half of his time was spent dealing with bureau-
cracy. He'd been to the army office responsible for Hong
Kong operations three times. Each time he'd been turned

away by officials with light smiles of sympathy. 'Look,' they would say, 'you have to understand that we just don't have the resources to handle messages for civilians. Have you tried the Red Cross?'

The Red Cross office was staffed by kind volunteers but the message was similar. 'We can't do anything for now, but leave us a message and we'll send it to India and Free China on the chance that things will open up.'

The papers were full of bad news about Asian shipping channels. Nothing was getting through and even Australian waters and harbours were at risk. The country had only a few warships with which to defend its shores, and most of its and New Zealand's soldiers and resources were committed to war zones on the other side of the world.

He had to make a decision. He took out the map again. He could probably get to India. He'd heard that people were making it out of southwest China that way, and it looked to be the only route not blocked by the Japanese. He calculated it would be possible to get there by July.

In India, maybe even in Kunming, southern China's closest city and airport to India, he'd be able to get information from people coming out of Hong Kong and Free China. He might be able to get messages back in and make plans to rescue Marie and the children. He felt increasingly desperate to do something. Anything was better than this living hell of relying on official channels and finding himself always at the bottom of lists.

Where could he get the money to go to India? His father had warned him when war started to leave as much money as he could in Hong Kong and at Marie's disposal in case something happened while he was away. People like his father had lived through the Great War and knew inflation made life

difficult for anyone who wasn't able to work. It was unlikely
he could get money from these accounts: he'd already tried
and failed.

He watched attentively as two men entered the restaurant.
They appeared to be a father and son out celebrating. The son
was in a new army private's uniform. The men sat close
enough to Vincent that he could follow their conversation.

'It comes down to king and country before all else,' the
older man said. 'You'll see. You'll come back a bloody hero.'

'Dad!'

'That's just the way it is.'

Vincent got up from the table and paid his bill at the door.

37.

'Mr Broom—'

'Please, just leave me alone. Close the door behind you.'

Vincent held his head in his hands. 'Christ almighty, why?
What the hell have I done to deserve this?'

He closed his eyes and tried to think rationally. With the
Kenilworth already loaded and only a day away from leaving
for a nine-month contract around the South Pacific, the chief
engineer had slipped on the gangplank and broken his leg.

Vincent's dedication to the codes of conduct and honour
of the merchant navy had never been so tested. Everything
told him he had to take the man's place. There was no one
else capable of ensuring the voyage ran smoothly without
unnecessary danger to the crew. Normally many young men
in New South Wales would have jumped at the opportunity
to take on the job but they were now in the army or navy.
The voyage would take him not only further away from his

family but further away from the first-hand information that might arrive with the streams of escapees and refugees from Asia.

He spent the first days of the voyage alone in the engine room, fine-tuning the newly serviced engines and worrying about his family. He listened religiously to news broadcasts and at each port he went straight to a library to read the newspapers. Any talk among the men about the Japanese had been banned by the captain: he knew accounts of what they might be doing with female prisoners and other women in Hong Kong would be too much for Vincent to bear.

On October 26, news came over the ship's radio that the Americans had bombed the power plant at North Point. The captain knew Vincent's home was only 100 yards from the plant, close enough to have been flattened. He gave the order to turn off all radios on the ship but it was too late: Vincent had been listening in his cabin.

MARIE

38.

A week after learning that Lofty and Harris had been interned in the camp at Stanley, Marie was summoned to her flat by a smartly dressed Japanese soldier. The colonel was leaving Hong Kong the following week and the Imperial Japanese Army would no longer have a need for her home, the translator said. The colonel was thankful for her generosity, and extremely regretful he had caused so much inconvenience to her and her family. 'The colonel would like to offer you a favour in thanks for your kindness. Anything reasonable that is in his power.'

She immediately considered asking him to help her make contact with Vincent, but quickly thought better of it. Divulging any information about her husband could put both of them at risk.

'Please ask the colonel if he might help me visit the Stanley camp,' she said.

The colonel paused for a few seconds while the request was translated, then gave a rapid response. 'The colonel says he will do all in his power to honour your request. He says you should prepare yourself each morning.'

That night she and Jane and Tony debated whether Marie
should put herself in this position. Jane and Tony, who had
not met the colonel, were worried that she had misread the
situation. Could his agreement be just a ploy to get Marie
on her own and unprotected? Marie was prepared to take
the risk. She went to a small shop nearby and bought some
packets of her friends' favourite brands of cigarettes.

Next morning there was a knock on Jane's door. The
colonel himself was standing there. As they walked down the
hill towards a small black car, Marie suddenly felt anxious
about being seen with a Japanese officer. The colonel,
perhaps sensing this, quickly opened the back door for her.

As they drove up the hill and across the island towards
Stanley, Marie was acutely aware of the large number of
soldiers stationed at road blocks and lookouts. Marie
wondered if they thought she was a courtesan.

At the first four barriers the car was saluted and allowed
to pass, but at the fifth they were stopped. A young soldier
signalled to the colonel to open his window. He approached
the car and asked where they were going. The colonel said a
few words. The soldier disappeared into a roadside building
and emerged a few minutes later with an older soldier with
grey hair and an array of medals on his uniform. The man
slid into the front passenger seat and talked quietly with the
colonel.

The car moved on. There was little on the roads apart
from Japanese army traffic. The car wove around and
between a succession of trucks, stores and soldiers marching
in formation before encountering a group of exhausted-
looking Canadian soldiers. They were standing as if on
parade. Some had their hands on their heads. Others seemed
to be filling in a bomb crater in the road. Marie was sure she

recognised the boy she'd danced with. He looked ill. Marie smiled at him. He responded with a look of confusion and hopelessness.

On the final stretch of the road, Marie suddenly felt nervous about entering the camp. What if this *was* a trick and she wouldn't be allowed back out? A soldier stood defiantly in the middle of the road with his legs well apart and his hands on his hips. The car stopped. The colonel and the other man seemed agitated as the soldier strode to the driver's window. Marie's hands began to shake. She stared out the window and tried to examine the security measures around the perimeter of the camp.

Suddenly the older man erupted, spewing forth a loud torrent of words. The soldier snapped to attention. The colonel pointed at his watch. He was giving Marie an hour.

The school grounds seemed larger than she remembered. She could see people at windows. Others were sitting on the steps of the buildings and bungalows. A few British people walked awkwardly past her. She didn't recognise any of them.

She carried on towards a small wooden building and knocked on the door. Someone murmured, 'Come in.' She was sure she knew the voice.

'Marie! My gosh, what are you doing here?' Lofty stood quickly and kissed her on both cheeks, transferring the large cigarette he had been holding to his left hand so he could grasp her wrist.

'Mrs Broom.' The woman with him also got up. Marie recognised her as Williamson's secretary. The two women hugged and stood back to look at one another. 'I was so lucky to find you,' Marie said. 'I've only just come in. You

both seem to be doing all right.' She tried to hide the shock
she felt at seeing them imprisoned like this.

'Why have they put you in here, Marie? Where are the
children?' Lofty said.

'They're fine. They're at home. I've been allowed in to
visit. I am so happy to see you both.'

'You're joking. You could talk your way into anything.'

'You know Mr Williamson is here too,' the woman said.
'He's in one of the bungalows down the hill. I'll go and find
him. How long are you here for?'

'Just an hour.'

'Good, wait here.' She rushed out the door.

There were no chairs in the room. Lofty gestured to her to
sit on the edge of the mattress. He extinguished his cigarette
and placed it carefully on a book on the floor, beside the roll
of clothes she assumed he was using as a pillow.

'Can you believe it?' he said. 'Smoking old tea leaves.'

She could see the sadness in his eyes. She handed him
three packets of cigarettes and told him to hide them before
Williamson arrived.

He told her about their last days of freedom after dropping
off the rice, and small details of their lives in the camp. As he
scratched at the skin of his wrist she noticed how lose his
watchstrap had become. 'It's so good to see you,' he said.
'You're a breath of fresh air. But how did you do it?'

Marie told him how she'd had to give up her house to
the colonel and move to Jane's. 'They're not all bad, are they,'
he said. 'There've been a lot of Chinese women coming
to the wire the last few days – girlfriends, wives, the odd
exceptionally dedicated amah. Sometimes the soldiers make
a real fuss, sometimes they don't. I suppose if people bring
food it's less they have to find for us.'

'What about Arthur?' Marie said. 'Is he here?'

'No, he hasn't been so lucky. Last I heard he'd been sent to the soldiers' camp in Kowloon.'

Their conversation was interrupted by heavy steps up the wooden staircase. Williamson helped Marie to her feet and they kissed each other on the cheek.

'How are you, Marie?' he said.

'I'm doing fine. But you, how are you? I was so worried.'

'We're not doing badly. Have you had any word from Vincent?'

'No. But I know Singapore has fallen.'

'Yes, we heard.'

Williamson told her the last news they'd had from Vincent was five weeks earlier: he'd sent a telegram to the office to say the workshop in Singapore had been destroyed. They had replied via the two local staff that he should try to get to Sydney. Since then the Hong Kong office had been closed.

'Vincent wanted us to come and find you, to see how you were. I'm sorry we couldn't do that. We were put in here so quickly. Now we're relying on Vincent to get us all out of here.' Williamson laughed.

'If he got away in time.' Marie fought to hold back tears.

Williamson offered to give her a list of people he knew were still free and from whom she could borrow money against his name. She carefully wrote down the names and addresses.

After Williamson left, Lofty seemed almost elated by the news of Vincent. 'You must be relieved to know he's not in a place like this,' he said to Marie.

'Mr Williamson didn't say for certain that he'd escaped.'

'Vincent won't fall into any traps. You'll get word soon. He'll be doing all he can to make sure you're all right.'

Marie paused. 'Yes, I know,' she said.

'Keep your chin up.'

'Of course I will.'

They said goodbye on the verandah, shaking hands under the gaze of the men waiting for her in the car. She walked down the path and quietly slipped into the back seat. As the car passed through the gates, the older man turned and looked at her. 'Is the tall man your husband?' he said in perfect English.

'No,' she replied. 'He's just a friend.'

'I have been hearing about your family and your home. Your girls. We will make another gesture to you. From tomorrow there will be a sign in front of your door making it off-limits to all soldiers. In your home you and your girls will be safe.'

39.

Marie watched over the girls as they ate. As a child she'd politely eaten everything that was put in front of her except the wok-sautéed cabbage her father's cook used to prepare, which she detested. Now such cabbage was all her girls had to add to their rice. Baby Vincent was the only one to get an egg. She was careful not to waste a drop as she spooned it into his mouth.

An idea came to her. 'Lizzie, Lizzie,' she shouted in the direction of the kitchen.

Lizzie entered, still chewing a mouthful of the rice she had been sharing with Ah Sup.

'Lizzie, I am going to go out after lunch. Can you get some lessons ready for the girls.'

It took Marie an hour to walk to Lofty's home. She felt a certain urgency. She was already picturing the flat without its clocks and silver; even an amateur thief would be able to get in.

The front door had been forced open. There was not a single grain of rice left in the pantry. The living room, where she and Vincent had spent their last Sunday before Vincent sailed for Singapore, stank of urine and whisky. Marie walked carefully around the smashed bottles, glasses and crockery. Even the frames from photographs of Lofty's family and friends had been taken. The photos lay scattered on the dirty floor. After a quick look in all the rooms, the only useful items she found were some pulp novels in English. She decided to take them with her. She could read them and then use them as fuel.

The scene upset her more than she could have imagined. It was terrible how fragile their lives were, how impossible it seemed that only months earlier they had been oblivious to the misery ahead. She started to leave, but halfway out the door she forced herself to go back inside. She searched under Lofty's bed and behind his bookshelves for something, anything, that might be important to him, even if just for its sentimental value. After ten minutes she had found only a small shaving kit.

40.

'Who is it?' The voice from behind the door was heavily accented.

'My name is Marie Broom. My husband Vincent works for Williamson's Shipping. Can I come in and see Mr Martin?'

'I'll go and ask if he will see you.'

She tried to pull Cynthia as close to the big front door as possible so they would be less conspicuous from the road.

'My master says he can't help you.'

'Please, I just need a loan. I have a note from Mr Williamson.' She stopped and listened for any noise from inside. Perhaps the amah had already left. 'Look, can you let me in at least. I don't like being out in the open like this.'

'My master says no.'

'But I have a note from Mr Williamson. He says he will cover any money that I borrow, that he will pay back Mr—'

'My master says he can't help you.'

'Mr Williamson gave me his name. Did you tell him that? Mr Williamson. From Williamson's Shipping. Please can you let us in. I'm here with my little girl.'

'No, I can't let you in. My master says no.'

'But I have a note from Mr Williamson. Did you tell him that?'

'I told him exactly what you said. He said that Mr Williamson's word wasn't worth anything to him. Now can you please leave our property.'

Cynthia started to cry. She had walked a good four miles and the final part of this hill was too much.

'Just a little further, Cynthia. Come on, Mummy is too tired to carry you.'

They had had to pass through five Japanese checkpoints. The only things to have generated any attention from the guards had been the pretty ribbons at the ends of Cynthia's plaits.

'The next one will be the last house, I promise you. Just a little further.'

Finally, they reached the front gates of another mansion on
the Peak. After double-checking the address, Marie banged
with the palm of her hand on the painted green metal. She
stopped and listened but there was no answer, not even the
sound of someone moving inside.

'Hello! Is anyone home?' She banged again, this time with
her fist. Still no answer.

'I'm hungry, Mummy. Can we go home?'

'Wait!' Marie picked up a stone and started to tap on the
metal. 'Hello. Is anyone there?' Nothing.

She checked her watch. She knew if they didn't leave
soon they wouldn't be back home before the curfew. If they
missed it, she'd have to find some floorspace at a friend's
for Cynthia and her to sleep, and even that couldn't be
guaranteed. Anyone caught in the open after curfew was
forced to stand in the middle of the street until the curfew
was lifted.

She gave a final bang on the door. Still nothing.

Making her way further up the hill towards the tram, she
looked back. At a window of the house a man was watching
them. She shook her head in anger and disbelief.

41.

It was April 17, Vincent's birthday. Margaret insisted a
place be set for him at the head of the dining table. Lizzie
brought out a small bun with sweet coconut in the centre.
The children crowded around, ready to blow out the single
candle.

Margaret turned to her mother. 'We have to sing "Happy
Birthday".' Marie nodded. Marie, Marie junior and Margaret

started singing loudly. Cynthia, though, had forgotten the English words.

'Who should cut the cake?' Margaret said.

'You do it, darling. Just cut it into three – I'm not hungry.'

Marie went into her bedroom. On top of the wardrobe there was an old leather satchel. She retrieved a small photograph of Vincent, placed it on the bedside table and stared at it. From one day to the next, her sense of where he might be changed. Today she saw him in a hotel restaurant in Sydney, surrounded by his work colleagues, all of them drinking to his health. Yesterday she had pictured him stuck in a camp in Singapore, skinnier than usual, but still tanned and dignified. Maybe he had started smoking again, maybe even tea-leaf cigarettes.

42.

At the bank Marie sat next to a woman who was also waiting to see Mr Hyde, another man on Williamson's list. The woman believed her husband had abandoned her, she told Marie. She had had no word from him, but she knew he had made it safely to Vancouver with his business partner because the partner had sent a message to his wife via a friend in China. Her mother might have been right, she said. 'You can't trust a gweilo.' She thought he had probably started a new family in Canada already. 'All those lonely women must be easy pickings,' she added.

Mr Hyde was a little older than Vincent, but he had the same gentle way about him. Marie had heard the Japanese hadn't sent him and his wife and son to an internment camp because of the vital role he was playing in keeping the bank functioning. The Japanese wanted maximum spoils of war.

He'd be able to give her a small amount each month from Vincent's two bank accounts, he said. Marie calculated this would cover about half the cost of rice and vegetables.

'Why are you doing this for us?' Marie asked him. 'Surely there's a risk?' They both knew the Japanese were watching everything.

'It is normal,' he replied. She sensed he couldn't say anything more.

To make up the balance of the money they needed to survive, Marie began to sell things: clothing, appliances, even furniture. Some days she took small items around to a shop in Causeway Bay. Other days a shop would send a staff member to negotiate a price for larger pieces and two coolies would take them away. The living room was starting to look bare; the armchairs had already gone. There was a short list of things she would never sell, such as the crystal and china she had chosen with Vincent and on which they had enjoyed many good dinners.

Hunger was now a constant sensation but Marie marvelled at how little food she needed. Before the invasion she'd rarely had a meal of fewer than four different dishes, with two or three bowls of rice. Now she'd discovered she could manage on one small bowl of food: a soup of vegetable scraps, some herbs, and chicken or pork bones or fat for flavour.

The children, though, needed more. They were growing rapidly. Marie junior was able to wear Margaret's old clothes and Cynthia could wear Marie junior's, but Marie was having to dress Vincent in Cynthia's old frocks.

He could pass for a girl, especially as he'd never had a hair-cut. He was now walking around the flat by himself.

Nine-year-old Margaret had started to wear some of Marie's clothes, but the problem was her feet. They were now the same size as her mother's, but Marie had few shoes without heels. Margaret could barely keep her balance, even on the lowest of them.

43.

Marie walked to the waterfront and through the last check-point, where she was again patted down thoroughly. On the Star Ferry to Kowloon she looked around at the faces of other passengers, Chinese and Japanese. Everyone seemed to be staring at her.

At the barracks, Arthur was standing in the shade. He looked even thinner, but there was still a bit of a skip in his step as he came up to their meeting point. As usual, they made their way along the tall barbed-wire fence towards the parade ground. Marie was late: they would have time to go around only once.

'No stopping, no passing of anything through the wires, one time only.' Sometimes these rules were enforced, sometimes not. If you were there just before ten in the morning when the guards changed, you could go around twice because the new guards didn't know how long you'd been there. On Marie's second visit she'd managed to pass a skinny mattress compressed into a tight roll through the wire. It was bulky but the guards hadn't said anything. Now she brought food if she could.

Marie and Arthur reached the place where they usually paused. Here the top of one of the barracks blocked the view from the main guard tower. The trail to and from this spot had been worn into a noticeable track.

Marie handed Arthur a thermos of vegetable broth. He passed back an empty thermos.

'Thank you so very, very much for this,' he said.

'Don't be silly, Arthur. It's nothing.'

'What's new?'

'Nothing. Nothing nice anyway.'

'The children?'

'They're fine. I've found someone who's happy to tutor the two big girls in English.'

'That's wonderful. They're great children.'

'If only Vincent was here to see junior growing. He'd be so proud. He's just like his father, excited by anything with an engine.'

As they made their way back along the wire they wove around a few other couples. Marie could see men standing in the shadows, out of the fierce June sun. 'Everyone looks so sick,' she said.

'A lot are very sick.' Arthur looked solemn. 'Things are not going well. Summer's turning out to be as tough as we feared. There's barely enough water to drink and everyone is beginning to stink. Various infections and diseases are rife.'

He smiled, trying to make light of the situation. 'How are you off for money?'

'I should be all right for another couple of weeks. Shall we try for one more turn?'

'No. Not today. The little cretin there has his eye on you. Say hello to the girls and Lizzie for me. And to Lofty too if you see him.'

'Of course. God bless.'

44.

Marie guided the girls through a maze of back streets, desperate to avoid as many checkpoints as possible between their flat and the French Hospital.

Marie junior had taken it upon herself to act as scout, running ahead to each corner and signalling if there were soldiers. Suddenly she screamed and rushed back towards them.

'What is it?'

Gasping for air, unable to speak, she pointed to the corner ahead.

'Quick,' Marie said. 'Come back this way. We'll find another street.'

'What was it?' Cynthia was determined to find out what her sister had seen.

'The bodies, they–'

'Shush.' Marie guided the children back to the corner they'd just passed, then realised there was no other way forward.

'Margaret, hold Vincent's hand. And don't move, any of you.'

The children huddled in the doorway of a boarded-up workshop. The shadows of the buildings on the narrow road and the pipes, cables and clotheslines overhead gave them the feeling of being in a cave. A ray of bright sunshine cut across the opening to the main street.

Marie walked twenty yards, crossed the road and peered around the corner. There was an outstretched hand on the pavement five yards away. A body. She stood upright and proceeded slowly.

'Oh, God have mercy.' She took in fully the sight that had terrified her daughter. A knife lay beside the naked corpse of a middle-aged woman. But this was not a murder scene. The colour of the skin and the state of the body showed the woman had most likely died of hunger or disease. She had then been butchered for meat. Her right thigh had been sliced into and was hanging half off the body, exposing bones, tendons and flesh. It was covered in a blanket of flies.

Marie hurried back to the children, took Vincent's and Marie junior's hands and led the children back the way they'd come. They would find another route, even if it was twice as long.

By the time Dr Selwyn-Clarke had examined all the children they had been in his surgery for over two hours. Doctors like Selwyn-Clarke had been allowed to remain outside the internment camps to tend to locals and foreigners with papers from neutral nations.

Marie rolled up her sleeve and presented her arm for a blood pressure test.

'What was the matter with Marie junior?' the doctor asked as he strapped on the inflatable cuff.

'We saw something on the way here. People are butchering the dead to eat.'

'Yes, I know. You shouldn't bring the girls here unless you absolutely have to. I'll give you enough medicine to take care of them at home next time they have a relapse of malaria. I'm sure there'll be a lot of it about later in the summer.'

The doctor stopped pumping. 'No word from Vincent?'

'No. Mr Williamson released him from his post in Singapore at the end of January and told him to get to Sydney.'

'You've heard nothing else?'

'No.'

'Have you sent messages?'

'How? Not even the Red Cross is doing anything.'

'Can you wait after this? I have someone coming in I think can help you.'

'Someone who's going to escape?'

'He's getting out through official channels. An exchange or something. He's going to New York.'

He checked Marie's chest with a stethoscope, then wrote notes on her file. 'You know, Marie,' he said quietly, 'I don't want to be a scaremonger, but we have to prepare for the worst. You have to manage your affairs as if this is going to go on for years.'

'Of course.'

'Keep your hopes up, but also keep in mind that Vincent could still be in Singapore. A lot of ships never made it out.'

'I know.'

'The good news is that you've all done well to stay in reasonably good health.' He returned to his desk. 'You still have some help, don't you?'

'Two amahs have agreed to stay on without pay. They help with Cynthia and the baby and do the cooking mostly. Margaret does a lot of the housework. I think it makes her less anxious. The girls collect firewood up the hill behind us, mostly just bits of bush and scrub.'

Selwyn-Clarke stood, placed a hand on Marie's shoulder as he walked past, and abruptly left the room. After a minute he returned. 'Don't open this until you get home.' He handed her a sealed envelope.

Marie studied his face.

'I know Ginger Hyde's helping you out,' he said, 'but there's only so much he can do at the bank. Come back next month on your own. I'll try and give you the same again. If it gets to the point where I can't help you any more, you may have to see about getting yourself interned in a camp. At least they'll feed you and the children.'

'I could never be interned. What if Vincent wants to get hold of us?'

'Never say never, Marie. The children are all right at the moment, but they'll be in trouble if they get any less food than they're getting now. The Japs are good to children, at least.'

'I've heard rumors about repatriation ships, but only for pure-blooded English passport holders. Do you know anything about that?' she said.

'As far as I know there's nothing in the works for Hong Kong families, just the odd non-residents who've found themselves here at the wrong time.'

After Marie and the children had sat for some time in the waiting room, Dr Selwyn-Clarke emerged with a tall man Marie assumed was the American.

'What do you want me to tell your husband?' the man said.

'Just tell him we're well, that we're still in our home if he wants to contact us. But we need help. We need money.'

'That's all?'

'That's all I can think of. I don't know what else to say.'

Her hand shook as she scribbled on the small sheet of paper the doctor had given her Vincent's full name and his sister's address in Hamilton, New Zealand. Hamilton was a small city. Mail would surely get there more quickly than Te Puke.

45.

Marie approached the barbed wire and walked along it with her carry-bag carefully turned to face the men. With time at the wire restricted, most of the women visiting the prison camp at Kowloon had started embroidering the names of those they wanted to see on the sides of their bags in anything from coloured cotton thread to sequins. The logic was that the roman lettering would look like any other emblem or pattern to the Japanese guards.

A young man saw Arthur's name and ran to get him. Marie stood well back from the fence until she saw her friend coming out of the barracks.

Another woman started to move towards the wire. Marie recognised her as the wife of an Australian. She was beautifully dressed in a tight cheongsam that showed off her youthful figure and slim legs. The woman held up her bag and pointed towards the letters stitched on it.

A guard watching from the gate rushed out, grabbed her arm and pulled her towards the entrance. Another guard marched briskly towards Marie. The guards pushed the women into a room in a small building inside the gate.

An officer and a translator were sitting behind a large British army desk.

'My commander wants you to know that you are in very much trouble,' the translator said to Marie.

'For doing what?'

'The Imperial Japanese Army forbids that anyone has contact with prisoners of war.'

'You don't have enough to feed them. We are helping you.'

The woman next to Marie began to sniffle.

The translator gestured with his eyes towards the officer. 'I will not translate what you are saying. It shows a lack of respect, and my commander would beat you for it. Our prisoners have a level of comfort better than in any other part of the world.'

The officer uttered a barrage of short phrases. Like most other Japanese soldiers Marie had faced, he made eye contact just long enough to assert his power over her, not long enough to take in a plea.

'The commander will be gentle with you this time,' the translator said, 'but you must help us show the rest of the world how well the prisoners are being treated here.'

The two women looked sideways at each other. What did this mean? Marie thought about the meagre supplies of food left in her house. What would the children do if she was held here or sent to a camp?

She and the other woman were ushered out of the office to an area of the barbed-wire fence behind the command buildings. A soldier with a camera on a tripod scurried out from one of the buildings.

'You are to wave and look happily through the wire,' the translator said.

'There is no way I'm doing this,' the woman whispered to Marie, 'not after what they've done to my husband.'

'Me neither.'

'Quiet! Smile! You understand? Smile and wave with your right hands. Smile! One, two, three…'

Marie and the woman stared stoney-faced at the camera as the shutter clicked open and shut.

The officer stomped towards them, raised his hand and slapped their faces. 'That was very stupid. This time you obey.'

The women stared expressionless at the camera. The commander hit them again. Then, apparently realising he was not going to get what he wanted, he walked back into his office. After hesitating a few seconds the translator followed.

Guards manhandled the women back to the main gates. In the scuffle, as the guards shoved them down on the gravel Marie heard the distinctive sound of her thermos smashing to pieces.

46.

Lizzie's Mary was to be married. Her boyfriend had money and connections in China: his family had owned some successful businesses in Shanghai.

Lizzie was a nervous wreck. She was happy for her daughter's good fortune but convinced the young couple would be killed the moment they tried to flee Hong Kong. They'd told her they were going to try to get as far away from Japanese-occupied areas of China as possible – going first to Guilin and then maybe on to Chiang Kai-shek's capital in Chongqing.

There had still been no word from Vincent, and there were no official channels through which people on the island could communicate with people on the outside. Despite this, some people had managed to get news. Arthur reported that a man in his camp had even received divorce papers. His wife had found out he'd had an affair before the war.

Mary had promised Marie she'd do all she could to take a letter out for her and send it to the Williamson office in Sydney. Hopefully it would get to Vincent.

Marie's progress writing the letter had been slow. Two weeks of practice had done little to increase the speed at which she found each key on Vincent's old typewriter. She had to hit the keys with just the right amount of force. Too light and the toilet paper wouldn't absorb the ink, too hard and the paper would rip. She knew she wouldn't be able to use thicker paper even if she could find it: the note had to be light so Mary could swallow it if she was searched.

Where to start? She wanted to sound tender, to let Vincent know he was greatly missed, but she was also desperate for him to send money. Her envelope now contained only a few notes, barely enough to last two weeks. With only the small amounts she got from the usual sources – Ginger Hyde, Dr Selwyn-Clarke and Arthur – it was a struggle to keep up with the skyrocketing prices. A week earlier she had sold the malaria medicine. It was the only thing of interest to the black-market trader who'd come to the flat. Mosquito nets and prayer would now be their only protection from the disease.

Mary was ready to go. Marie's eyes blurred with tears. The sheet she had laboriously prepared was messy and full of errors. Vincent would laugh when he read that she'd been practising her typing in the hope of getting a job when the war ended. Her mind was still on the letter two hours later as she walked down the hill to the markets. She'd written that she hoped he would never go to sea again, that they'd make do on whatever money he could earn from onshore work. Living permanently in Hong Kong, he could be with their children through all their phases and special moments. He could see his son's curiosity, his combination of his father's good looks and his mother's temper. Writing this, she'd smiled to herself.

She'd also shared gossip about pregnancies in the camp at Stanley among the fine upstanding British expatriates. How, she wondered, did they have the energy to do it on a diet of cabbage soup and teaspoonfuls of rice?

47.

'Marie! Marie!'

Lizzie's shouts snapped Marie out of a trance. She'd been awake from her afternoon nap for twenty minutes, lying motionless on the mattress in the living room contemplating, as she often did, the decisions she had to make.

She got up quickly and went into her bedroom. Lizzie and Ah Sup were standing over Cynthia. She was lying in the bed all the girls now shared, sleeping under the single mosquito net they'd been able to buy. There was a strong smell of vomit.

'Malaria?'

'Yes.'

'Get her dressed. Girls, we have to go to the hospital. Get ready. Lizzie, you and Ah Sup stay here with the baby. Don't let anyone in.'

'I can't believe you've used everything I gave you already.' Dr Selwyn-Clarke looked hard at Marie.

'I'm sorry, I sold it.'

'That was stupid, Marie. I didn't give it to you for that.'

'We were down to our last sack of rice.'

'You're damn lucky we have some. Cynthia should be all right with what I've given her. I'll give her another dose in the morning. But you have to consider going into the Red Cross's Rosary Hill camp.'

'I know.'

'You won't be able to leave once you're in there, but I've been seeing the children there and they're in good health. I know you'll all be fed. And I'll be able to look after you on the visits the Japs let me in for.'

'Perhaps,' Marie said. 'Can you give me the other dose. I can carry Cynthia home.'

The doctor frowned. 'It's too late, Marie. It's not a good night to be outside. It'll be dangerous. You need to stay here. I'll have the nurses find you some mattresses. I can give you a little more cash but I won't be able to give you anything for a while after that, maybe never. I doubt you'll be able to get by on the outside for much longer. Please think seriously about the camp.'

'But Vincent—'

'Marie, there's a chance Vincent's locked up somewhere. And even if he isn't, what can he do for you? You are just going to have to wait this thing out. Who knows, maybe the Japanese will allow everyone to go back to living normally soon? If they really want Hong Kong as a colony like Taiwan, they can't keep so many people locked up indefinitely. Your priority needs to be the health of the children.'

Next morning Cynthia had barely enough energy to keep her eyes open. Her head bounced and rolled as Marie carried her home. Her two sisters walked behind in silence.

After they turned a corner they found themselves back in the open, beyond the network of small streets near the docks at the end of Causeway Bay. To their horror, black smoke was rising from behind Fortress Hill, exactly where their flat was. Margaret and Marie junior started running, screaming for Lizzie and Ah Sup as Marie struggled to catch up with them.

Coming around the final bend she gasped in relief. Despite the rubble, smoke and flames in front of it, their building was untouched. Margaret and Marie junior were standing with Jane beside the crater of an unexploded bomb.

'It's American,' Jane said.

'You think it might still go off?'

'Who knows?'

'Shouldn't we stay away?'

Jane shrugged. 'Look at that.' She pointed to the lettering on the side of the bomb. It read 'Ohio'.

'Do you think it's meant to be a joke? Ohayō means good morning in Japanese.'

'I don't know.'

Marie paused. 'We've been at the hospital, Jane. Dr Selwyn-Clarke thinks I should be putting our names down for Rosary Hill.'

'You think that's wise? You'll be stuck there. Vincent might send money to the flat, maybe enough to help you get out. Locals have been getting to the mainland. It might be an option.'

Jane looked intently at her friend's face. 'I don't know what you should do, Marie. I'm sorry.'

VINCENT

48.

Vincent had grease on his arms and was in need of a wash. He'd rushed straight to the office when the ship docked. He held up the fine sheet and carefully placed it on the lightly glued piece of white typing paper. He'd read the letter twice already. Gluing it would ensure it would stay intact as he read it again that night and handed it around the people he planned to see next morning.

He put the letter in the top drawer of the desk and walked through the outer office and past its silent staff to the toilet. He found a clean cubicle, pulled down the toilet lid and sat behind the locked door. As his chin began to spasm he leaned forward and covered his face with his hands. He was exhausted. He'd barely slept on the ship after the news of the American bombings in Hong Kong. His lungs sucked in half breaths, almost painfully and beyond his control, one rapidly following another.

Mary had been able to get to Free China and send Marie's letter to Sydney. It seemed Marie and the children were well, or at least they had been when the letter was written four months earlier. Lizzie was still with Marie. But they were broke and starving. Mary had enclosed a note saying she might be able to act as a go-between if Vincent wanted to send them anything. She had signed the note 'the Brat', Vincent's nickname for her.

From the news reports he'd studied, Vincent knew the closest he could get to Hong Kong by ship was India. India was a long way from Hong Kong, but at least there were civilian flights – or, if need be, trucks – crossing the Himalayas into China. And in India there might be escapees from Hong Kong he could talk to, perhaps even people who had seen Marie.

Vincent arranged to meet the captain of his ship for a beer. The captain had been his closest confidant during the nine months they'd been at sea. He was well aware of Vincent's anguish at his wife and children living in Hong Kong under Japanese occupation.

'You have enough money for the journey, you think?' the captain said.

'I don't know.'

'I suppose you can't be sure these days. What about contacting your wife through the army, now you know she's still in your home?'

'They say it's not possible.' Vincent paused. 'I really don't think they give a damn.'

'They are always so bloody young, the soldiers. You should try and see someone more senior tomorrow.'

'I don't think it'd be worth the trouble. They always assume I've come to enlist. Before I open my mouth they direct me down the hall to the office.'

'That's understandable. You look fit enough.'

'It's the last thing on my mind. What about you?'

'I'll probably see if they can use me. I've already lost so many friends around the Pacific. I know we've been useful to the civilians we've been provisioning, but now I feel obliged to do something to help stop all this.'

He paused. 'I'm not making a judgement, but you have to be ready for a lot of people finding it strange that you're not joining up, not particularly patriotic.'

'I don't feel particularly patriotic,' Vincent said.

'No?'

'It's not that simple.'

'No. If I was in your shoes with no word for over a year...' He was silent for a moment. 'It's normal you want to find a way to help your wife and children, but–'

'But?'

'I was going to say, "But I don't know how far you can expect to get." I know you well enough to know you have to try.'

49.

Vincent's parents had emigrated to New Zealand from England when he was a child. The combination of his English birth, New Zealand education and Hong Kong residency confused the bureaucrats, but everywhere the word, spoken or implied, was that he should sign up. 'Our boys are dying all over the world for lack of skilled technicians like you to back them up in their landings and pushes,' one army officer told him.

The newspapers were full of it. Australia and New Zealand had sent their best to Europe and North Africa, leaving the South Pacific vulnerable to the Japanese.

Vincent pushed his way through the crowds on Sydney's streets. The voice in his head constantly told him he should already be in India or even Free China. His family had to come first. They'd been on the brink of starvation five months ago. What state were they in now?

He put the papers into a manila folder: his maps, his hand-scribbled notes, Marie's letter, Mary's letter, and a letter from a man in New York he'd received when his ship docked in Dunedin on the way to Sydney; his sister had somehow managed to find out the route of his ship and redirected it.

He had carbon copies of his letters to the British Army, the Red Cross and several embassies. Most had gone unanswered; there had been short replies to the others. It seemed that even if the Japanese were willing to negotiate exchanges, Marie and the children would not have priority. They had Portuguese papers and looked Chinese. It was felt they should be able to look after themselves better than others. Various officials had told him face-to-face that Marie should not reveal his nationality and should use her own papers to get to Macau.

'You know you'll be the only person wanting to go *into* China.' The middle-aged man with the empty right sleeve of his uniform strapped over his shoulder spoke with a bullish tone.

'I doubt I'll be the only one,' Vincent said.

'I can assure you that you will be. I've never heard such a thing in all my days here. We'd all like to go off and rescue our loved ones like bloody knights but that's what the army's for, and it works a lot better if everyone sticks to what they're good at, no matter what they might want to do.'

'Perhaps.' It was hard to argue with a man who'd obviously sacrificed a lot. His injury was probably why he'd been given this desk job.

'There's no "perhaps" about it. You'll be wasting your time and every cent you have, just to sit out the war in some hot-as-hell infested dosshouse two thousand miles from Hong Kong. There's famine throughout China right now. Do you have any idea how many refugees are processed every day escaping the place?'

'No.'

'A bloody lot. And not nearly as many as those who've died trying to get out of the occupied territories.'

'But I'm free to go?'

'There's nothing we can do to stop you. But think things through a bit more, would you.'

At the Chinese consulate in Sydney, dozens of people were trying to get in the door. Vincent was eventually directed to an office where his details were taken, and then into a waiting room. He stared at the large map of China on the wall. The distances looked vast.

'Mr Broom.'

The young man was impeccably dressed in a Western suit despite the midday heat. He offered Vincent his hand and introduced himself. 'Your request is rather unusual,' he said.

'I don't know if you can help me,' Vincent said, 'but there is so little trustworthy information about my chances of getting into and across China right now. I've been told I won't get further than Kunming.'

'Who told you that?'

'Why – it's not true?'

'Not in the least. The Japanese control only a tiny stretch along the coast of China. The Generalissimo's armies are currently preparing with great speed and efficiency to retake those areas.'

Vincent was silent, unsure what to say.

'You think that I am exaggerating. I am not exaggerating.'

'I thought about getting to Calcutta, flying to Kunming, then taking the train to as close to Hong Kong as I can get.'

'It sounds like a reasonable plan. You will be able to get within a hundred miles of Hong Kong. Then it will be easy for you to send a message to your wife.'

Vincent was in disbelief.

The man continued, 'I respect greatly your desire to help your wife and family, Mr Broom. You will succeed if you are careful.'

'I'm sorry if I seem dubious. It's just that you're the first person to tell me my ideas aren't completely mad or misguided.'

'I assure you that you have a very good chance. My brother works in our office in Calcutta. If you like I will prepare a letter of introduction for you. You can pick it up tomorrow. He will be happy to help you.'

'Thank you. Xie-xie. Thank you very, very much.' Vincent stood, shook the man's hand and attempted a perfunctory bow, which was returned.

'Really. Don't mention it.'

50.

Vincent leaned against the railings of the SS *Querimba*. The ticket to India had cost him a third of the money he'd saved.

He knew that sometime during his journey he might run out of cash, especially if inflation was as bad as people said. He would then have to survive like any of the thousands of other penniless refugees.

In Sydney he had started to lie about his plans. When he told people what he intended to do, many said he was crazy or selfish and this had eaten into his confidence. On the ship there were no such judgements. The passengers were a group of people with a worldly outlook. When he told them he was going to try to get across the Himalayas and half of China to attempt to get his family out of Hong Kong, they wished him all the best.

The ship was due to arrive in Bombay by May 18. From there he would get the next train to Calcutta. His maps showed he would be travelling along the Tropic of Cancer at the beginning of summer. It was not going to be easy, but not too difficult either. He'd often been stuck in the engine rooms of coastal trading ships in Asia in July. Out there on the Indian Ocean, with its calm sea and gentle breeze, everything seemed possible.

51.

Vincent had lost a lot of weight and was bone-thin but in India he felt obese. On the train from Bombay he watched emaciated peasants working the land. In Calcutta it was even worse. The skin of the beggars who surrounded the train as it pulled into the station seemed to be painted on to their bones and ligaments. He knew the few pieces of loose change in his pocket would be needed for some steamed rice and vegetables in China. He should keep as much of it as he could. Nonetheless, he couldn't resist helping a mother and her child. Maybe he'd need such charity himself later on.

The sea of faces around the marketplace near his cheap hotel included many British and Chinese. As he sat in front of a stall he found himself focusing absentmindedly on a Chinese woman in dusty clothes leaning against a wall across the street, seemingly oblivious to the flies swarming over her. He was amazed to see her face light up when she noticed him looking at her. As she rushed towards him he recognised her; she was the wife of a British doctor in Hong Kong.

She had not seen Marie for over a year, she told him. She had come across China from Canton. There could still be trucks arriving from southern China, she said, but there was little traffic going the other way. The famine was shocking, she said. She had seen more peasants dead beside the road than she could count. The price of food was exorbitant, even by European standards. 'You'll need a lot of money,' she said as Vincent explained his plan.

From the moment they'd started talking Vincent had sensed she was holding something back. Now she said she had a favour to ask. She was stuck in Calcutta, 'just another bloody Chinese'. She had no papers with her, so she couldn't be evacuated on British Army transport trains or ships, no matter how many of their friends' names she dropped. Could he put in a word for her with the army?

'Look, Vincent, I'm sure you'll make it close enough to have some local fisherman take Marie a message,' she said as they walked back from the army's offices. 'That moral support will mean the world to her.'

Vincent decided not to tell her any more. 'That's all I'm hoping for, realistically.'

'Good. Because I'm sure no one is getting out through Canton now.'

'No,' he said, 'that's not surprising.'

They shook hands outside Vincent's hotel.

'Thank you for all you've done,' she said. 'You've really saved me.'

'It's nothing. Good luck with the rest of it.' He looked at her carefully. 'I feel there's something you're not telling me.'

'It's nothing. I want to wish you good luck too, but I also want to tell you…' She paused. 'You understand – just don't get your hopes up too much.'

'In what way? Do you know something?'

'No. I last saw Marie over twelve months ago. She was faring well enough then, but horrible things are happening in Hong Kong. Women are treated dreadfully and there's not enough food. Many of my friends have already lost a child.'

'That bad?'

'Just be reasonable with what you hope to find. They've been on their own for eighteen months. It's a long time, Vincent.'

52.

'It's not your lucky day, sir.'

'But I was told in Bombay that I could buy a ticket here for Kunming.'

'Nobody in Bombay would have known about this turn of events. Orders came through yesterday. No more civilian traffic.'

'What are they all waiting for then?' Vincent gestured at the dozen or so people sitting around the room.

'They've been told the same thing, sir. They're staying in the hope that things will change. But I have to warn you, sir, I doubt very much they will. Events have been leading up to this for a long time.'

'What do you suggest I do?'

'I don't know, sir, but unless you have official army business in China I am not permitted to issue you a ticket.'

A visit to the British consulate confirmed the bad news. A soldier in an immaculately ironed and starched uniform insisted there was nothing he could do. They weren't making any exceptions, otherwise every trader and war profiteer in Calcutta would be tying up their time with every excuse possible as to why they had to get across.

Vincent cast an eye at the other men at their desks. He lowered his voice to just above a whisper and moved his chair closer.

'Look, I've come all the way from Sydney for this.'

'I understand, sir.'

'Please let me finish.' Vincent took a deep breath as his voice rose uncontrollably. 'My family are in Hong Kong. They have been there for almost two years under the Japanese. They are starving and not even the Red Cross is helping them.'

'Sir, it's for your own protection.'

'Please, don't you think ...' Conscious he was on the verge of tears, Vincent paused.

'The Japanese airforce, sir ...' The man seemed at a loss for words.

'I understand all that. But don't you think I can make a decision for myself?'

'Yes of course, sir, but that is not the issue. We cannot—'

Vincent interrupted. 'There must be a way.'

'Maybe in other posts, sir. Maybe with other commanding officers. But there is absolutely no way any exceptions are going to be made here.'

'I don't want to be disrespectful, but can I please talk to your commanding officer.'

'I'll see. Please wait here.'

Vincent took a handkerchief from his pocket and pressed the cloth firmly against his eyes. Dealing with army bureaucrats in Asia had never been easy.

The soldier returned and sat down. 'I'm truly sorry, sir, but there is no way we can put civilians on these flights any more.'

'Thank you for your time,' Vincent said. He shook the soldier's hand, turned mechanically and walked towards the exit.

Back in his hotel room, with his fingers locked behind his head, he watched the faint shadows of people passing the window, projected on to the white ceiling. Time advanced without him noticing it. His mind raced from one idea to another until finally all the tasks, the negotiations, the distances walked carrying his luggage, the constant heat, all the things that had been easily put to one side in the blind hope that everything was working out, caught up with him. He slept for sixteen hours.

53.

The likeness between the Chinese diplomat in Calcutta and his brother in Sydney was disarming. Vincent stared as the man rose to greet him. Like his brother, he moved with the ease and dignity you expected of a diplomat.

He listened carefully, even though Vincent was merely repeating what he'd written in the letter he'd dropped off the day before. He then politely but firmly dismissed Vincent's latest idea, which was to hitch a ride on supply trucks over the Himalayas.

After this he sat perfectly still.

Vincent filled in the silence. 'Is there anything official or even unofficial your government can do to get me on a plane?'

'I assure you there is nothing unofficial we can do. And unfortunately nothing official either. But tell me, as an officer in the merchant navy you must have a uniform. Did you bring it with you?'

'Yes, actually. I thought I might need it if I stayed here longer than expected and had to find work.'

'Why not go back to your hotel and put it on. And then try for this afternoon's flight. The staff people on the desk may just think you look military enough for them to sell you a ticket.'

'You think that will work?'

'Who knows. This is India. You can only try.'

'And if it doesn't work should I come back to see you — to see if we can find another way to handle this?'

'Of course, of course.'

The same men were sitting around the ticketing office when Vincent returned that afternoon. He placed his two small suitcases on the floor beside one of the vacant chairs, took care to straighten his back and smooth the creases out of his sleeves, and approached the counter.

The same Indian clerk was manning the desk.

'Hello.'

'Yes, sir.'

Vincent braced himself for a challenge. 'I was here yesterday.'

'Yes. Mr Broom, isn't it?'

'Yes.'

'I'd like to buy a ticket for Kunming please.'

'May I have your papers?'

Vincent handed him his civilian visas for entry into China.

'Everything appears to be in order.'

Vincent fished his wallet from his satchel and passed over the required cash. He then put his papers and wallet back into the satchel and took a seat next to the waiting men. He scanned the details on the ticket and double-checked the time. There was just half an hour until take-off.

54.

Far below them a tangle of lines threaded and crisscrossed the river plain to become a single meandering line as the plane climbed east, away from the delta. Gradually the scrappy patchwork of small brown fields grew larger and the fields greener. In some places the river was the width of a small lake. Steep mountainsides rose beyond the top of the plane's window to elevations well above cruising height.

There were no spare seats between the men in their various uniforms. Each man looked steadily out at the remote land. Vincent doubted many of the people tending their crops far below were aware of the war.

The passenger sitting next to him was the only one not in uniform. His age and well-tailored suit indicated some sort of senior advisory position. What might be taking such a man into China?

Just as Vincent was studying him, the man turned and offered his hand. 'John Keswick.'

Vincent recognised the name. John Keswick was the head of Jardine, Matheson, a large trading company based in Hong Kong.

'Vincent Broom.'

Keswick smiled. 'I watched you come on board and was curious as to what a merchant navy engineer might be doing heading into a largely landlocked state.'

Vincent chose to use the noise of the engines as an excuse to pretend he hadn't fully heard him. He wasn't sure Keswick could be trusted. 'I was wondering if you could answer a question,' he said finally.

'What's that?'

'How cold does it get on this flight? I saw a dozen people at the airport trying to get on the plane. They were dressed for a polar crossing.'

'It gets extremely cold and tough on the system thanks to the height, about 20,000 feet, but they hand out thick jackets on the next leg. The men you saw were probably merchants doing a little smuggling. The price of fabric is fifty times in China what it is in India. They like to wear three or four extra suits that they can sell when they get across. It's your first time?'

'Yes. What about you?'

'Too many times to remember.'

Keswick gave Vincent an account of some of the difficulties and horrors of running a business in China over the previous two years. He himself had fled Hong Kong after the surrender and moved to Ceylon. He was now working as an adviser on Chinese affairs for Louis Mountbatten, the

man Winston Churchill had appointed Supreme Allied
Commander South East Asia in August. He was on his way
to see China's Nationalist leader Chiang Kai-shek.

'You didn't answer my question,' he said. 'Forgive me for
being nosy but I can't fathom why a merchant seaman might
be heading into China.'

'To be honest, the uniform's a ruse,' Vincent replied. 'They
wouldn't sell me a ticket otherwise. Although it's likely I've
been quietly helped by someone at the Chinese consulate.'

'That wouldn't surprise me,' Keswick said. 'The great
unseen workings of China. But why the visit? You don't
strike me as a businessman.'

'My wife and family are in Hong Kong.'

'Oh God, I'm sorry to hear that. Many of my friends are
too. You want to get them out?'

'I want to try.'

'It's going to be difficult for you to get close to Hong
Kong. Few of the railways in China work any more. The
roads are diabolical and fuel supplies have been completely
disrupted. Then there's the problem of getting communications in and out of Hong Kong. There's no way you
could get within a hundred miles of that part of the coast.
Sadly, your height and blue eyes are going to be extremely
disadvantageous.'

'But Chinese still seem to be able to get out,' Vincent said.
'Marie is Macanese and our children, depending what they're
wearing, can look the part.'

'Even so, from what I know of the activities of the
communists and the nationalists, things are in a pretty poor
state in that part of Canton. There's almost as much antag-
onism between the different Chinese factions and the Allies
as with the Japanese.'

He stopped. 'Look, anything is possible though. How much money do you have?'

'A few hundred pounds. This ticket took most of what I had.'

'You're going to need more. Even half-decent digs and basic food now cost the earth. The one thing I can do is give you a letter. Whenever you get to one of our offices, you can borrow whatever you need against it.'

'I don't know what to say.'

'As I said, it's all I can do. I wish I could do more. It's just a loan, I'm not being all that generous.'

'Thank you,' Vincent said. 'Thank you very much. I feel like my luck is finally changing.'

'The luck of a Chinaman.'

'Perhaps.'

Before reaching the lowest saddle of the Himalayas, the plane landed in Ledo. It was the last stop in India. The next stage – the flight over 'The Hump' – had to be made under cover of darkness to avoid enemy planes; by now the Japanese occupied most of Burma and its skies.

As they took off and flew between the mountains, Vincent was astounded by the grandeur of the scenery. Against the blackness of the rocky slopes, he spied a campfire a good three hundred miles from any other sign of civilisation.

The plane was flying at a high altitude. Vincent felt the stress on his body first as pain in the joints. The pain worked its way from the back of his neck up into his head. He experimented with pressing against different parts of his skull with his hands, but raising his arms and keeping them in place became unbearable. He saw a number of heads in front of him flop as men passed out.

There was an announcement: the plane would need to go even higher because of exceptional cloud cover. At the front of the cabin a soldier vomited into a paper bag. Seconds later, another did the same.

Eventually, after more than five hours, they touched down at an airstrip in Kunming.

55.

As the sun rose, Vincent travelled in a taxi along streets lined with tall trees and finally around the curves of a small lake surrounded by delicate willows and gold-roofed pagodas. He was overcome by the feeling of being back in China, in the culture that had absorbed so much of his adult life. He was shown to a high-ceilinged room in the Hôtel du Commerce with a glorious view of the lake. He removed his shoes and lay face down on the bed, adjusting his neck and head several times before finding respite from his headache and plunging into a deep sleep.

The clerk behind the front desk asked in broken English to see Vincent's papers and then searched the register. He pointed to 'New Zealand', which Vincent had scribbled in the column headed 'Nationality', and ran his finger down the page to the details of another guest.

He came around from behind the counter and indicated to Vincent to follow him. Passing through a set of large doors towards the back of the hotel, the two men entered a bar. The room was cool and pleasant. Hotel guests were sitting at low teak tables, sipping five o'clock sundowners.

At a table occupied by a Chinese man about Vincent's age

and an older European man dressed in a loose shirt, open at the top just enough to show burn scars, the clerk bowed and gestured to Vincent. 'New Zealand,' he said. He smiled broadly and left the room.

'Sorry to intrude,' Vincent said. 'I was showing him my papers and he pointed to your name on the register. Mr Whitehead, is that right?'

'Ronnie. And this is Mr Wong.'

They rose and each shook Vincent's hand.

'I didn't want to disturb you,' Vincent said. 'I was just on my way out to get something to eat.'

'You're new?'

'Yes. I arrived this morning.'

'Have a drink and then we can go out together.'

Mr Wong explained that he worked for Wallace Harpers, the Ford agents in Hong Kong. Like Vincent, he had left Hong Kong before the invasion and hadn't been back. Ronnie Whitehead was a pilot who'd trained in Britain and New Zealand. Flying was his passion. Before the war he had signed up with Colonel Claire Chennault of the Flying Tigers, back when Chennault's operation was just a small foreign mercenary airforce created by Chiang Kai-shek and his wife when the Japanese were attacking Shanghai.

In December 1937 he had been shot down and terribly wounded. After three months in hospital he had partially healed but was not allowed back in the air: his sight and judgement of distances were impaired. He had, he told Vincent, missed out on all the 'excitement' when President Roosevelt sent a hundred fighter planes to help the Nationalists hit the Japanese harder.

Soon afterwards the bombing of Pearl Harbour had dragged the US into the war. Unable to contribute to the war effort from the air, Whitehead had set up a trucking business, running supplies around the region.

Both men had been in this south-west corner of China long enough to be able to answer Vincent's general questions. Over dinner they gave him information about the best options. He should go directly to Guilin, eight hundred miles to the east. It was still over four hundred miles from there to Hong Kong, but Guilin was the last large city being held convincingly by the Chinese: it had a natural defence in the form of steep limestone pillars that prevented Japanese planes getting close. Once there he could get up-to-date information.

Postal trucks were the only regular transport; many of the train lines between Kunming and Hong Kong, especially those near the coast, had been torn up to make life difficult for the Japanese. The postmaster in Kunming was 'not a bad fellow'. If he struck him in a good mood Vincent might be able to hitch a ride about halfway. From there there should still be a train to Guilin.

'Tell the postmaster what you're trying to do,' Wong said. 'He's originally from Hong Kong or Macau, I think. His name is Smith.'

Vincent headed back to the hotel for an early night. He wanted to be at the post office first thing in the morning.

56.

Vincent immediately recognised Smith as a similar mix of Portuguese and Chinese to Marie. The postmaster was being besieged from all angles. He couldn't invite Vincent into his office, he said. He suggested he follow him around the depot while he did his rounds.

As Smith gave his staff directions, Vincent told him his story. It was only when he said he hadn't been in Hong Kong when it fell because he was a ship's engineer working in Singapore that the postmaster stopped walking and gave him his full attention.

'Which company do you work for?'

'Williamson's. It's one of the larger ones in Hong Kong.'

'I know Williamson's.' Smith turned abruptly and steered Vincent back towards his office. 'You must know a chief engineer called Alphabetical Smith.'

'I do. I've sailed with him many times.'

'It is a very small world, Mr Broom. Alphabetical, as the people at Williamson's call him, is my brother.'

For the next half hour, despite frequent knocks at the door, the two men exchanged information. By the end Smith had offered Vincent passage on postal trains and trucks right through to Guiyang. He'd initially need to take the train that came through Kunming from the south on to Kutsing. From there he would have the much coveted seat beside the driver on a postal truck that left at five the next morning. The wait for such a lift would usually have been at least ten days.

That night Vincent again dined with Mr Wong and Ronnie Whitehead. In a small schoolbook he'd bought, he wrote down the place names and facts they mentioned. From time to time he asked Wong to render place names in Chinese characters so he could show them to local villagers when he had to.

The men said they had encountered dozens of escapees from Hong Kong but the numbers had definitely begun to trickle off. Vincent should prepare for what might be a difficult few weeks, they said, and ordered him an extra dish of noodles. It might be a while before he found another good place to eat.

57.

Once the postal truck emerged from the maze of streets on the edge of Kutsing, they made quite good time. The landscape was a mix of plains and gentle hills and the roads were relatively straight.

Regular stops for servicing were necessary: the truck's engine suffered from carbon deposits formed because of the fuel, a mixture of locally distilled alcohol and diesel.

These stops, along with the driver's nervous navigation of potholes and untended landslides, prevented Vincent slipping into a traveller's trance. The truck's suspension was non-existent. After two hours he was feeling every knock and bump of the road. His arms and legs were aching. It was impossible to sleep. No sooner would he lean his head against the door frame than a sudden jolt would shock him awake. From time to time he even envied the other passengers, who were lying fully exposed to the sun on mail sacks on the back of the truck.

As the hills increased the truck stopped even more frequently so the passengers could head towards the open latrines on the side of the road. Vincent, deciding he was too heavy to stand on the narrow planks arranged across open ponds of sewage, found trees to pee behind. Flies buzzed around the makeshift noodle stalls and sat undisturbed on the raw vegetables and offal left lying in the sun before being put in the stockpots. On the first few stops Vincent bought only tea but later hunger got the better of him.

At about ten at night they stopped at a small town. Vincent raced to a guest house to arrange a room, but the owner loudly berated him from behind a closed door. At a second guest house the owner stood with crossed forearms, indicating there were no rooms left. Seeing the driver of the truck enter a flophouse, he followed him inside, handed a few coins to the proprietor, and took his place on the wide communal bed. The planks lay less than a foot above a dirt floor. There was barely enough space to squeeze in between the migrant Chinese workers and refugees. Straw stuck out of the bed roll and through his clothing, making it impossible to get into a comfortable position without disturbing the men on either side. Eventually, exhausted, he fell asleep.

When he woke he noticed that the candle at the entrance to the room had burned down barely an inch. There was a painful itch on his left ankle. With men so tightly packed around him, it was hard to sit up or bend over to scratch the spot. He looked around the room; no one was moving.

A sting on his calf muscle made him sit up abruptly. He touched his leg. It was wet: he was being attacked by bed bugs and bleeding through his trousers. As delicately as he could he crawled off the bed.

He carefully checked his shoes for insects, snakes and scorpions and finding none slipped them on and went outside. The street was dead quiet. Under big-leafed trees at the side of the road he made out the bodies of a dozen people who couldn't afford the luxury of the flophouse. He climbed up on to the mail sacks on the back of the truck and tried to sleep.

58.

On the second day they began to weave up the Burma Road, which had been built by hundreds of thousands of Chinese and Burmese labourers during the second Sino-Japanese War just a few years earlier. Travellers had come this way since the time of Marco Polo to cross between China and towns lining the Irrawaddy River.

Vincent stared at the corpses lying in drains at the side of the road, bodies left where they'd fallen or been dragged out of the way of the traffic. In one place a giant road-working roller sat on the verge. By the size and placement of its harnesses it was obvious it had been built to be pulled by coolies. Human energy was still the least expensive kind in rural China.

At one point the way was blocked by a caravan of nearly thirty small horses. The riders were not Han Chinese. They looked Turkish. Many were red-haired and freckled. Vincent guessed they were Uighurs, Muslims from the desert basins of the Gobi and the Taklamakan far away to the north.

As the truck pushed up the side of the Yunnan–Guizhou plateau the air became cooler and the views even more spectacular. Vincent felt as though he could see all the way down the Indochinese Peninsula. On a good day, he thought, Saigon might be visible.

In the evening they reached a town called Annan, where Vincent treated the driver to a dinner of vegetable soup and noodles. Afterwards he elected to again sleep on the mailbags. Next morning he walked along paths between paddy fields to stretch his aching limbs. The town looked straight out of a Chinese watercolour. Even the simplest and smallest houses had ornate grey tiled roofs and neat brickwork. At the end of an alley between the houses at the north end, green rice fields touched the outer walls of the village's last houses, like sea lapping at coastal ramparts.

Despite Vincent's five small meals the day before, he noticed his belt had become loose again. It would soon need a new hole.

59.

Vincent had doubted he would encounter any Europeans on the way to Guilin, but as the truck rumbled past the entrance to the marketplace in Guiyang he saw three priests in heavy black robes walking along the road. He paid careful attention to the truck's route and after shaking the driver's hand at the depot he lifted down his small suitcases and walked back towards them.

He knew from experience not to expect an automatic affinity with other Europeans but the priests were friendly. They were from France, spoke English and had lived in China a long time. They were curious: where was he from and why was he travelling in the wrong direction? He gave them an honest answer. He was still worried he'd be prevented from carrying on, but he was learning to read people and recognise those who might help.

The priests suggested he go directly to a Major Hemingway, who lived nearby. Apparently the major handled some sort of logistics function for British army doctors in Guilin.

Hemingway's smile put Vincent at ease immediately. After listening to his plans he said he'd been lucky to find him: his commanding officer, Lindsay Ride, had been one of the first people to escape from an army detention camp in Hong Kong. Rather than getting as far away as possible, Ride had stayed in Guilin to set up and manage an organisation he called the British Army Aid Group. The group included some young men from Hong Kong, mostly former medical students of Ride's when he was professor of physiology at Hong Kong University. Its members, dressed as peasants, were able to run messages in and out of the colony.

'I was sure such an organisation would exist,' Vincent said.

'Nothing is that evident,' Hemingway replied. 'I assure you that you are very, very lucky.' He banged two knuckles down on the table. 'Up until now all the activities have been based around military operations: intelligence, emergency supplies, reconnaissance and the retrieval of the odd downed flyer. You'll have to ask Colonel Ride if he can help you with a civilian matter, or even if Chongqing will allow it. The question has never come up before to my knowledge.'

'You think there's a chance he won't?'

'I can't say for certain. He's a fine and friendly man, don't get me wrong. But around here you can never be certain. Between the Japs, the Chinese Nationalists, the Communists, the Americans and even some of the British, there can be a lot of politics involved.'

'I hope to God he appreciates my case.'

'Well, you've been damn lucky so far. Someone's looking out for you. It can't all be to just let you down at the very end, can it?'

After a dinner prepared by his resident cook, Hemingway asked if Vincent had found a place to stay. When he said he hadn't, Hemingway directed him to the operating table in the surgery behind his office. 'It may seem a bit strange,' he said, 'but I assure you it's quite comfortable. I've slept there myself a good many times.'

'It looks like a bed at the Ritz,' Vincent said, 'the way I'm feeling.'

60.

Vincent now had a guaranteed place on a British Army Aid Group supply truck leaving that afternoon for the railhead. He took the morning to wash his clothes and walk around the town. Guiyang, a crossroads with a small river port, was bigger than he'd imagined. He was surprised he'd never heard of the place before. Traders going east to west, or north to Chongqing or Xian, China's ancient capital, had probably exchanged goods here for centuries.

Seated at a table in the compound of a Buddhist temple garden at the top of a hill, Vincent took his map from his pocket, and using his finger widths measured the distance he'd covered so far. He had come well over three hundred miles in three days. If all went well with the trains, he should cover the next three hundred to Guilin just as quickly. All the trouble he'd had getting to China, all the misfortune that had kept him in the Pacific for so long, were being wiped away.

61.

The giant army truck bumped down into dry paddy field that had been turned into a makeshift parking yard just outside the walls of the town. Hemingway introduced Vincent to a man who was getting on the same truck. Li had been a dean at Lingnan University in Canton and had had to flee when the Japanese occupied the city in 1937. He spoke impeccable English and had a vocabulary that would have put most British people to shame. Vincent could tell he would be an affable travelling companion.

Li suggested they find somewhere to eat. At a small restaurant nearby, he had a long exchange with the proprietor in what appeared to be a mix of dialects. The only meat on the menu was tortoise, he told Vincent finally.

When the truck left, they tried to make themselves comfortable, using blankets Hemingway had given them to cushion themselves against the bare metal of the cab. Next morning, as they drove alongside the railway line, Li turned to Vincent and grinned.

'Have you ever heard of the Blue Train?' He pointed two hundred yards down the track.

'Of course.'

'There she is, or two of her carriages at least. We are going to arrive in Guilin in style.'

Vincent laughed. 'My wife's been on at me for years about taking a trip on the Blue Train.'

Inside the cabin the brass and the rosewood veneers were pristine. The monogrammed sheets and pillow cases were brightly bleached and ironed. Vincent stowed his two suitcases in the small wardrobe and changed into trousers and a long-sleeved shirt.

The train travelled at about twenty miles an hour. As night began to fall Vincent watched people coming out of their villages to wash in the streams beside the tracks. Children jumped from low hillocks of dirt into the shallow waters and splashed each other.

Next morning he woke to subtle changes in the landscape. The straight parallel lines, lanes, canals and terraces of the paddy fields were giving way to large mounds of earth and rocks. With each mile the mounds grew higher. Giant rocks thrust upwards, rupturing the blankets of grass and plants. As the rocks grew to the heights of houses and barns, their tops retained berets of dirt and small trees, while their sides became vertical rock faces. The famous limestone pillars were starting to reveal themselves.

The pillars soon towered hundreds of feet above workers in the fields. They were high enough and large enough that they separated villages from each other. Rivers disappeared into a wall of rock only to emerge from another, until finally the whole countryside fell away in a steep downward slope.

As the train began to descend to the plain Vincent got the sense that Guilin couldn't be far off. He fell into a deep peaceful sleep.

62.

By chance, the headquarters of the British Army Aid Group were a short walk from Vincent's hotel. He arrived early enough in the morning to witness a steady stream of uniformed soldiers entering a cavernous room decorated with British, Chinese and American flags and taking their places at desks and meeting tables.

He was directed to a group of low teak and wicker chairs and instructed to wait for Colonel Ride to finish his morning briefings. He took out his notebook and started writing a list of questions. He wasn't sure how much time he'd get to make his case.

He and Ride recognised each other at once: their paths

had crossed at social events in Hong Kong. Vincent had heard a little of Ride's story. When the invasion began, he had coordinated the colony's field ambulances, but after the surrender the Japanese had refused to allow him to continue to search for injured soldiers in the hills. Instead, like most military personnel, he had been interned at Sham Shui Po.

Recognising it would be increasingly difficult to escape once the Japanese army secured the camp, he had arrived with a few items he could need to rapidly get himself out of captivity, none of which would generate undue attention if he were searched.

During the first week he had selected three men to go with him and weighed the merits of various plans. Finally, on January 9, 1942, he and the other men had managed to get away from a pier next to the camp on a small sampan. Over the following weeks they had worked their way north to safety, far beyond enemy lines.

As Vincent talked about what life might be like for Marie, their children and the amahs under the occupation, Ride looked thoughtful. What Vincent was asking was a completely new type of request. Given his limited resources, he knew he had to carefully balance the pros and cons of taking on such a risky civilian mission.

'We'll need a code name,' he said finally, 'something only your wife will recognise as coming from you.'

'You can help me then?'

'We can only try.'

Vincent's hands started to shake as he closed his notebook.

'You should probably get some rest,' Ride said.

'I'm fine, really. You have no idea what this means to me, to have your help.'

'I'm sure you'll be able to find a way to help us while we wait for some news. You'll need all your strength though. You'll eventually have to travel to Samfou, our last post in the south. It's a hard trip – no Blue Train, I can assure you. Just a lot of time on small boats and a good sixty miles of walking.'

'Of course. How long do you think it'll take to get some news?'

'Who knows, a couple of weeks. A month. If Marie is still at your old address it will be sooner. We'll have to wait and see. As we get more information out we'll have to ask you for more details, but we have enough to start on. Have you thought of a code name?'

'Nasty.'

'Nasty?'

'Nasty. It was my nickname for my wife when we first met. She's very direct – too direct for some.'

'That should work,' Ride said. 'Write two copies of a small note to her on tissue paper, two inches by two inches, which my assistant will give you. We'll send the notes in with two different runners. They'll leave tomorrow. One will go via Huizhou and then down through Fanling into the New Territories. The other will go through Samfou, around Jiangmen and on to Macau. At the moment Macau will probably be the best place to get her out from. Most of our runners are still making it through.'

'Most?'

'Let's first send in a message and we'll weigh up the odds as we go.' He paused and looked straight at Vincent. 'I should have mentioned this from the start, but I'll have to get approval from a number of people: my superiors, the Chinese and so on.'

63.

Lindsay Ride quietly entered the hospital room. Vincent
was wreathed in sweat, with only a sheet covering his body.
He was barely recognisable as the man the colonel had met
two weeks before. His cheeks were sunken and his skin
wrinkled and dry. The dark grey patches under his eyes gave
him the look of a corpse.

Dr Elizabeth Bacon stopped at the door behind him.

'He hasn't even been able to get to the shelters,' she said.

'Can I ask him some questions?'

'He hasn't talked for two days. When he wakes he barely
has the energy to roll his neck and move his eyes. You'd
better come back later.'

Almost on cue, sirens started to sound.

'Where's your shelter?' Ride said.

'There are some caves in the pillar behind the hospital.'

'Can I help you get him out?'

'Thanks, yes. I'll send a porter with a stretcher.'

When Vincent woke there was a young nurse in his room.

'How do you feel?' she said.

'The colonel – he was here, wasn't he? My wife, did he
say anything about my wife?'

'Lie back. Don't get excited.'

'What did he say?'

'He said he hadn't heard anything yet. He said that's to
be expected. He should normally know something in a few
more weeks.'

'He wants me to go south.'

'You're not going anywhere for now. I'm going to organise
you some rice and soup. Please do your best to eat it. You

must build up your strength. There is a medicine that will see you well again. We are waiting for it to arrive.'

'When will that be?'

'I can't be sure. Just promise me you'll try to eat something.'

Elizabeth Bacon walked briskly under an archway into the garden in front of the hospital. Two senior nurses were trying to help the pitifully sick refugees who had been left on the front steps during the night. Half of them would be taken directly to the makeshift hospice near the railway yards.

'Any luck with the pills?' she asked as she entered her office. Her assistant was arranging files in an old wooden cabinet.

'No.'

'I thought they said the package would be on the next plane.'

'They couldn't find any of the pills, even in Calcutta. Did you manage to weigh him today?'

'A hundred and forty pounds. That's thirty-five pounds he's lost now.'

'Is he in pain?'

'He's still sleeping.'

They both knew Vincent would be dead within the week if the medicine didn't arrive.

The corridor outside his room was completely silent. It was either extremely early, Vincent thought, or he had slept through an evacuation. With a lot of effort he manoeuvered himself up on to one arm and looked out the window. Judging from the light, it must be early morning.

His eyes were swollen and sore. Warm vapours rose up around his face from under the sheets. They smelled putrid.

The knots and cramps in his intestines, the way the pain raced from one part to another, made him feel a worm the size of a snake was moving around inside him. He tried to imagine which meal could have caused this agony.

Each afternoon just before supper, one of two nurses, or sometimes both, ended their rounds in Vincent's room. Over the weeks they had watched his energy level, the amount of fight he had in him, progressively weaken. On the rare occasions when he could speak, they listened to his stories about Marie and their children. In turn they told him about some of their adventures. They had both been kidnapped by bandits. They had visited remote villages. In some they had found that cannibalism was still practised as a traditional punishment for enemies.

It was during one of these storytelling sessions that an American pilot poked his head around the door and handed them a package. The nurses rushed to the pharmacy to prepare its contents for administration.

MARIE

64.

'May I see Mr Hyde please?'

'He's not here today, Mrs Broom.'

'Will he be here tomorrow? He gave me this appointment a month ago.'

The receptionist's eyes flicked nervously around the massive room. Soldiers were standing in each corner. They were watching her closely.

'I'm sorry, I don't know when he'll be back. I'm sorry. I'm very busy, I have to get back to my work. I hope you understand.'

Marie looked at the woman's eyes. There was no expression.

'But—'

'Look. I'm very busy today. I'm sorry but I have to go.' She spun round and disappeared through the doorway to the managers' offices.

Marie turned quietly and walked out the revolving door.

'What's the matter, Marie? You look worried.' Arthur was standing close to the fence, talking quietly so the guards wouldn't hear.

'Ginger Hyde wasn't at the bank on Friday, Arthur.'

'Maybe he's sick.'

'No, I think it's worse than that. We had an appointment. He was supposed to give me this month's money. You know him, there's no one more reliable.'

'I'd go and say a prayer for him if I were you. It might be all you can do if they've found out about his charity work.'

'I don't want to even think about it,' Marie said.

'How are you off for money then, without Ginger's help?'

'Not good. Really not good at all. I'll go to the hospital tomorrow. I'll see if Dr Selwyn-Clarke knows anything.'

65.

'Don't look directly at me.'

'Sorry.'

Marie moved in the same direction as the woman, circling a table piled with old marrows.

'Is anyone following you?'

'Who would want to follow me, Mrs Hyde?'

'There are spies everywhere, Mrs Broom. Who knows who they followed to catch Ginger out?'

Marie paused, unsure how to respond. 'How is he?'

'He's all right. They let me take food to him.'

'Which camp is he in?'

The women moved around a large group of people and further into the market, detouring in different directions.

'He's not in a camp. The kempeitai put him in the police cells.'

Marie tried not to flinch. She'd heard this was where the Japanese were torturing people. She knew that David Loie, a New Zealand chemist who was a leader in the resistance, had recently committed suicide there. He had taken cyanide.

'Can't I take him anything?' she said.

'No. Only I'm allowed in.' She moved away and signalled with her eyes towards a table of tinned goods on the other side of the market where they could converge again. They took several minutes to zigzag there through the shoppers, not looking at each other. Now they were out of sight of the guards.

'You'll be needing some money.'

'That's not why I wanted to see you.'

'Don't be silly, Marie. Of course you need money. Go to this address.' She placed a piece of paper on the table. 'I have to go now. God be with you.'

'Mrs Hyde …' Marie's words were lost as the woman rushed away. She wanted to say, 'God bless you and Mr Hyde.' The bank manager had kept her children alive for months. Without him she was sure at least one would have succumbed to an illness brought on by malnutrition.

When she left the market, Marie noticed a young man buying a packet of cigarettes from the window of a wooden shack at the entrance. He didn't look at her, but she was certain she'd crossed paths with him in a lot of places recently. Was he following her? Despite the heavy food she was carrying, she took a long detour via wide open streets where she could see clearly behind her for a good long distance.

66.

Marie took Cynthia with her to the address on the Peak. The letterbox had the name of a Frenchman, but a young

woman with an English accent answered the door. She
quickly asked Marie if she thought she'd been followed.
Since noticing the man in the market, Marie had started
paying more attention to people around her. She was confident she hadn't been followed.

Satisfied with Marie's answer, the woman invited her in
and disappeared. The room was sparsely furnished, but there
were no unpolished squares of floor space where furniture
was missing, as there were in Marie's flat and those of most
of her friends.

'Sorry, what did you say your name was?' The woman had
returned. She addressed herself directly to Marie, ignoring
Cynthia. Marie thought there might be someone else in the
next room who needed to be consulted but didn't want to
be seen.

'Broom,' she said. 'Marie Broom.'

'Good. Top of the list. Have you any papers on you,
anything to prove who you are?'

'Just my Portuguese papers. Will they do? I don't like
carrying my British passport.' Marie's hands shook as she
pulled the papers out of her handbag.

'Of course. Good.' The woman handed them back. 'Look,
we can't repeat this. We're going to give you everything he's
allotted you in one go. And I have to ask you to destroy any
pieces of paper you have with this address on them. And
don't tell anyone about us.'

'Of course.' Marie had become used to the fact people
behaved as if they were characters in a spy novel. She took
the envelope from the woman and opened it in front of her.

'It's all there,' the woman said. 'I'd prefer if you left now.'

'Yes, of course. I'd just like to hide some of the money
in my daughter's shoes. The Japanese rarely search children.'

'Please be quick.'

Marie placed money in each of Cynthia's shoes, then laced them up.

'Thank you for doing this.'

'It's nothing. It's Mr Hyde who really deserves your thanks.'

'How is he?' She pulled up Cynthia's socks and looked at the woman.

'We don't know. No one's been allowed in to see him for a few days.'

'Your husband works at the bank?'

'We'd rather not say anything.'

'I'm sorry. It's just that I'd like to be able to thank you in some way.'

'That won't be necessary. Please, you must go.' She moved to the door and opened it partially to look outside.

'Thank you. And please thank Mrs Hyde.'

'She's been interned, Mrs Broom. Both she and her son have been put into Stanley. Turns out they were just keeping Mrs Hyde out as a ploy to make her husband talk. Now I'm afraid they're using plain old torture. Goodbye, Mrs Broom.'

VINCENT

67.

Vincent got back to the hospital from his rented room near the British Army Aid Group headquarters after the hottest three days on record in Guilin. There were fifteen sick peasants on the steps. The nurses had identified five they could help. The others would have to go to the hospice.

Vincent and two porters lifted the men on to hospital carts and wheeled them as gently as possible across the town. Under the trees around the railway yard and the overhangs of the old warehouses, more than a hundred emaciated Chinese refugees lay waiting to die. Vincent could do nothing more than offer them water.

He was still horribly thin, but most of the strength had returned to his legs. He had taken to walking around the town every morning to ready himself for the day that Lindsay Ride sent his next agent downriver. He looked for food scraps for the hospital and talked to anyone who could have come from Hong Kong. The reports were both good and bad, but with luck on their side Marie and the children might make it out. To think otherwise was too painful.

Vincent had visited every hotel, hostel, hospital and refugee camp in Guilin in the hope of finding Lizzie's daughter Mary. Perhaps she had stayed on in the town after she posted her letter to him ten months earlier. Careful to get the accent right, he asked the clerks if they had a Miss Ah Yuk – Mary's Chinese name – registered but found no trace of her.

By chance he passed the Chinese wife of a British friend in the street. She had just escaped from Hong Kong with the couple's teenage son but had no news of Marie. Like the doctor's wife he had met in India, she needed to be vouched for with the British Consulate and Vincent was happy to help. He was also able to give her hopeful news: he had seen her husband a few months earlier, working on a ship out of Bombay. The relief on her face was something he would never forget. Before they parted, he inquired if she had enough money to fund her voyage out of China. She showed him two large solid gold coins; they would be almost priceless against the mixed and changing currencies.

Vincent turned to walk back to his hotel. Suddenly the woman called after him and ran back. 'I don't want to panic you, Vincent,' she said. 'It doesn't seem fair after the good news you've brought me.'

'What is it?'

'I know nothing of what Marie's been through, but if she is still in your flat I should warn you that the whole area around it has been taken over by the Japanese army.'

'What do you mean exactly? Please be frank.'

'Just keep an open mind.' She studied his face. 'It's important you understand how difficult life has been in Hong Kong. She may have given up and asked to be put in a camp.'

68.

The time had come to leave Guilin. Vincent's money was running out. He decided to use John Keswick's letter at the local Jardine, Matheson office to try to get a loan for the next part of his journey. Within fifteen minutes he had a roll of banknotes in his wallet.

He arrived at the riverside wharf soon afterwards. The hot dry spell had been broken by three days of heavy rain. The calm river along which he had walked in the evenings watching boatmen and cormorant fishermen had turned into a torrent of swirling brown water and debris.

Lindsay Ride and a young Portuguese man were waiting. 'You might just break our record,' Ride said. He seemed in good spirits despite the problems that had delayed the mission three times already. 'Young Anthony here and the punt master are confident you won't be in any real danger. You can swim of course?'

'Of course.'

The journey was expected to take from five to twelve days, but Anthony thought they might be able to do it in three. With his manner, posture and high level of English, the guide reminded Vincent of many of the young Macanese seamen he had worked with and trained. Anthony had been a student of Ride's at Hong Kong University. With the Japanese invasion he'd had to halt his studies, and he and his wife had fled to China. He had turned his intelligence towards memorising every stream and trail between Guilin and the towns near the coast and trying to outthink Japanese search patrols. He told Vincent the Japanese were everywhere along the coast, but he should be safe inland at Samfou.

Anthony was clearly in awe of Ride. Before the surrender, he had worked for the doctor's ambulance service. Afterwards he felt he had no option but to leave while he was still fit enough to get out and be useful somewhere else. Since making it to Guilin, he had been running messages and coordinating couriers and spies going in and out of Hong Kong. He told Vincent the group had chosen the motto *Spes Salutis*, Hope of Salvation.

Vincent and Anthony sat as comfortably as they could with their luggage on the bare wood at the punt's bow. Vincent had transferred a few items of clothing into a small suitcase and reserved a second suitcase for currency, medicine and other provisions destined for the British Army Aid Group outpost at Samfou.

He quickly gained confidence in the skills of the punter, who had their lives in his hands. Steep rock faces and spectacular scenery raced past; each towering column had its own distinct shape and patterned cliffs. After a few hours the limestone mountains grew smaller and by early afternoon the men could see only bamboo forests and small villages along the river.

Still moving downriver at nightfall, they decided to continue on to Wuzhou, the next big town on the map. The night was black with barely any stars. They could make out only a few cooking fires near the riverbank.

Vincent watched the punt master closely, unable to work out how he was managing to navigate through the river's turns and channels without any visibility. As they rounded the final corner he gasped: a huge neon sign pierced the gloom. Anthony smiled. 'It's a café. Last good meal you'll find.'

The two men stepped ashore and climbed the steps to the town's main street. Apart from the neon sign there was little to the café: a menu nailed to a tree, a covered area for when it rained, and eight tables on the roadside. Vincent began to regret sitting at the best lit table as one beggar after another emerged from the darkness. They looked as close to death as the men and women he had seen lying on the ground at the hospice.

An old woman appeared, dressed in a ragged Chinese army coat. She held it open to reveal her wasted body. Vincent and Anthony decided to eat quickly and go back to the punt to sleep. As they walked away Anthony tried to assuage their guilt. They would need to keep all their funds for their own food, he said. And they would cause a violent riot if they started handing out money.

Next day they made good time, passing the town of Zhaoqing and arriving at the wide muddy road where they would start their journey overland from the Xi River to the Tanjiang.

It was now mid July and steaming hot. Vincent stripped to his shorts and swapped his shoes for a pair of sandals with soles of old tyre rubber, which he'd had made to his size in Guilin. He and Anthony walked single file on compacted dirt paths that wove around the edges of long-abandoned paddy fields and the wooded hills dotted between them. At several points they handed over money at barriers set up by local protection gangs.

At midday, across a wide expanse of gently descending fields, they saw a group of Sikhs dressed in pristine white tunics coming towards them. As they got closer one of the Sikhs grinned. 'This is very "Stanley and Livingstone",' he said and laughed. He had been the radio operator on a ship Vincent had worked on.

He and his friends had been waiting in Macau for fifteen months, he told Vincent. They'd finally concluded that things weren't going to get any better and decided to flee north, regardless of the danger. Both men were keen to talk but the exchange was brief: their travelling companions wanted to keep moving.

After an exhausting day's walk of about thirty miles, Vincent and Anthony found a small inn, washed as best they could and went out to look for a meal. The village's night market had a paltry selection of overpriced food, and a section full of goods that the men strongly suspected had been looted from Hong Kong by fleeing Chinese. Cocktail dresses, dinner jackets, elaborate hats, makeup boxes and furs lay on the bare clay of the road. Vincent realised with a shiver they were the sorts of items that could have come from his home.

Back at the inn, he lay on the wooden planks of a bed shaped to human form by travellers over hundreds of years and massaged his knees. They looked skinnier than when he was a teenager. His shoulders ached from carrying not just suitcases but a parasol to protect himself from the merciless sun.

Their goal the following day was to cover the same distance. After two hours they stopped for a quick breakfast of rice and vegetables. The rice was full of small stones, which they spat into the grass beside their table. Merchants had started to mix rice with anything they could find to increase the weight.

69.

Anthony had warned Vincent he wouldn't wait around once they reached Samfou, but the goodbye was even more rapid than Vincent expected. He was standing surprised and alone in the courtyard of a large house when a tall slim Englishman walked briskly out of the main door. The man shook his hand. Anthony always left quickly, he explained. His wife lived nearby. He hadn't seen her for a long time and was understandably keen to check she was all right.

'You must be Vincent Broom,' he said. 'Shiner Wright. You're to stay here. There's a room prepared upstairs. Take up your things and I'll bring you water. You'll be wanting a wash I imagine, and a good meal. We don't have a lot of food but it should be a bit better than what you've been eating on the road.' He looked carefully at Vincent and in a softer tone added, 'When you come back down I'll introduce you to my wife.'

Over dinner, Wright's wife told her story. She and their children had just got out of Macau. She trembled as she described the final part of their escape. They had crossed a massive expanse of water in a snake boat. Such boats, used by smugglers, were swift and low with enormous long oars. At any time Japanese patrol boats could have caught up with them. 'I'm not sure I would have done it if I'd known what it was going to be like,' she said, and touched her husband's hand thoughtfully.

Vincent sensed that the years apart had made Wright's wife stronger and more independent and that both of them were negotiating these changes carefully. She and the children were leaving soon for Guilin. She knew little about what was happening in Hong Kong, she said, but she'd seen a massive exodus to Macau in recent months as the food situation on the island became ever more desperate.

In normal times Samfou would have been airy and pleasant. The town had arisen from the amalgamation of three ancient villages, each established on one or other side of two converging rivers. The large bridges that spanned them allowed the town to function as a single municipality. However, the thousands of people who now filled the streets were in as bad, or in some cases even worse, condition than those Vincent had seen up north. Perhaps the people who'd stayed here simply lacked the energy to go any further.

Shiner assigned Vincent a job: he was to search the markets for any reasonably priced scraps of food from which they could make soup to feed everyone at the base. He warned him not to buy fish: the fish farms at the edge of town were doubling as public latrines. He also told him to take a hard look at any meat before buying since it might contain body parts of humans, both children and adults.

On the first day Vincent watched the locals haggle and slowly got a feel for the market's norms and bargaining language. Keen to be fully occupied, he assisted Shiner to set up a public soup kitchen to help feed the many starving villagers and refugees. That evening he scrubbed, cut down and positioned two 44-gallon drums over a pile of stones. Between the drums the men could light a fire to cook the soup.

At the end of the week, Shiner Wright's wife and children were ready to head north. Vincent and Wright went with them upstream to where they'd begin their journey overland with a British Army Aid Group guide. They watched as

the small children set off in sedan chairs, carried by pairs
of coolies walking in a well-learned rhythm, with Wright's
wife walking alongside.

Next night Wright took Vincent to visit General Lee,
the leader of the Nationalist army for the area surrounding
Samfou. Lee had organised a six-course banquet, starting
with oysters especially brought up from the coast. He and
Wright had an animated conversation in Cantonese. Shiner
turned to Vincent every few minutes to explain what they
were discussing.

Vincent knew it was thanks to such meetings that the
British Army Aid Group was able to stay abreast of Japanese
troop movements. Relations between the group and the army
had been mostly effective and mutually beneficial. There had,
Wright told him, been just one temporary setback when two
escaping Royal Scots had taken it upon themselves to train
communist soldiers in return for food and shelter.

On the way back to the compound, Wright related a
strange dream he'd had the night before. He'd dreamed that
Marie and the children got out safely but that Vincent was
not there to welcome them. The story reminded Vincent
of the fears he'd had while lying in the hospital.

70.

On the first day the soup kitchen was operating over two
hundred people filed through the courtyard. Next day there
were more than three hundred. Thanks to Wright's profi-
ciency in Cantonese and the respect he'd gained in the town,
most people moved past quietly and with surprising order
as Vincent ladled the soup into bowls.

In the afternoon a boy came running into the compound screeching excitedly and rattling off a few sentences in Wright's ear.

Both the boy and Wright turned to Vincent.

'What is it?'

'There's a boat with a family in Western clothes coming up the river,' Wright said.

Vincent slid his feet into his sandals and ran ahead of Wright to the town's main jetty. A crowd of locals had assembled. A middle-aged couple and their children were coming up the river in a punt. Vincent looked further down the river to see if there was another punt. There wasn't. Wright consoled him with a hand on his arm before warmly greeting the arrivals and offering to carry some of their bags.

71.

The soup kitchen had begun to run smoothly. The broth was prepared in the mornings, so most afternoons Vincent was free. Wright could see that the spare time was torturing him. 'We have a treat for dinner tonight.'

Vincent pulled himself up off his bed. 'What's that?'

'Beef. The cook has evidently had a lucky day in the market.'

'Beef. You're joking.'

'See you in the mess in five minutes.'

As they waited for the meal, Wright started to talk. 'I thought I'd look after the broth tomorrow on my own, with the help of the boys.'

'I appreciate your concern,' Vincent said, 'but I feel better if I stay busy.'

'Yes, I know,' Wright said, 'but I have something else for you to do, a mail run to a town. It's about thirteen miles away. Lee has given us the green light. He says there aren't any Jap patrols near here at the moment.'

The cook came in with the beef. The men stared at the white mound. Wright asked the cook what it was. When the cook waved her arms expressively around her stomach, Vincent gathered it was the inside of a cow's udder.

The men poked at the mound with their chopsticks and gingerly tasted it. 'I thought I'd reached the stage where I would eat anything,' Wright said, groaning. 'Now I realise I'm not quite there.'

72.

Vincent followed the short tracks zigzagging between barren paddy fields. A few low forested hills and walled groups of farm buildings were the only places where you could take cover or hide. In open areas a Japanese patrol with binoculars would be able to see Vincent's silhouette more than two miles away. He had no choice but to cross these places. He walked as fast as he could.

Wright had given him a general description of the route, but with a lack of landmarks Vincent often had to resort to asking directions, wielding a piece of paper with the name of his destination in Chinese characters. Locals who stared from their doorways at the tall foreigner passing through their village were generally happy to point the way. Farmers were better off for food than the refugees, but they were taking extreme measures to safeguard it. In one village Vincent saw a young boy whose responsibility seemed to be to follow his father's pig around and guard it from bandits.

Vincent was to deliver medicines to a group of Maryknoll priests who ran a mission and hospital in Taishan. For generations, people from this town had been migrating to the United States and sending back money to family members. Vincent figured this explained the high quality of the houses.

On a large table in the main kitchen the mission's head doctor unpacked the medicines. He was polite, but Vincent could see the shipment was far smaller than he had hoped for.

Vincent returned to Samfou just in time to serve the next day's meal. He'd hoped there would be news of Marie. Two British Army Aid Group runners had been through but neither was assigned to his case. Wright assured him it was normal not to hear anything.

Over the next weeks Vincent was sent on other delivery runs. He became accustomed to the landscape and knew the fastest routes in all directions. On one run, while waiting his turn to cross a narrow bridge, he was surprised to see among the group of farmers coming the other way an unusually tall European woman and a girl he assumed was her daughter. The woman smiled warmly as she came down the ramp at the end of the bridge. She told him she was Australian, married to a Chinese man she had met in Sydney. They had moved back to his home village twenty years earlier. Her daughter couldn't even speak English. As they parted she warned him she'd seen Japanese patrols in the area a month before. She had recognised him as a foreigner from miles away. He should be very, very careful.

On his way back to Samfou there was a torrential storm. A flash flood in the hills destroyed the bridge he had crossed earlier in the day. Stranded between towns he was forced to settle for the night in an empty barn. He was now more wary than ever of enemy patrols. Should any approach, they would be completely hidden by the stand of trees behind him. From a lean-to shelter attached to the barn, he watched the river's rushing brown water. The wreckage of a sampan and the bodies of two men sailed by. Fording the river was clearly impossible.

MARIE

73.

Vincent junior stood on his chair with his eyes fixed on his mother as Ah Sup fed him his weekly egg. The young amah seemed nervous. Her hand shook just enough to dislodge a quarter of the yolk from the tiny porcelain spoon. Marie got up from her chair, picked up the piece of yolk, brushed off the specks of dust and put it back on the spoon. Then she left the kitchen, put on her most comfortable shoes and went out the front door without saying a word.

The walk along the quay gave her time to think. Her instincts were leading her towards the Red Cross office, to ask to be interned in the organisation's camp. They'd be prisoners, but at least they'd be secure, have food and medicine, and there would be less risk of the children starving. The benefits had begun to outweigh the loss of freedom and any chance of escape from Hong Kong.

As she came to the crossroads at Wanchai, she found herself heading towards the home of her preferred fortune teller. She was confused to the point of tears when she left the old woman's flat. The giant steel door clanged shut behind her. It was too late to turn around and ask another question.

She had been told to wait for a message.

74.

'It's time to be reasonable, Marie.' The lines on Arthur's face seemed like knife cuts, deep and defined.

'But what about you?'

'I'll miss your visits of course. But if you don't go into the camp and one of the children gets sick, how will you feel? How will I feel? It's not the time to be believing some mumbo jumbo from a soothsayer who's making money building up people's hopes without thinking of the danger she's putting them in. How much money do you have left from what I last gave you?'

'Enough for two weeks.'

'And then what are you going to do? I don't have a penny left.'

Marie rounded the last corner of the barbed wire fence. They had made only one pass along it, but the guard change was late so they would not be able to do another.

'You'd better go,' Arthur said. 'God bless.'

The sun forced the women returning to the island from their visit to the camp into the fine line of shadow beside the ferry building as the Japanese guards checked everyone's papers. The women exchanged solemn smiles – they recognised each other now, perhaps taking some comfort from the fact that every one of them was the girlfriend, wife, friend or mistress of an incarcerated British soldier.

At last they were allowed to trickle down, one at a time, into the waiting room at the end of the wharf. Sitting on the hard wooden seat, Marie contemplated again the choice she had to make. Everything she'd owned that was not in daily use had been sold. All their silver and china had gone. The only valuable thing she'd kept was her diamond wedding ring. How was she going to buy next month's food?

The ferry was late. Marie gazed up at the high-vaulted roof, back around at the other women, and out the windows towards the Peak across the water. How did these other women keep it together? Some sat gossiping, as if they had just spent the afternoon at a pleasant lunch.

She could hear two women speaking quietly a few seats in front of her. One, she knew, was Emily Hahn, an American journalist. She had seen her about a year before the invasion in a bar that often doubled as an opium den. Now she was sure she heard her say the English word 'nasty' in the middle of a Chinese sentence. She pricked up her ears.

'Nasty,' Emily Hahn repeated. 'How am I supposed to know who Nasty is?'

Marie froze. She tried to pick out other words, but the sound of the approaching ferry, its chugging engine and the splash of its wake against the wharf, drowned them out. As she stood in the queue to get on the boat she fixed her eyes on the back of Hahn's head. Once on board, she pushed ahead of other passengers and sat beside Hahn and her companion. She forced herself not to stare at them. Once the boat landed she followed Hahn out of the terminal and along a succession of alleys and streets. In the open she kept her distance, but on the smaller streets she increased her pace so as not to lose the trail.

She waited until she saw Hahn enter a grocery store where

there were no other customers. 'Excuse me.' She talked softly, staying hidden behind shelves where she pretended to be looking at a selection of tinned fruit, products she had not been able to buy for months.

'Yes?'

'On the boat, I heard you say something about Nasty. Someone called Nasty.'

'Please go away. Don't say another word. I don't know what you're talking about.'

Hahn looked frightened. Marie turned and left the shop, but lingered on the other side of the road. As Hahn came out she saw Marie and turned away. Marie followed her until she entered the foyer of a hotel.

'Please. Can you tell me if there was a message for someone called Nasty?'

'Look, I don't know who you are.'

'My name is Marie Broom. I have four children here. My husband – he wasn't here when Hong Kong fell. He used to call me Nasty.'

Each of them looked around the large room. They were completely alone, but conscious that someone could come around the corner at any moment.

Hahn moved closer. 'Please leave me alone,' she whispered. 'Things are very dangerous. They are executing people who pass messages. There was a message from outside to someone called Nasty, but I destroyed it.'

'What did it say? You must remember what it said at least.'

'I didn't read it, I'm sorry. It's too dangerous now for such things. I have a child too. Do you know how many messages I've had to pass on to people? I'm sorry but you're just too late. I can't risk it.'

'But when was it? When did it arrive?'

'Yesterday. That's all I can tell you. You must go.'

'If you need to reach me I'm up on Fort Street. I can write down the address.'

'Don't write anything. Just go.'

75.

Marie walked into the flat. Without even greeting the children, she told Lizzie she wanted to talk to her in the bedroom.

'What is it? Was there a problem at the camp?' Lizzie feared for the children and herself every time Marie left the flat.

'Someone is trying to contact us for Vincent,' Marie said. She made a circuit of the room, then knelt down to open the loose floorboards where she'd hidden documents and money.

'What do you mean?' Lizzie said, uncertain whether Marie was even rational. 'What do you mean "trying"?'

'Someone sent a message from the outside addressed to Nasty. They sent it to Emily Hahn, the American journalist.'

'But this one word – Nasty – that's all you know? What about the Red Cross? What did they say?'

'We can't go into the camp now.'

'But what are the children going to eat?'

'I don't know. We'll find something. Vincent's alive. He must have made it to Sydney. I know he'll try to get us out.'

'Marie.'

'What?'

'I'm sure he's alive, I know he is, but the children are getting weak.'

'We'll find some way. Leave me alone to freshen up. I don't want to tell the children anything for now.'

76.

Marie was still in her room when there was a knock on the door of the flat. Lizzie and Ah Sup opened it just enough to see a fisherman on the landing.

'Go away. We don't have any money for fish,' Lizzie said.

'Please open. Quickly.' The old man's voice rasped with frustration.

'I'll get my boss. Stay here.' Lizzie ran to Marie's room, gesturing for the children to go to their rooms.

'What is it?'

'A fisherman.'

'Let him in. Let him in.'

The three women stood in the entrance. Marie asked Ah Sup to open the door again a little. As she did so, a second man, younger but also in peasant clothing, shoved the door, pushed past the old man and entered the room.

'I have a message for Nasty.' He looked behind him into the hallway and told the old man to knock if anyone came up the stairs.

'Yes, yes, that's me. That's me.' Marie was breathless.

'I can't stay long,' the man said.

He produced a tiny folded note from the cuff of his sleeve. Marie took it. Her hands were quivering.

'Why didn't you hide the note better?' she said.

'The Japanese don't search in the most obvious places. Read it please. I must go.'

The short note was in Vincent's unmistakable handwriting. Marie should prepare to escape, it said. She must trust the instructions in the other message.

'What was in the other message?' Marie said angrily. 'It was destroyed by the woman who received it. Do your people know she's no longer reliable?' She paused, fighting back tears. 'Where is he? Where is my husband?'

'I don't know.' The man was agitated. 'I don't know anything about this. I was given the message to bring here as a secondary mission. I blew up the Fanling bridge last night. Now I have to get back to China. I was told there was a plan for you to go to Macau. Go to your usual Mass when you are there. You will be contacted. I have to go. Good luck.'

The door closed. The three women stood in stunned silence.

77.

Marie took shelter under the eaves near the gates of the Star Ferry. While visiting Arthur, she had seen Emily Hahn at the wire talking to her boyfriend, an officer, but she'd avoided making eye contact. She thought of Arthur and his selfless response to the news that she was leaving for Macau and wouldn't be able to bring him any more of her broths.

A Japanese soldier started yelling at the hundreds of people pressing to get into the building. A man waiting near the entrance gave up. He passed Marie and the other women on his way out, shaking his head and mumbling to himself.

'What's happening?' Marie said.

'They are searching everyone. It's going to take forever. And they've cancelled most of the later ferries. Some resistance saboteurs have blown up the Fanling bridge.'

As Marie repressed her desire to ask more questions, she noticed Emily Hahn standing next to her. With a discreet movement of her eyes Hahn asked permission from the women behind to join the queue.

'I'm sorry for the other day,' she said quietly to Marie.

Marie turned to look at her. 'I understand how scared you must have been.'

'Did you get another message?' Hahn said. 'Usually they send two.'

The women stopped talking as a soldier walked past them.

'Yes. Someone came to my home last night.'

'Are you going to leave?'

'Maybe. Yes, I think so.'

'Can you do me a favour, if you can forgive me for what I did?'

'What is it?'

'I'm supposed to be exchanged out. Madame Chiang Kai-shek is arranging it. I don't want to be sent to Guam,' Hahn went on. 'I want to go to the US.'

The story sounded incredible. 'I don't know what I can do but I'll try,' Marie murmured.

'Thank you. I'd better leave you. Goodbye, and good luck.'

78.

On the ferry to Macau with Lizzie, Ah Sup and the children, a woman Marie vaguely recognised sat next to her and asked her question after question. Marie didn't want to be impolite but at the same time she didn't want to divulge any details of her plans. Every extra person who knew might cause them problems, whether intentionally or accidentally.

'How much money do you have with you?' the woman asked.

'Not very much.' This at least was not a lie.

'They stole so much of what I had in the house,' the

woman said, 'things my husband and I had worked for for years.'

'I'm sorry,' Marie said. 'It's the same for us. We had to sell a lot too, but that was also like theft.'

'I hid my jewelry.'

'You have all your jewelry with you?' Marie cast an eye over the woman's meagre effects.

'Well hidden.'

'But where? They searched all our bags.' Marie thought about the wedding ring she'd hidden in her cold-cream.

The woman moved closer to Marie. 'I swapped all the gems for gold and had the gold melted down. Feel my handbag,' she said.

Marie picked it up. The woman leaned in closer. 'Solid gold. The black bamboo handles. They're solid gold wrapped in black leather. They say it costs a fortune to bribe your way out.'

'I don't know anything about that,' Marie said. 'We're just visiting my family in Macau.'

79.

Lizzie and Ah Sup watched over the children as they played in the large bright living room of Marie's cousin Julia as Julia and Marie hurriedly got ready to go to Mass. The girls took turns holding Vincent junior and stroking his newly shaved head. His blond curls had been sacrificed to avoid any last-minute problems processing the children into Macau as Portuguese descendants.

The girls had always been uncomfortable visiting Macau. Family relationships were awkward and they had difficulty eating the oily food. But for now they seemed happy to be away from Hong Kong. As soon as they arrived they'd noticed the absence of Japanese flags and soldiers. Macau was largely as it had been on their last visit, but with less food in the grocery stores.

The Mass was like any other Marie and Julia had attended. The elderly Macanese women who walked up the hill to the church each day were managing to keep up appearances, but their worn and frayed clothes would have been replaced in better times.

Afterwards, as the two women turned a sharp corner to head home, a man walking closely behind them spoke in a deep whisper, just loud enough for them to hear.

'Mrs Broom.'

They stopped under a tree.

'Yes.'

'My name is Dr Gosano. I have a message for you. For Nasty.'

'Yes?'

'There is a teahouse just down the hill. Do you know it?'

'Yes,' Julia said.

'Go there tomorrow at three. Wait downstairs. A man in a grey suit and dark glasses will enter and signal to you to go upstairs.'

'Do you know where my husband is?' Marie said.

'Sorry, I know nothing more. A word of caution though: stay away from the British consulate.'

'Why?'

'It's not prudent to let them know anything. Good day, ladies.' The man tipped his hat and walked off down an alley.

'Why do you think he said that about the British consulate?' Julia said.

'Maybe it's just a matter of politics. Or maybe if the Japanese see us there they'll guess we're British'

'You must take the risk. I've heard they're giving food money to anyone with British papers.'

At ten that night Julia went to Marie's room. A woman waiting in the living room said she had a telegram for her.

Marie quickly got dressed. She recognised the woman as the Portuguese wife of a marine engineer who worked for Williamson's. The woman was apologetic. She had tried to send Marie the telegram a number of times over the past eighteen months via people going to Hong Kong. Nobody had been willing to risk it. As soon as she heard from her sister that Marie had been at Mass, she'd rushed over.

Marie grabbed the telegram. Mr Vassoura had made it safely to Australia, she read. Her eyes fillled with tears. All that time ago, when she was feeling so alone, Vincent had been thinking of her. She pictured him now in Sydney, waiting for them.

80.

Marie and Julia sat for an hour on the uncomfortable wooden stools of the teahouse. There were only two other women. The room was full of middle-aged and elderly men continuously smoking. They were conscious of many eyes on them.

On two occasions men appearing to be Japanese in civilian suits came in, looked around and went back outside.

At last a young Chinese man who looked to be in his late twenties stopped halfway up the stairs and gestured for them to follow him.

'It is you, Nasty?' he said at the top of the stairs.

'Yes. Marie Broom. This is my cousin Julia.'

'Please, quickly. My name is Leung. Take a seat. Where are you staying?'

'With Julia in a flat up by São Paulo.'

'Ah, it's too far. You have to be down by the docks. I'll give you the card of a hotel. You must move there this afternoon.'

'When do we go?' Marie tried to sound calm.

'We don't know exactly. It could be tomorrow; it could be two weeks. It depends on the roster of the Japanese guards on the patrol boats. They are trying to stop people getting to Free China. If the Japanese guards are not there, there will be Koreans on duty. That is when we'll go. We can bribe the Koreans.'

'I don't have much money left.'

'I have an envelope for you to pay the hotel. Everything else I will pay for. You must be ready to leave each morning at four o'clock. It will be me who will come to get you.'

'What if you don't come?'

'If I am not there before the sun comes up, you can go back to bed. Pack only the things you will need for the voyage. We will be walking a lot, so no more clothing than is necessary. Bring some food, some bananas. You have two amahs with you and four children I understand.'

'Yes. Sorry to ask so many questions but how will we get across China? Will it take us long to get all the way out? You know, I haven't seen my husband for two years.'

'You must miss him. He is a very nice man, even though he has eaten almost all of my wife's chillies.'

'I don't understand.'

'You know he's here, don't you? He's just north of here. He hitchhiked and walked halfway across China.'

Marie let out an uncontrollable sob.

'Don't cry. People will look. I must go. Just be ready each morning.'

'Goodbye. God bless you.' Julia spoke as Marie stood in silence, digesting the news.

81.

Marie junior was excited to learn her father was so close. 'Mummy, you'll cry when you see him. You won't be able to stop,' she said. Marie smiled. Her daughter was probably right.

Their small room in the hotel looked out on a narrow dark lane. While Ah Sup and Lizzie arranged pillows and mattresses around the floor, Marie went outside. As she wove through the streets towards the cemetery she noticed dozens of familiar faces. Many of them were women she hadn't seen since just before the Japanese attacked. She'd heard that when the British authorities had insisted 'non-essential' expatriates leave Hong Kong for Australia via the Philippines, many women had decided to go only as far as Macau in the hope they could see their husbands on weekends. Later, when their husbands were interned, they wondered if they had made the right decision.

Turning a bend near the central post office, Marie came face-to-face with Kay Ma. She'd last seen her when the pair had searched the hospitals for Kay's sons and Marie's friends. The women hugged. Each asked the other what they were doing on Macau. Both gave the same evasive answer: they were just there for a change of scenery. Marie realised she had not been alone in reaching the end of her tether in Hong Kong. Almost two years after the invasion, with cash running out, conditions deteriorating, and the knowledge that another winter could be deadly for children, many women had fled with them to Macau.

She left the shopping area and made her way to the cemetery. At the four-year-old grave of her father, on a rise above a tiny chapel, she bowed her head and said a short prayer, then a last goodbye. She loved him, she whispered, but she was not sure when she would be able to visit him again.

82.

At half past three in the morning Marie was woken by Lizzie. Silently, she turned on a small light. The two women dressed in the clothes they had taken off a few hours earlier and shook the children and Ah Sup awake. They had one change of clothes for everyone and a small bag of bananas and sweets packed into two small suitcases.

They sat on the edge of the mattresses and watched the hands of the clock tick over. Four, four-thirty, five. Finally, Lizzie pulled the blankets back over the children and unstrapped the four pairs of sandals.

A week passed. Some mornings Marie was convinced she could see the guide from the window, but every time the person walked right past the hotel. With three adults and four children in one small room, the air was almost unbreathable by the time everyone awoke for the second time each day.

The children quickly became frustrated. Ah Sup and Lizzie found a circuit to take them on. It included the gardens, harbourside paths and temples. Marie would have a nap and then wash before they returned with food that Lizzie had managed to find in the markets.

On the eighth day Marie visited the British consulate. She was determined not to give away her reason for being in Macau, but she desperately wanted to know if there was any truth to the stories that civilians with British papers were being given money.

From deep within the side pocket of her handbag she took out her British passport and the children's papers. The Macanese woman at the desk took them and asked her to sit in the waiting room. After ten minutes, when only three of the dozen people ahead of her had been called, the clerk summoned Marie back to the front desk. 'I've made an entry for you in the register, but you won't be able to collect any money until next week. Otherwise...'

She lowered her voice and leaned closer to Marie. 'My supervisor has asked that you go to the Pan Am building tonight at midnight. Don't try to go in. Just wait in front.'

83.

The night was black and moonless. Although she had grown up in the area, Marie made a few wrong turns on her way to Pan Am's flying-boat port. It was just after midnight when she arrived. The car park was amost empty, with just three cars lined up along the wall.

She stood near the entrance to catch her breath. After checking her watch, she realised she was late and began to worry that the walk had been for nothing. Just then a young Englishman carrying a gun at his shoulder appeared from a dark corner.

'Mrs Broom.'

'I know you.'

'Yes. I'm Jim. We were neighbours in Fort Street before the invasion.'

'What are you doing with that thing? I remember you when you were a boy.'

'Mrs Broom!' Another man's voice sounded from the shadows. The figure who came towards her appeared to be in his late forties and was dressed in a light tropical suit.

'It was you who wanted to see me?' she said.

'Yes. I understand you are wanting to escape into China.'

The loudness of his voice was unnerving. Marie detected a strong smell of Scotch.

'No,' she said. 'I'm Macanese. I grew up here. I wanted to bring my children over. There's no food in Hong Kong. I'll go back when things quieten down.'

'I'm sorry. I must have my wires crossed. I was just wanting to offer you some help. That is, if you ever did want to escape.'

'Thank you, but I couldn't take such a risk with my children. We are just going to stay here, as I said, until things settle down.'

The man took out a packet of cigarettes and offered one to Marie. After she declined he took one himself and then offered one to the guard. 'We have quite a system being set up,' he said. 'I just wanted to let you know. God knows if things will ever quieten down again, as you put it.'

'Thank you. I'll keep that in mind. But for now we're all right.'

'Good.'

'I should be getting back to my family.'

'Of course.'

'Sorry about the misunderstanding,' she said. 'I hope it didn't put you out to come here tonight.' She turned in the direction of the young man. 'Goodnight, Jim. Be careful with that gun.'

'There is something I should warn you about, Mrs Broom.' The older man reached clumsily for Marie's arm. 'Don't take these things lightly. The more help you can get, the better. It's a very tough trip and a lot of people die. I don't know of one family that has reached China and then crossed it without losing at least one child. There are many risks.'

'Why are you saying this?' She was angry he was speaking so loudly.

'I'm just pointing out the risks so you don't do anything half prepared. Without involving the right people.'

'Good night. I have no such plans.'

84.

They started up a little later each morning, leaving little Vincent and Cynthia asleep while they performed the ritual of getting dressed and ready to leave. Marie was having increasing difficulty getting to sleep. Always in the back of her mind was the uncertainty of what might happen the next day, and the worry that they were losing valuable time when Vincent was so close. He might leave, thinking they weren't coming.

Two weeks passed without word from Leung. Marie doubted he would have left them waiting so long without even a visit to reassure them. He must have been captured.

By now the children were tiring of their daily walks and visits to gardens. They resisted noisily whenever Lizzie wanted to take them out and then when she wanted to bring them back to the hotel for a nap. Marie was going to Julia's for lunch every day and then to Mass, partly in the hope she would see Dr Gosano again and ask him what to do. Should she be asking people around the docks to see if there was a way they could get across the narrow band of water to the mainland?

'What is it? Is he here? Is he here?' Marie was still half asleep.

'No, it's Margaret,' Lizzie said. 'Malaria. She's vomiting.'

Margaret was lying on Lizzie's bed with a bowl beside her head. The bowl was full of green bile and half-digested scraps of food. Marie sat down and stroked her daughter's hair. Marie junior watched them from her mattress on the other side of the room.

Lizzie handed Marie a cleanly rinsed face cloth for Margaret's forehead. 'We'll take her to Dr Gosano tomorrow,' Marie said. 'It will give me an excuse to find him. I'm going to try to get some more sleep. Please wake me if she gets any worse.'

'What if the man comes?'

'He won't. It's been too long already. It's time to make new plans.'

Marie opened her eyes. Lizzie was standing over her again. All the lights in the room were on.

'What is it?' she murmured groggily. 'Is Margaret worse?'

'He's here,' Lizzie said. 'The man, Mr Leung, he's here. He's waiting outside for us to get ready.'

'What time is it?'

'Just after four.'

Marie got up, pulled on the clothes by her bed and went out into the corridor.

'Did Lizzie tell you my eldest daughter is sick?' she said to Leung.

'Can she walk?'

'I doubt it. She can't even lift her head up. It's malaria. She's been getting these bouts off and on for years.'

'It doesn't matter,' Leung said. 'I'll have to carry her.'

'She's too big. She's almost as tall as me. We have to postpone leaving for at least another night.'

'You don't know what you're talking about.' Leung's voice cracked with urgency. 'People have risked their lives to organise this today and a lot of money has already been spent on bribes. Please, hurry and get ready.'

It was half past four when they finally made their way down the stairs and out into the narrow alley. Leung, carrying Margaret, told everyone to follow him in single file and match the line he was walking perfectly. In less than a minute they were out of the shadow of the buildings and on the edge of a seawall. Eight feet below a small sampan was rocking slightly. A woman was standing in front of the cabin. A man was holding on to the bottom of a rope ladder, attached at the top to a metal ring.

He was waving frantically at Leung. 'No, no. It's too late,' he shouted.

'No. We go. You've been paid, we go. Marie, get in the boat quickly.'

'No, no, it's too late,' the man on the boat repeated.

Marie clambered down the ladder on to the boat. Lizzie handed her the suitcases, and she and Ah Sup followed.

Lizzie and Ah Sup stood near the bow and steadied themselves to take Margaret from Leung and help Vincent junior
and Cynthia down the ladder. Seconds later Leung was on
board. He placed his foot on the stone wall and forced the
bow of the boat out towards the open water.

They were soon well away from the wall. A slight glow
in the eastern sky showed they were completely alone. They
could see only a few lights from houses on Macau and on
the coast of a nearby island.

'Do you have hats for the children?' Leung said.

Marie took hats from the pockets of her padded jacket
and handed them to Ah Sup.

'It's important you cover the blond stubble on the boy's
head. Go to the back in the cabin with the children.'

'But when do we turn? We're heading to the open water.
The whole of Macau will see us.'

'We have to get further away.'

'No. Turn around. If I'd known you weren't going straight
across I would never have come. Turn around. Please, it's
too dangerous.'

'It's too late to go back now. This is the way we always
come. It's the only way. These patrols can be bribed.'

Marie looked towards Lizzie for moral support. Both
women knew Macau well from the years they'd lived there.

Marie moved to the back of the boat and started to pray.
About a quarter of a mile from shore, she saw a light near
the island growing larger. Given the speed with which it was
moving and the hum that had started to drift over the water,
it could only be from a patrol boat.

She waved to Leung, who was still at the front of the
sampan, to get his attention. He had already seen it. 'Just
remain silent,' he said. 'Let me do the talking.'

The sampan owner and his wife looked angrily towards Leung and then Marie. Marie forced Marie junior and Cynthia to put their hands together and pray with her. When she opened her eyes, the patrol boat was almost right beside them. She could make out the faces of armed Korean guards standing on the deck.

The guards signalled to the sampan owner to stop and tie his craft to theirs. Leung stood to indicate it was him they should be talking to.

'Papers!'

As the sampan owner busied himself with the ropes, Leung handed an envelope up to the senior guard, who was quickly joined by two younger colleagues. The three of them stared down at Marie and the children.

'No! No! Not enough!'

Marie tried to follow what was being said. Leung was still trying to hand over the rejected envelope.

'No! Look!' The guard jumped down on to the deck of the sampan, walked towards Cynthia and Vincent and pulled off Vincent's hat.

'Not Chinese! You said Chinese! Not enough money! Not Chinese!' he shouted.

There were now more lights on in houses near the shore. It was possible they'd been heard. Marie knew that if the Koreans were seen by their Japanese controllers, there would be no further possibility of negotiation.

The sun would rise soon, too; the buildings and trees around the old fort were beginning to take shape under the brightening sky.

'Mrs Broom, I will have to give him more money. Do you have anything else of value?'

The image of her diamond wedding ring submerged in

her jar of cold cream came to mind. If things got even worse she might need it. She shook her head.

With the barrel of his rifle, the guard pushed open the hampers on the deck. Leung knelt down to protect the dried fish and other provisions. Then with one last look towards Marie, he passed over some of the food. With a loud grunt the guard stepped up out of the sampan. The owner pushed the bow of the craft away from the side of the patrol boat and they turned again, with Macau behind them.

Marie bent her head and said a prayer of thanks. When she opened her eyes she saw other boats moving across the open waters of the harbour. She said another prayer that they wouldn't be stopped again before reaching the beach in front of them. It was now very close.

'Do you have any other warm clothes for the children?' Leung's voice was higher than before. Marie realised he was afraid.

'No. Only what they have on.'

'The colours are too bright.'

'I thought it would still be dark when we arrived.'

'It should have been. But now we're much, much too late. We'll just have to move fast as soon as we touch the beach. I'll carry the sick girl.'

Moving along the open deck and around the cabin, he assigned each of them loads. Marie was to take only Vincent so she could run with him. Lizzie was to take one suitcase, Ah Sup the other suitcase and what was left of the food. Leung handed an envelope to the sampan owner just as they heard the sound of sand scraping under the bow.

With Margaret in his arms, Leung was the first to make it over the mound at the top of the beach. From there they followed a trail through the scrub and long grass and found themselves on a larger cart track. They were now well hidden from Macau and the waters in between. With Marie at the back of the line, they kept up with Leung. Margaret's arms and head swayed limply over his shoulder.

Far away from the coast they asked to have a rest, but Leung insisted they keep going. Marie put Vincent down on the ground and he walked beside her, keeping a firm grip on her hand. It was not yet light. The few houses on the side of a hill about a mile away were quiet and dark. As the group passed close to a village not even a cock crowed.

At last Leung stopped. He walked behind a clump of small trees, laid Margaret on the ground and whispered to Marie. No one was to move from the clearing, he said. He had to leave them for five minutes.

Marie sat on a tree stump and had Vincent junior sit down between her ankles while Ah Sup watched over Margaret. Lizzie, Cynthia and Marie junior crouched in the grass. There was no sound over the hum of their heavy breathing. After about five minutes a dog barked nearby and they heard bicycles clanking on rough ground, apparently heading in their direction. The women looked at each other and held their breath.

Suddenly Leung appeared on the track with two other men. Each of them was pushing two bicycles.

Marie coaxed Margaret, sick and only half awake, on to the back of Leung's bicycle, then she, Lizzie and Ah Sup each took a bicycle. The three other children and the luggage were distributed between the two hired men.

The stony muddy path was only faintly visible. Frequent potholes and small streams made the going difficult. Vincent, sandwiched between Marie junior and one of the men, smiled and giggled with each dip and rise of the track. Marie watched anxiously as Margaret leaned first to one side of Leung's bike and then to the other. It often looked as if she would fall, yet her hands remained clasped around Leung's waist.

The route overland kept them away from the coast. They wove in and out of wooded areas and passed between flooded rice fields until they reached the outskirts of a village. Here they took shelter in a barn, sitting among dry rice straw. The village looked empty, but as the sun broke through people began to emerge. Leung walked out into the narrow streets and returned with two large bowls of steaming black noodles. Vincent gulped down the fingerfuls of food offered to him, but Cynthia and Marie junior refused: they'd realised the 'noodles' were wok-fried earthworms.

Marie bribed them into eating, promising they would be allowed to share one of the bananas she'd brought, then she wandered away to find a quiet corner. Her underpants were saturated with menstrual blood. Her thighs were chafed and painful. She did what she could to wipe away the blood but it kept coming. Sensing her distress, Lizzie cut a sleeve off her blouse and gave it to her to use as a pad.

After the children had slept for three hours Leung insisted they move on: there were a few miles to go before the next village, which was on the coast. They wearily pushed the bikes along roads and small tracks between rice fields. When the sun warmed their backs and drew steamy heat from the ground, they stripped off their jerseys.

At the coast Leung paid the men and they left with the bicycles. While Marie and the children and amahs sheltered in a barn Leung went into the village. He returned with news: he'd organised a sampan to take them across the channel. First, they would have to wait another hour for the regular Japanese patrol boat to pass.

Much of the discomfort and nausea Margaret had felt in the morning had passed and she fell back to sleep. The rest of the group sat silently. Marie and Lizzie peered through the knots in the barn's walls for any activity that might indicate they had been betrayed, their presence signalled to the Japanese.

After a second visit to the boatman, Leung returned. He looked worried. There were extra patrols on the water. There was no way they could leave as planned.

'Does that mean we have to go back? Are they looking for us?' Marie fought to stay calm.

'It's unlikely. We will continue further overland to the next bay. It's a bit more secluded.'

'But what about all our other rendezvous? We won't be there in time.'

'Mrs Broom, please don't worry. Nothing ever runs perfectly smoothly. We are going to be all right.'

'Can't we stop here and wait? Margaret is too sick for all this movement.'

Leung paused. He looked at Marie for a long time.

'Please just do as I say,' he said finally. 'We are a long way from being safe yet.'

The new route was steep. They avoided walking along worn paths and instead zigzagged so they were always on the far side of the hills, out of sight of nearby villages. Ah Sup held Vincent's hand and walked in a steady rhythm, wary that any stop might cause him to try to struggle free or stop completely. Margaret lay like a rolled-up carpet in Leung's arms. As she walked behind, Marie watched her daughter fall in and out of consciousness.

After two hours they stopped in a clump of trees with a view of the sea. From here it was almost impossible to distinguish between islands and bluffs around river mouths and peninsulas of China. As Marie junior and Cynthia leaned against her, Marie asked Leung which of the brown grassy hilltops was closest to their planned landing spot on the mainland. He pointed to one. It seemed impossibly far away. Conscious the children were listening, Marie didn't think it was wise to ask him if he knew where they might find the next boat, or any of the other questions weighing heavily on her mind.

After another long march they descended towards a village by the water. As Leung went on ahead, they shared the final drops of water in their one remaining bottle. Marie went behind a knoll and threw away the soiled piece of Lizzie's sleeve. Lizzie rose angrily, followed her and picked it up. Marie obviously had no idea how expensive food and clothing would be in China in these hard times, she said. She could wash the sleeve and stitch it back on her blouse.

Leung returned with good news: they would be able to make the next part of the journey to a bay opposite without difficulty. At that time of day patrols were apparently rare.

They walked quickly down to the village and through its central marketplace, doing their best to ignore the wide-eyed stares of the locals. The sampan was waiting. The water was calm. The glow of the late afternoon sun was reflected in the murky yellow water. Marie junior and Cynthia rested their chins on the gunnel and smiled broadly at each other. The boatman took the sampan directly out from the ramp, around a headland and across the water towards a bluff. It would be a good time to give the children something to eat, Leung said. After a nod of agreement from the boatman, Ah Sup distributed warm tea from a large metal kettle.

'Damn. How could you not have seen them?' Leung passed Margaret to Ah Sup and stood up.

There was a fast-moving craft on the horizon. A look of fear had come over the face of the elderly boatman. He was taking long sweeps with his oar in an attempt to turn the sampan towards the coast.

'What should we do?' Marie stood to get a better view.

'Quiet! Sit back down please.' Leung turned to the man. 'Keep the same course.'

'Mister, we have to go back.'

'If he sees you change course now, he'll turn to investigate.' Reluctantly, the man steered the boat back on course.

'Marie,' Lizzie whispered across the boat, 'what do we do if they come? We don't have any more money.'

'Just pray.' Marie rocked and made the sign of the cross. Lizzie crouched down on her knees and leaned forward. Ah Sup, with Margaret's head on her lap, bowed her head and squeezed her eyes shut. The only sounds were the rippling water around the boat's oar and the gentle thud of the distant engine. All ears were focused on the noise, trying to discern if it was getting stronger or weaker.

'We're all right.' Marie opened her eyes to see Leung still standing beside the boatman. 'We're all right. But stay where you are.'

Marie strained her neck and looked around the bay. The patrol boat had disappeared. She silently promised to make a large gift to the church for this deliverance.

85.

The sampan owner pulled into a small busy bay next to a large junk. 'We're changing boats,' Leung said after paying the man. 'Be quick and follow me.'

He carried Margaret up the gangway of the junk and the others followed. The wife of the junk master was preparing them a meal of fish and rice. Cynthia and Marie junior asked if they could walk around on the beach. No, Leung said. No one was to leave the space under the boat's roof. With few windows on the sides, they were well hidden there.

'Just eat and rest,' he said. 'We'll set off close to dusk.'

Marie was shaken awake by a forceful hand on her shoulder.

'Get everything together.'

'What time is it? How long have we been asleep?'

'Just half an hour, forty-five minutes. We have to go up into the mountains.'

'I thought we were going to Vincent on this boat.'

'There are too many patrol boats going up and down the coast.'

'Can't we wait until morning? Everyone is exhausted. The girls will all get sick.'

'By tomorrow morning a dozen reward hunters will have given us away. Please hurry.'

The short nap had made Marie drowsy. With a lot of effort she quietly woke Lizzie, Ah Sup, Marie and Cynthia, letting Vincent junior and Margaret continue sleeping until the last moment.

For the first mile as they trudged back up to the ridge everyone was silent, battling against their aching shoulders and the blisters on their toes and heels. They rested for a few minutes on the crest of the hill, just long enough to take in the shadows of the setting sun on the dips and peaks of the ridge across the water, along which they had walked only hours before. In the other direction, they could see the hills that lay between them and the relative safety of the river mouth on the mainland.

Marie walked behind the rest of the group, holding Vincent's hand. Twice they passed groups of young men sitting beside the path clutching rusty smallbore rifles. Each time Leung gave the men a handful of coins.

It was almost dark before they started downhill to a beach. They could now see only their feet and the back of the person in front of them. At one point Lizzie slipped and bloodied her knee but kept walking. Leung gently touched their shoulders when, from time to time, he stood back from the lead and let them walk past. But his fear was obvious. Marie realised things had strayed far from his original plan. This was probably their last chance.

A few hours after dark they reached a shack by the water, lay on the dirt floor and rested.

'Why don't we just go back?'

'You think that's best?' Leung's whispered response lacked his usual confidence.

'You seem scared.'

'No,' Leung said. 'Things are going to be fine.'

He went outside the shack to listen again for any activity on the water. Marie checked the others were still asleep and followed him. They could see nothing beyond the faint whiteness of tiny waves breaking on the sand.

'What if your friends don't find us here? What if we are still here when the sun comes up?'

'These men are smugglers. They know this coast better than anyone. I've never been this far, but this has always been our back-up place to leave from. Get some rest. Everything is going to be all right.'

'But dawn can't be far away.'

'Don't worry.'

'I think I heard something.' Marie sat bolt upright.

'Quiet.'

At first it seemed like a slightly louder lapping of the waves, then came the sound of water trickling off the ends of oars.

'Please wake everyone and get ready,' Leung said. He walked out and down to the water's edge.

By the time Marie emerged from the shack, the bow of a very long low boat was resting on the beach. The oars were floating on the water, stretched far out from the boat's sides. Ten men were standing in the boat, ready to set off. Marie recognised it as the sort of snake boat used by smugglers.

'Is everyone ready?' Leung called out. 'The boss says we have to leave immediately. He thinks we're already too late to get to the river mouth.'

'They're ready,' Marie said.

Leung followed her into the shack and picked up Margaret. Lizzie, Ah Sup and the three other children climbed on board and wove past the oarsmen to the bow. The tillerman darted around, roughly pulling and pushing them into positions on the floor where they wouldn't obstruct the oars of the two front rowers. Leung, Marie and Margaret sat on the floor at the back. There was precious little room.

Leung craned his head around the two oarsmen next to him. 'Everyone has to be completely silent when we get out on the water,' he said. Seeing the fatigue on Marie's face he added, 'Just remember, Vincent is at the end of this.' For the first time Marie perceived a nervous smile on the young man's lips.

The order to cast off was given. Silently the oarsmen chipped out from the coast, then dug their oars down further as the water got deeper, pushing hard to pick up speed. A man near the back, slow to find the rhythm, received a sharp slap from the tillerman.

As the speed increased the rowers' strokes became longer, starting far back and ending with the men leaning forward until they were almost horizontal. Everyone in the group had to stay low and sway in time with the men or get a bruising oar handle on their head.

Lizzie, near the bow, was having difficulty bending at the waist enough to protect Vincent from the oars. 'Leung,' Marie whispered. Without disturbing Margaret, who was sleeping in his arms, Leung spun around and moved his fingers to his lips. His eyes directed Marie to the tillerman. The man was staring down at her. Marie pointed to Lizzie. Leung shrugged.

The sky turned from black to blue as the stars disappeared and the ridges of the mountains around them began to appear. Marie noticed they were gaining on a sampan about half a mile in front. From the way the tillerman was watching a man at the back of the sampan, Marie decided the man must be the smugglers' boss, looking out for patrols.

They were now in the centre of a smooth expanse of water, a gulf about five miles wide. Cooking fires and lamps were flickering to life along the coast. Marie realised that a barking dog in a village could alert a Japanese sentry to their presence.

With sacks wrapped tightly around the oars, there was no sound of wood straining on wood, only that of bubbles trickling under the boat. For the first time Marie allowed herself to properly picture her husband. She smiled.

Suddenly the silence was broken. Disturbed by Lizzie's movements, Vincent had begun to cry. As the toddler gasped in more air, each cry became louder.

Leung and Marie looked at each other, then at the tillerman.

'Silence the child.' The tillerman's sharp whisper carried along the length of the boat.

Marie noticed the sampan was stopping and turning.

'How much further is there to go?' Leung sounded worried.

The tillerman flung out his arm and pointed to a dent in the coast where two bluffs appeared to overlap. It looked to be about three miles away.

The man in the sampan was now frantically gesturing.

'You have to do something, Marie.'

'What? Please tell them to go faster. You can't make a child stop crying when he has oars going everywhere around him.' Her voice cracked.

'Do something, Marie. He won't risk his life for a child. He'll kill him if you can't stop him crying.'

Marie furiously waved her hand to get Lizzie's attention. The handle of an oar dug into her ear as it swung back. She winced in pain.

'Be quiet, Marie,' Leung said.

Vincent's cries echoed across the lake-like basin. Lizzie put her hand loosely over Vincent's mouth and nose. When he started to make choking sounds she removed her hand and tried to bury his face in her jacket. His cries got even louder as he turned and gasped for air. Lizzie's face was streaked with tears.

Marie desperately crawled under the oars and wove around
the men between her and Vincent. Halfway down the boat
she glanced at the tillerman. His eyes were flaring. She
crouched beside Lizzie and scrambled to find something in
the bag beside them that would pacify the baby. As Vincent's
cries turned to loud wails, the tillerman gestured for Lizzie
to put her hand on his face or around his throat.

Fishing around the bottom of the bag, Marie found
a sweet. With trembling hands she unravelled the paper,
held the sweet between her fingers, bit it in half and put a
piece in Vincent's mouth. As if by magic he fell instantly
silent. Marie took the other half of the sweet from her
mouth, put it back in the wrapping paper and placed it in
Lizzie's hand.

The river mouth was still more than two miles away. Every
detail of the land was now visible. The sky was turning to
gold around the fading moon.

'Harder!' The voice came as a shock. None of them had
dared speak above a whisper and now the tillerman had
screamed.

'Patrol boat!'

Marie stood up and looked behind her. A Japanese boat
was rounding a headland near the beach they'd come from.
Its movement along the horizon seemed improbably fast.

'Get down!'

Marie remained standing, transfixed. 'Are we going to
make it?'

'I don't know, Mrs Broom. Please do as the man says.'
Leung looked terrified. 'All I know is that for half a mile
out from the river mouth the water is too shallow for the
patrol boats.'

Marie tried to gauge how far that might be. Another mile maybe. Another four minutes.

The patrol boat seemed to have covered half the bay since she first saw it. She knelt down, closed her eyes tightly and began to chant in Latin, 'Hail Mary, Mother of God.' Over the creaking of the boat she could hear Margaret crying faintly behind her. 'Hail Mary, Mother of God. Hail Mary, Mother of God.'

'It's turned. It's turned. Keep going. It's turned away.' The joy and excitement in Leung's voice was palpable. Marie sat and prayed again, this time in thanks. She didn't want to see for herself if the patrol boat was moving away or only zigzagging. She didn't move until she heard the tillerman order the men to slow their speed. She felt the boat turn sharply.

86.

'Marie. Marie Broom. Thank God, Marie, thank God you're here.'

Marie was overwhelmed by the emotion in the tall stranger's voice. At first, as she'd watched him moving through the crowd around the boat landing, she had mistaken him for her husband.

She turned to Leung.

'This is Mr Shiner Wright,' Leung said.

'Marie, I'm so happy you're here.' Tears were forming in the man's eyes. Suddenly he noticed something behind her. 'What's the matter, Leung? What happened? What's the matter with the girl?'

'Malaria. She'll be all right.'

'Thank God.'

'My husband,' Marie said, 'do you have news? Is he all right?'

'No, I have some bad news. I dreamed it would happen this way.'

'What bad news?'

'He's fine. He's in good, very good, health. It's just that I had to ask him to go to a monastery near here to take food to a sick priest.'

'He's here?' Marie could hardly believe what she was hearing.

'Yes. We're expecting him back tomorrow.'

'But he's all right?'

'He's fine,' Wright said. 'Really.'

Marie pulled Cynthia and Marie junior close as they walked up the clay track. Halfway to the top, she turned around and walked back down to the snake boat. Leung was handing a large sum of money to the tillerman. For the last terrible hour of the journey Marie had hated this man as much as she had ever hated anyone. Now she wordlessly shook his hand.

While Leung's wife took care of Margaret, Marie made her way upstairs to the room where Vincent was staying. She picked through his few possessions: two pairs of shorts in a drawer, some basic items in a shaving kit. His suitcase was etched with mud and covered in scratches.

When Wright called up the stairs to see if she needed anything, she asked for some water to wash in. She looked in the mirror at the dirt caked around her eyes and her rough sun-baked skin. What must Wright think of her? She must smell terrible.

'After you've bathed we can call Vincent on the phone,' Wright said. 'He'll be at the mission by then.'

The telephone was one of the earliest models imported into China. Wright stood in front of Marie and shouted into the mouthpiece, gripping the speaker firmly against his head.

'They're getting him. Here.'

'I can't hear anything, just a crackling noise.'

'It's not the best.'

'There's someone. Hello. Hello. Vincent. Vincent, is that you? I don't know if it's him. Hello. Vincent? We're here. We're all here. We're with Shiner. All the children. All the children are here. Hello, can you hear me?'

'It often goes dead,' Wright said.

'I can't hear anything. Hello...' She was crying.

'Don't worry. You'll see him tomorrow. You need to get some rest.'

'I couldn't even tell if it was him. It was crackling too much.'

'I know. Don't worry about it. You'll see him tomorrow.'

MARIE
&
VINCENT

87.

Thanks to the fine mist from the rice fields, it was possible to look directly at the rising sun. Vincent could see the vapour of his breath. The morning temperature was cooler than usual and he was walking fast. When he passed the last marker before Samfou and saw the buildings ahead of him, he broke into a run.

A little girl with her hair in plaits was playing on the stairs below his room. She leapt up and ran up the stairs into the room. 'A gweilo man is chasing me,' she called out.

Marie pushed past her. Vincent was coming up the stairs. Marie barely looked at his face. She fell against him. He was weaker and thinner than she remembered. He swayed slightly as she clutched on to him.

Lizzie had rushed to get Vincent junior. Marie hugged their three-year-old son and passed him to Vincent. 'Do you recognise him?' she said. 'He had beautiful long hair until a month ago. I promised myself I would never cut it until you saw him but...' She stopped, overcome with emotion. Then in Chinese, the only language the child knew, she said, 'Vincent, this is your father.'

88.

Marie pushed her wedding ring back to the bottom of her jar of cold cream and put the jar on top of the clean clothes and soap in her suitcase. She had been able to wear the ring for the last few days. Now her finger felt naked without it.

She closed the case and sat down on the mattress. Part of her would like to stay in this bare small room in this quiet little village. Vincent had gone over the details of the journey that all eight of them would be making north to Guilin, and then across China to Kunming and India. Marie had learned enough from the others at the base to know that adults and children had died on this route. Between here and Kunming lay weeks of travel in wartime conditions. Boats on the rivers got bombed by Japanese planes. Snipers picked off people walking along the rice paths. Bandits killed for food. Disease was everywhere.

89.

Shiner Wright escorted them on the three-day walk north to Shuihing, where he would pick up funds and provisions sent down from the British Army Aid Group's headquarters. He and Vincent had been through a lot together, but when they parted it was with a simple handshake.

The sampan carrying the family with Lizzie, Ah Sup and Jackie, their guide, cast off smoothly from the shore. The boat turned quickly upstream.

'What did she say?'

'She says she remembers you now.' Margaret translated as Cynthia sat on her father's lap, speaking a mixture of Cantonese and barely remembered English.

'She said Te Puke, didn't she?'

'She says she remembers New Zealand and Ma and Pa and a long white beach.'

'We'll be there soon. Ma and Pa will be thrilled to see you all.'

'Is it spring there now?'

'Yes, it will be summer by the time we arrive.'

'That's good. I don't like the cold.'

'I know, Blossom. You never did.'

'You seem to have a natural touch with children, Jackie.'

'I like them very much. You are fortunate, Mr Broom.'

'Can I ask you a question? When we are on the river or on the train, what happens if a Japanese plane swoops down on us? Do we stop and take shelter?'

'There's no time. All we can do is pray.'

'That's not very reassuring.'

'No. But why would your luck change now?'

'Nor yours.'

'I haven't really been so lucky.'

'After two years of doing these runs unscathed, you don't think that's lucky?'

'The Japanese killed my father.'

'Oh, I'm so sorry.' Vincent wanted to touch the guide on the arm but resisted.

'They found out who I was and what I was doing. Then they found my family in Hong Kong and asked them to betray me. When they wouldn't, they tortured and killed my father.'

'Why don't you stop? You've already done so much.'

'I wanted to stop but Colonel Ride suggested I stay. Now he gives me missions like yours. I think it's better than being alone with nothing to do.'

'Perhaps you're right.'

'And nobody knows these routes better than me.'

The journey upriver took much longer than the descent that had brought Vincent south three months earlier. The sampan made slow progress against the currents, and to get to Guilin they were forced to make a detour using a second river network and then small local trains. Vincent tried to lift Marie's spirits by talking about the Blue Train, which had made a small part of his journey from Kunming quite comfortable. One day when the war was over they would take that train together, he promised.

Marie smiled, but worry was taking its toll. Her hair had started to fall out in clumps. On their last night in Samfou she had woken everyone with a loud scream. A rat had got into their room and was climbing up on to the hanging food bag. Afterwards she'd felt foolish. Vincent must think I'm weak, she thought. She doubted he could truly imagine what she'd been through, what she'd had to do to keep their family safe.

90.

'Mummy, there's a stranger on the riverbank. A man with a beard.' Margaret tugged on Marie's arm.

Marie had noticed him too. 'Vincent,' she said, 'there's a priest on the shore. He looks as though he's looking for someone. Do you know anyone here?'

Vincent had been dozing at the front of the tied-up sampan. He looked over his shoulder towards the rough shanties and jetties along the riverside. A broad-shouldered man with a long grey beard and wearing the heavy black tunic of a priest was weaving his way along the path towards them.

Using broken English, the man introduced himself as the senior Jesuit priest of the town. Marie did her best to interpret, relying on the few French words that were similar to Portuguese.

'We should ask him if he wants to come up to Guilin with us,' Vincent said.

The man shook his head and grinned.

'He said thank you but he will never leave,' Marie said. 'He has lived here for forty years. He heard from one of the villagers that there was a foreign man travelling with his family on the river. He is inviting us to dinner.'

'Please thank him, but tell him we can't leave the children.'

'Of course you can leave the children, Vincent.' Jackie sounded determined. 'The amahs and I will be fine. This is one of the safest towns in the area.'

Vincent glanced at Marie, then nodded to the priest.

'Thank you. Yes. Merci.'

At six that evening a smartly dressed boy came to the boat to escort Marie and Vincent to the priest's house. As they strolled behind him they noticed most of the shops in the town were boarded up or had almost empty shelves. The place seemed abandoned, inhabited only by people who, like them, were just passing through, or who lacked the energy to go back or further on. In Samfou, although the town was closer to the Japanese forces, the stream of refugees had created a sense of hope. Here there was nothing to raise the spirits.

The priest occupied the only stone house in the town. He suggested they might enjoy a tour around the buildings and courtyard before dinner. Marie thought how ridiculous

she must look. She made a futile effort to smooth out the
creases in her blouse. After a few minutes, though, all thought
of the outside world had vanished. She and Vincent were
dazzled by the deep saturated colours as the late afternoon
light streamed through the windows of the house. There
was fine craftsmanship everywhere, especially in the wooden
beams smoothed into strong perfect curves.

'You comprehend better now perhaps why I cannot leave,'
the priest said.

Dinner was served in a wood-panelled room at one end
of a long table that could have seated two dozen people.
The boy who had guided Marie and Vincent to the house
placed Limoges dishes of food carefully in front of the priest,
and handed him silver ladles to serve with. The food was
rich and delicious. Wine was poured from a crystal decanter.

Vincent gripped Marie's hand tightly under the table as
he described his journey across China from the base of the
Himalayas. In turn, Marie told the priest what she had seen
and lived through during the previous two years. Vincent
looked sad, horrified, tearful. Some of these things Marie
had not yet had time to share with him.

The moon was glowing faintly on the water as Vincent and
Marie made their way back along the riverbank. Cormorant
fishermen were lighting their lamps and casting off into the
middle of the river as their birds stood on the bows of their
boats. Marie and Vincent were silent, deep in their own
thoughts. When the sampan came into view, they stopped
and held each other. Then they cried, great wrenching sobs
that felt as though they would never end.

EPILOGUE

Marie, Vincent, their four children and Lizzie and Ah Sup
arrived in Guilin in time for Marie and Marie junior to
celebrate their late October birthdays in the mess of the
British Army Aid Group. For three days the compound was
the centre of their life as intelligence officers debriefed Marie
on what she had seen and heard during her visits to the
internment camps in Hong Kong and in her daily struggle
to survive. Marie passed on the message Emily Hahn had
wanted delivered to Madame Chiang Kai-shek. However,
Hahn had already been repatriated to the United States on
September 23, 1943, leaving Hong Kong with her young
daughter Carola and 120 other civilians in an International
Red Cross prisoner exchange.

Marie, Vincent and Lizzie found no trace in Guilin of
Lizzie's daughter Mary. Marie and Vincent were not able to
convince the British Army to provide transport for Lizzie
and Ah Sup across China. They were told that flights over
the Himalayas had limited spaces and they could not set
a precedent by allowing Chinese people with no family
connection to Britain aboard. Marie left her diamond

wedding ring with the two women so they might have some advantage over the tens of thousands of other dispossessed people around Guilin.

The British Army Aid Group arranged transport back across China for the Broom family and other Hong Kong refugee families with papers that permitted them to leave the country. For twelve days they travelled on the back of supply trucks, facing immense discomfort and ever-present risk of disease and enemy attack. Rats stole much of their meagre food and bedbugs made their nights long and painful. Finally boarding the plane in Kunming, Vincent and Marie were horrified to see that what they'd been told about the lack of places wasn't true. The aircraft was empty except for them and a Frenchman and his two dogs.

The plane took them to Calcutta. Here they had a long wait for a ship. On December 24, 1943, two years after the British had surrendered Hong Kong to the Japanese, the family set sail for Sydney on the SS *Querimba*, the same ship on which Vincent had travelled to India six months earlier.

Margaret recovered from malaria in Guilin, and the Broom children remained in good health throughout the arduous journey through China and India to Australia. Along the way they visited people who had helped Vincent on his trek into China, including Salvation Army doctors and nurses.

While the family waited in Sydney for a ship to New Zealand, Vincent signed on to the United States Army's transport service as a marine chief engineer, a position carrying the rank of colonel. He served two and a half years on armed supply ships in the Pacific war zone and was awarded three Second World War medals. By the end he had managed to pay back most of the debts he'd accrued travelling into China.

During this time Marie and the children lived in a rented house in Tauranga, a small city on the east coast of New Zealand's North Island. The stress of what she'd endured continued to cause Marie's hair to fall out and for a year she took to wearing a scarf around her head.

As the only children of Asian heritage at their school, the Broom children stood out. They struggled to come to terms with the horrors they had experienced during the war. It was years before they could watch a war film without fearing the bombs exploding onscreen were outside the cinema and fleeing to take shelter.

The Japanese forces in Hong Kong surrendered on August 15, 1945. The following year the Broom family returned to Hong Kong. Their ship stopped in Japan en route and they saw first-hand the devastation wrought on Hiroshima by the American nuclear bomb. Although saddened by the sight, Marie continued to carry a strong dislike and mistrust of the Japanese for the rest of her life. Margaret, then thirteen, became a lifelong opponent of nuclear weapons.

The family never returned to the flat on Fort Street. All their possessions had been looted, except a trunk of small items they had left with friends. From the late 1940s all flats in the street were demolished to make way for taller buildings.

Marie and Vincent had stayed in contact with some friends and neighbours but many had left Hong Kong, never to return. They discovered that the neighbour known in the story as Lily, who had confided to Marie that she and her daughter had been raped by Japanese soldiers, had committed suicide soon after the war.

Stewart Williamson had survived imprisonment in Stanley camp; Vincent went back to work as his marine superintendent. When the Korean War broke out in 1950 and there were fears of a communist attack on Hong Kong from China, it was decided Marie and the children would be safer in New Zealand. For the next four years they visited Vincent every Christmas. In 1953 Cynthia returned to Hong Kong to learn secretarial skills in her father's office; Marie, Margaret and Marie junior moved back the following year and Vincent junior after finishing school in New Zealand a few years later. The family lived in Kowloon surrounded by people who, like them, had survived the war and were determined to rebuild their city. Once a week Arthur came to dinner.

When Vincent took early retirement in 1959, the family moved back to New Zealand and began a new life in Auckland. Weakened by his wartime illness, particularly the chronic dysentery he had contracted in Guilin, Vincent had a heart attack in 1962 while on a visit to London. He lived more quietly after this, although he frequently visited Pacific islands as chief engineer on merchant ships and supervised engineering refits in Singapore.

Between these trips he fished in the Hauraki Gulf with his son-in-law and grandson, and tended his prized orchids at his home in the suburb of St Heliers. While he and Marie gave extravagant dinner parties, he was prone to sit quietly in a corner with a whisky in hand. He finally retired and left his beloved sea at the age of 75. Four years later he died of a heart attack after a day spent working in his garden.

One day when the war was still raging and Marie and the children were living in New Zealand, Margaret ran the three miles home from school to show her family a photograph in *The New Zealand Herald* of a woman nursing a dying person on the train tracks in Guilin as refugees climbed into carriages headed north to escape the Japanese advance. She was sure the woman was Lizzie. Marie asked the newspaper about the exact day the photograph was taken and confirmed the location, but there was no way of identifying Lizzie officially or providing any aid to her from New Zealand.

One day late in 1946, after the family moved back to Hong Kong, Vincent was walking through Victoria when he heard a woman scream. He turned, thinking there'd been a horrific car accident, and instead saw Lizzie running towards him. She had finally found her daughter Mary in China and, like many expatriates and locals, had returned to Hong Kong after the war. She confirmed that she was the woman in the photograph; the young woman was a friend who had been killed when she fell off the crowded train. Lizzie rejoined the Broom household, retiring in 1959 when the family went back to New Zealand. She died in 2010 at the age of 108.

Mary and her husband had left Guilin long before Vincent arrived. They had had a baby there and would have two more children in different Chinese cities during the war. They returned to Hong Kong late in 1945.

With the backing of her husband's family and her natural talent for languages and business, Mary opened a succession of factories in Hong Kong and China, becoming one of the region's most successful businesswomen and living in a beautiful home on the Peak. She retired from most of her corporate roles in 2012 and lived in Hong Kong with one of her sons. She died in April 2022.

The Broom family never managed to find out what had happened to Ah Sup.

Marie Broom died peacefully in Auckland Hospital in her ninetieth year in February 2002. Her son Vincent died in Auckland in 2019. Margaret died in September 2021, having read one of the final drafts of this book. Marie junior lives in Auckland; Cynthia lives on Canada's Vancouver Island, near her daughter and grandchildren.

Marie & Vincent, Hong Kong, c.1932

Left: Vincent, Marie junior and Margaret, Hong Kong, 1937

Below: Marie with Margaret, Marie junior, Cynthia and Vincent junior on their Hong Kong rooftop, October 1942, 10 months into the occupation

HISTORY NOTES

HOW HONG KONG BECAME BRITISH

During most of its first 3,500 years, the country now known to the West as China received few visitors in Hong Kong or its many other coastal settlements, even from its closest neighbours. Before the advent of large ocean-going sailing ships, explorers attempted to travel overland from Europe, only to be turned back by snow-covered mountain ranges and deserts too dry to cross safely in summer. This isolation enabled China to define its borders, develop largely effective regional and national bureaucracies, and create a common written language. Its provinces were linked under centralised rule.

From the thirteenth century, explorers such as the Venetian Marco Polo travelled along what became known as the Silk Route to trade with Yuan dynasty leader Kublai Khan, emperor of the Mongol Empire. News of these visits spread around Europe, and many countries saw the potential for trade. Countries such as Portugal invested in building ships and developing shipping routes to China and Japan. By the middle of the sixteenth century Portugal had even managed to establish the colony of Macau, just west of Hong Kong.

Over the next centuries many other nations, including
Holland, France, Germany and Britain, made trade with Asia
a priority. Britain's advantage came from its technological
and industrial achievements in boat building and navigation,
its military strength and its centralised development of trade
and diplomacy through organisations such as the private East
India Company.

By the middle of the nineteenth century, trade between
Britain and China's last dynasty, the Qing, had reached
staggering heights. Initially this trade, built on satisfying
Europe's love of products such as silk, porcelain and tea,
favoured China. The British were obliged to hand over large
sums of silver to the limited number of Chinese coastal
merchants allowed to have direct contact with them. Silver
was the only currency of interest to the Chinese, and the
British had to buy it from countries such as Mexico at a
high cost.

Effectively blocked from travelling inland and upriver,
they had no opportunity to directly market their goods to
locals. Their solution was to promote the use of opium,
an addictive drug they transported from their colony of India
and sold direct to Chinese addicts and den owners.

Chinese authorities recognised that the opium, the illicit
dens and the associated black market for the drug were
corrupting their population and weakening its resistance
to outside influences. They issued a set of decrees stopping
the importation of opium and went as far as destroying
stocks owned by British merchants and placing many of
the traders who ignored the new restrictions under house
arrest. The British government quickly retaliated, using the
might of its navy to violently overpower the relatively poorly
armed Chinese police.

The defeat of the Chinese led to the forced negotiation and signing of the 1842 Treaty of Nanking. The British government gained Hong Kong Island and was allowed to open five treaty ports in mainland China through which its merchants would in theory be free to conduct trade. In practice, the Chinese continued to resist Britain's desire to impose opium on the population, leading to a second opium war from 1856 to 1860.

When the British finally overpowered the Chinese empire's attempts to control their activities, the British ports prospered. However, political pressure at home against the immoral nature of the opium trade led British traders to look for more legitimate ways of growing their wealth.

Even with less opium reaching its people, the Chinese empire grew steadily weaker. The Sino-Japanese War of 1894 to '95 (fought over control of Korea), the undermining of centralised power during the Boxer Rebellion (during which a Chinese religious group attacked foreigners and Christian Chinese with the help of government insiders) and an overall failure to modernise all contributed to the fragility of the Qing dynasty. In 1912 the young emperor abdicated and a republic was founded. In October 1919 Sun Yat-sen, a revolutionary who had lived abroad for 16 years, became the leader and father of modern China as premier of the Kuomintang.

The process of replacing thousands of years of dynastic rule proved complicated. Until his early death in 1925, Sun Yat-sen struggled to keep the many revolutionary factions together and was constantly challenged by regional warlords. His successor Chiang Kai-shek initially did a better job, steering China away from communism and developing a nationalist ideology as a way of binding the country together around a free-market economy.

The progressive opening up and growing prosperity of China brought a tide of immigration. The effects of the Depression started by the New York stock market crash were felt across the world and many people were keen to try to improve their lot in the British colony of Hong Kong or the Chinese entrepôt of Shanghai. One was Vincent Broom, a New Zealander who had finished training as a marine engineer in 1929.

THE RISE OF JAPAN

For three hundred years successive Japanese emperors had sought to control more of Asia. By 1895 the Japanese had pushed China out of Korea and taken over control of Taiwan. Where China had largely failed to modernise its army, Japan had spent years buying military equipment and paying for military advice from countries such as Britain and France. The British government believed having Japan as an ally was the best way to curb Russian activities in the Pacific.

Under pressure from the United States, British support of Japan, set out in the Anglo-Japanese Treaty of 1902, officially came to an end in 1923, with trust between the two countries greatly damaged. Using spies and British traitors – among them Scottish lord and aviator William Francis Forbes-Sempill – the Japanese continued to appropriate technology to improve their air and naval capabilities, especially in the development of fighter planes powerful enough to take off from aircraft carriers.

From 1931 the Japanese army began to overrun towns and regions in north-east China, winning numerous battles and pressuring local leaders to join them. The parts of China under Japanese control steadily increased.

Chiang Kai-shek, Sun Yat-sen's brother-in-law, had become leader of the Nationalist government in 1928. In 1934 the communist movement under Mao Zedong undertook the 6,000-mile Long March from the south-east to Shaanxi in the northwest, gathering support from peasants along the route.

In 1937 the Communists and Nationalists briefly joined forces to battle the Japanese but even their combined might was ineffective. In August, Shanghai, with its large British, French, Iraqi and other expatriate communities, fell. Japan had gone from being considered an ally of the British Empire to being an enemy: in 1936 it had signed a treaty with Germany to link diplomatic and military efforts against their common enemy, communism.

In December 1937 the Japanese army reached Nanking, the capital of Nationalist China, and looted, raped and slaughtered hundreds of thousands of civilians (estimates of deaths range from 100,000 to 300,000), striking fear into the hearts of Chinese everywhere. Over the next four years it pushed on southwards, its progress, especially inland, slowed from time to time by Nationalist and Communist soldiers but never convincingly stopped. By the beginning of 1938 it had extended its territory from the north of China into not only Shanghai and Nanking but Xuzhou, Wuhan and vast swathes of middle and coastal China.

From 1936 the British had built defences on the Hong Kong peninsula. The most remarkable was a series of concrete trenches, tunnels, pillboxes and observation posts across the ridge of the isthmus; this became known as the Gin

Drinkers Line. No military expert believed Hong Kong could be defended indefinitely. It was hoped the defences would slow down an attack long enough for British residents to be evacuated by sea.

In March 1939, during an effort to secure Shenzhen, a city just over the border from the New Territories, the Japanese destroyed targets on areas of the Hong Kong peninsula closest to China. By mid 1941 the Japanese army controlled most of the Chinese coast and ports between Hong Kong and Beijing, and the islands off the coast.

British prime minister Winston Churchill and his war office had decided that Hong Kong was not a high priority. If they were going to dedicate more resources to its defence it would not be to save the colony but in the hope of hurting the Japanese army enough to slow it down. On November 16, 1941, just under 2000 Canadian soldiers arrived, but most of their equipment had been diverted elsewhere.

On December 8, 1941 Japanese planes attacked Hong Kong airport; the few British planes still based there were destroyed. This surprise attack, together with the ones on Pearl Harbour, northern Malaya and Thailand, as well as a bombing raid on Singapore, were part of a Japanese strategy to eliminate any possibility of the entire Asian coast being successfully defended.

By December 11 the Gin Drinkers Line had been breached. All British and Commonwealth forces were ordered to cross the harbour and defend Hong Kong Island. The odds were on Japan's side: its 52,000 soldiers well outnumbered the 14,000 attempting to protect Hong Kong, who included young inexperienced Canadians, Rajput and Punjabi Indians incorporated into a number of battalions, British troops including Royal Scots and the Middlesex Regiment, local colonial troops and the Hong Kong Volunteer Defence Corps.

On December 13 the Japanese demanded Hong Kong surrender. When this was rejected they began firing at targets on the island from the southernmost points of the peninsula. On December 17 a second demand for surrender was also rejected. The following night Japanese soldiers landed on the north-eastern coast of the island, not far from Vincent and Marie Broom's flat. Many of Hong Kong's defenders were rapidly killed or forced from their strongholds on the coast.

More Japanese soldiers made their way across the harbour on small boats. On the first night they executed around twenty gunners, even though the men had surrendered. Soon afterwards at the Salesian Mission, which was being used as an advance dressing station, they massacred defenceless prisoners and medical staff. Attempts were made by the British to counter-attack and regain key positions, but to no avail.

During the next ten days the Japanese gained important territory and key passes across the island such as the Wong Nai Chung Gap. This allowed them relatively easy access south to Repulse Bay and west to where the British forces were retreating.

From early on Marie Broom found herself far behind enemy lines. Unknown to her and those around her, within a short time all remaining troops defending Hong Kong Island had been chased from their pillboxes along the coast, bombed out of their anti-aircraft nests, and had made their way for a final stand on the Stanley Peninsula and the west of the island.

Most historical accounts of the battles in Hong Kong and their aftermath focus on the loss of over two thousand

British and Allied soldiers and nurses, but civilians suffered even greater losses. To understand the level of fear Marie Broom lived with, keep in mind that she looked Chinese. Rumours circulated among the local Chinese population that Japanese soldiers were allowed to steal food, alcohol and money and rape women, without fear of reproach from senior officers.

A major turning point was reached when the Japanese forces gained control of the island's reservoirs, enabling them to limit water supplies to civilians and Allied soldiers. On the morning of Christmas Day, December 25, Japanese soldiers entered the British field hospital at St Stephen's College, tortured and killed many injured soldiers and medical staff, and raped British and Chinese nurses. That afternoon the Hong Kong governor, Sir Mark Young, crossed the harbour to Kowloon and surrendered at Japanese headquarters on the third floor of the Peninsula Hotel. By then the death toll included around 10,000 Chinese civilians and 550 soldiers. As many or more had been injured, raped or tortured.

The people of Hong Kong now faced years of harsh occupation. Captured British, Canadian and Indian soldiers endured hard labour in prisoner-of-war camps in Hong Kong and Japan; many died of sickness and starvation. After the war, Takashi Sakai, who had commanded the Japanese forces in Hong Kong during the invasion and been governor until February 1942, was captured by the Americans. He was extradited to China, found guilty of war crimes and excuted by firing squad on September 30, 1946.

INTERNMENT AND PRISONER-OF-WAR CAMPS

In July 1940, the British War Office had set up a mandatory evacuation program for all civilian expatriate women and children. Many families had resisted evacuation; there was a general belief there was no imminent threat from the Japanese, and a desire not to leave husbands, comfortable homes and the good life in Hong Kong. The plan was also blatantly racist in differentiating between British passport holders of British descent and British passport holders of non-British decent.

Faced with an operation that was not rolling out as smoothly as they had hoped, the authorities softened the rules. Women could stay if they volunteered for nursing and other auxiliary and administrative roles. As a result there were many expatriate civilians in Hong Kong when the Japanese invaded. This was a massive cause of stress for both the British authorities and for the Japanese army, which had not planned for such numbers.

Enemy nation civilians were ordered, via an announcement in the English-language newspaper, to meet at the Murray Parade Grounds on January 4, 1942, almost a month after the invasion and ten days after the surrender. Only a thousand people made their way there; the majority of civilians were forcibly taken from their homes over the following days.

The Japanese kept prisoners in six different camps. The ones that contained most of Marie Broom's friends were Sham Shui Po Camp, where British and other Allied soldiers were imprisoned after the surrender in December 1941, Argyle Street Camp (from mid April 1942 until it was closed and officers returned to Sham Shui Po in 1944) and Stanley

Internment Camp, where non-military men, women and children from Allied nations were interned.

Eventually the Stanley camp housed more than 2,800 people. The site, on the south side of Hong Kong Island, made use of buildings and land that normally housed a school, accommodation for guards at a nearby prison and auxiliary buildings (but not the prison itself). Most people slept in cramped conditions in large groups, either in bungalows or flats normally used by teachers and their families, or in classrooms with sheets hung between families for privacy. Medicine was almost non-existent and meals were a bare survival minimum of rice and broth. With many doctors, dentists and nurses among the inmates, epidemics were avoided through careful hygiene. Morale was kept reasonably high because the prisoners were largely left to manage themselves. They organised classes for the children, lectures on various subjects and a programme of musicals, recitals and plays.

There were few such distractions at Sham Shui Po Camp. Situated a few kilometres north of the Star Ferry Building on Kowloon, the camp primarily housed British and Canadian prisoners-of-war. The huts had been built by the British as army barracks; under the Japanese each was crammed with 200 men, many badly wounded and exhausted. The Japanese-style bedding was often infested with bedbugs and most men preferred sleeping on the concrete floors. Latrines were filthy, cooking and eating utensils rare and food scarce.

Flies covered everything, there were epidemics, and the high death rate was increased by forced labour on projects such as the rebuilding of Kai Tak Airport. From mid 1942 some prisoners were sent to POW camps in Japan, from where they were used as slave labour in mines and other industries. Of the nearly 2,000 Canadians sent to Hong

Kong, a fifth never made it home and half of these died not in battle but in captivity.

Some things made it through Sham Shui Po's barbed-wire fences. Books were shared, the odd game of football was arranged and an effort was made by the men to remain positive, although there were limits to what even the bravest could endure. At the time of the Japanese surrender and the liberation of the camp, many of those who'd survived were unable to walk and would take a long time to recover.

Ginger Hyde was tortured over a duration of six months. The fact the people he was working with against the Japanese were left alone seems to indicate that he refused to divulge any names. He was executed on Stanley Beach on October 29, 1943, near the camp where his wife Florence and young son Michael were incarcerated.

Dr Selwyn Selwyn-Clarke, director of medical services in Hong Kong, was arrested by the Japanese on May 2, 1943 and condemned to death for sending food and drugs to prisoner-of-war camps. After a year and a half in confined isolation, including months of torture, he was given a second military trial and allowed to join his wife and daughter in Stanley camp. After the war he became governor of the Seychelles.

The Broom family have never forgotten the debt they owe these men.

Emily Hahn, China corrrespondent for *The New Yorker* from 1935, was a confidante of two of the Soong sisters, the wives of Sun Yat-sen and Chiang Kai-shek. In 1940 in Hong Kong she began an affair with Charles Boxer, a married British officer. Soon after their daughter Carola was born, Boxer was interned in Sham Shui Po Camp. After the war the couple married. Hahn wrote about her experiences in *China to Me: A Partial Autobiography*, one of her 54 books.

Eduardo (Eddie) Gosano, one of nine children of a Portuguese Macanese family, was a doctor in the medical unit of the Hong Kong Volunteer Defence Corps. In June 1942 he escaped to Macau and became an agent for the British Army Aid Group. He returned to Hong Kong after the war and in 1960 emigrated to the United States. In 1997 he wrote a memoir, *Farewell to Hong Kong*.

Lindsay Ride, a doctor and professor of physiology at the University of Hong Kong, was Australian. The commander of the Hong Kong Field Ambulance when the Japanese invaded, he was imprisoned in Sham Shui Po Camp. In January 1942 he escaped to Free China, where he formed the British Army Aid Group, which smuggled medicine, food and messages into Hong Kong. The organisation also smuggled out around 2000 people, including Marie Broom, her four children and amahs Lizzie and Ah Sup. After the war, Ride returned to Hong Kong, becoming vice-chancellor of the university and commandant of the Royal Hong Kong Defence Force. He was knighted in 1962.

F.W. (Shiner) Wright worked for the Chinese Maritime Customs Service, a British organisation set up after the opium wars to facilitate foreign trade along the China coast. When the Japanese invaded Hong Kong, he was interned in the Stanley camp. On March 18, 1942 he and three other men made a daring escape by boat to a small island, where they hired a junk to take them to Macau. From there, they managed to get to Free China.

From November 1942 to March 1944, Wright was in charge of the British Army Aid Group's forward post in Samfou. He developed a route for small groups of escapees from Hong Kong, aided by guerilla groups who had formerly been smugglers. After the war, he briefly rejoined the Chinese Maritime Customs Service; it was dissolved in 1950.

Many other people were involved in the rescue of Marie Broom and her children, and the journey through China of Vincent Broom. Most worked behind the scenes and many remained unknown to my grandparents. However, in his papers Vincent noted Captain R.D. Scriven; Captain P. Eardley; Captain Raymond Lee; Major J.D. Clague; Dr. R.H.S. Lee; Anthony Ngan; Jackie Lau; Rudy Choy and William Chong Gun.

THE FALL OF SINGAPORE AND
THE FATE OF SS *VYNER BROOKE*

A generation before the British government secured Hong Kong, it had identified Singapore Island on the southern tip of the Malay Peninsula as a potentially useful harbour and military base for activities in a region then dominated by the Dutch. It was also perfectly placed to be a reprovisioning station for ships travelling between India and China.

The town of Singapore was established in 1819 by Sir Stamford Raffles via a treaty with locals after he had engineered the return of exiled leader Sultan Hussein Shah. The town grew rapidly and by the 1890s had become the most important place in the world for sourcing rubber, a commodity of growing international importance.

The First World War had little impact on Singapore, but as part of a post-war re-think of its military strategy the British government decided to build a key naval base there. The base was impressive for its size and modernity and boasted the world's largest dry dock, but no British Navy ships were available for stationing there. The plan was to send ships from Australia and from Europe via the Suez Canal if they were required to defend British interests. This plan did not foresee the British military needing to be active in Europe and Asia simultaneously.

In the early 1940s, as the Japanese army was advancing through China towards Hong Kong, it was also moving down through Thailand towards the Malay border, from where its troops could move rapidly to Singapore. Although the troops were still a long way from Singapore on December 8, 1941, they were able to launch a pre-dawn aerial attack on the city from captured airfields in French Indochina, 1,000 kilometres to the north.

As well as their strategy to destroy all military bases in and near the parts of Asia they coveted, the Japanese had another reason for attacking Singapore. After Japanese forces invaded north-eastern China and French Indochina, the Allies had placed trade embargoes on the country, hindering its efforts to procure oil and fuel. Controlling Singapore would place Japanese forces on the doorstep of oil-rich Borneo and Indonesia.

The Japanese knew that in attempting to take Singapore they would be outnumbered, but they were confident of success. They had detailed information on the weaknesses of the island's defences, having cracked British military codes and received intelligence from spies. On top of this, the German army had passed on reports by military strategists from a British steamer it had captured in the Indian Ocean.

The first bombing raid on Singapore – December 8, 1941 – came just a few hours after the attack on Pearl Harbour and caught the Allies by surprise. Spotters saw Japanese bombers approaching Singapore an hour before they arrived but even basic measures, such as blacking out street lights, weren't carried out: the person with the key to the control room couldn't be found. Able to use the lights for navigation, the Japanese airmen easily attained most of their targets, killing sixty-one people and injuring 700, damaging the airfield and destroying three grounded aircraft. They left without losing a single plane.

In Singapore harbour the battleship HMS *Prince of Wales* and battle cruiser HMS *Repulse* had used anti-aircraft guns to dissuade the Japanese pilots from coming in any lower. Soon afterwards, fearing Japanese boats could be heading to Singapore from Indochina, they departed to defend the seas north of Singapore and the east coast of Malaya.

Although shaken, the inhabitants of Singapore remained relatively sure they wouldn't be invaded: there was dense unwelcoming jungle just across the causeway and large coastal guns had been put in place to protect the harbour. The news on December 10 that both the *Prince of Wales* and the *Repulse* had been sunk had a devastating effect on morale. The Japanese were clearly much better prepared than anyone had thought. Added to this, the aircraft carrier that was to have given the town air cover had run aground before the attacks. Many also knew that ships leaving Singapore would be exposed to Japanese torpedoes.

For a few weeks there were no more attacks and the residents of Singapore busied themselves training and preparing for air raids. In the middle of December there were minor raids but then, after two weeks of calm, came a frightening attack on the night of December 29. By then it had become clear that the hindrances the Japanese might face in attacking

Singapore by land had been massively overestimated. After
the two British battleships were sunk the Japanese landed
small tanks on the eastern side of the Malay peninsula. Using
these, together with their own and stolen bicycles, they
advanced south so fast the Allies had little time to take up
defendable positions.

Although British and Australian forces and Volunteers
carried out some successful ambushes and counter-attacks,
nothing really slowed down the Japanese. Many Allied
soldiers were newly arrived and undertrained. Commanders
made wrong decisions as they tried to out-think the Japanese
strategists. Although Singapore is relatively small, it has
approximately fifty kilometres of coastline along the Johor
Strait. In the 1940s many areas of this coast were overgrown
with wild vegetation around numerous creeks and inlets,
making it tough to defend. The question of where to deploy
troops and build up defences was complicated. On numerous
occasions Allied commanders wrongly guessed where the
main attacks would come from.

The first daylight air raid occurred on January 12, 1942.
A few days later ships began to evacuate women, children
and other civilians. On January 31 Allied engineers were
ordered to blow up parts of the causeway and prevent the
Japanese crossing it.

With all shipping channels now patrolled by a small but
growing number of Japanese boats and planes, Vincent
Broom was lucky to get passage on a boat heading south
on February 2. By the end of the next day Japanese soldiers
were close enough to be firing at targets on the island from
across the Johor Strait.

On February 8, less than a week after Vincent escaped,
the Japanese crossed the strait at night, using 150 barges and

collapsible boats to land on the north-west coast of the island.
Defences here were weak and spotlights on the beaches
had already been destroyed and not replaced or simply not
turned on, so they arrived largely unseen. Thirteen thousand
men came ashore and moved slowly inland.

From February 8 to 10 there were many battles. Most
were won by the Japanese, who were able to protect enough
of the coastline to bring in a constant stream of soldiers
and equipment. On February 10 the British prime minister,
Winston Churchill, sent a telegram to General Archibald
Wavell, American-British-Dutch-Australian Command's
commander-in-chief, in Singapore:

> I think you ought to realise the way we view the situation
> in Singapore. It was reported to Cabinet by the CIGS
> [Chief of the Imperial General Staff, General Alan Brooke]
> that [Malay command Lieutenant General Arthur] Percival
> has over 100,000 men, of whom 33,000 are British and
> 17,000 Australian. It is doubtful whether the Japanese
> have as many in the whole Malay Peninsula. … In these
> circumstances the defenders must greatly outnumber
> Japanese forces who have crossed the straits, and in a well-
> contested battle they should destroy them. There must at
> this stage be no thought of saving the troops or sparing the
> population. The battle must be fought to the bitter end at
> all costs. The 18th Division has a chance to make its name
> in history. Commanders and senior officers should die with
> their troops. The honour of the British Empire and of the
> British Army is at stake. I rely on you to show no mercy to
> weakness in any form. With the Russians fighting as they
> are and the Americans so stubborn at Luzon, the whole
> reputation of our country and our race is involved. It is

expected that every unit will be brought into close contact with the enemy and fight it out.

As this telegram reached Singapore a retreat of remaining aircraft to the Dutch East Indies (today's Indonesia) was already being organised. The Allies had fought some convincing dogfights over the city but the Japanese bombing had been successful enough to make the island's airfields largely inoperable. The Japanese advanced towards the main residential part of the island and quickly captured provision stores and the island's reservoir. As the Allied forces retreated, the civilian and military population of around a million found themselves constricted to buildings and main streets in the centre of town, where they were easier than ever to shell and bomb. Casualties were high.

On February 13 Japanese engineers finished repairing the causeway and Japanese tanks and other vehicles surged on to the island. Next day the Japanese broke through Allied lines near the hospital and killed around 250 patients, doctors and nurses over a period of twenty-four hours. Some of the few survivors had lain among piles of corpses pretending to be dead.

On the morning of February 15 the Allies held an emergency meeting to decide whether to mount counter-attacks against key locations controlled by the Japanese. The result of the heated debate, in which factions blamed each other, was that surrender was the only reasonable option. A meeting was held with Japanese leaders and conditions agreed upon: by 8.30 that night all hostilities would cease and Allied soldiers would surrender their weapons.

Winston Churchill would call this the 'worst disaster' and 'largest capitulation' in British military history. Desertion

among many in Australian and British army units was felt to
have been a major cause. Even the leader of the Australian
troops, General Henry Gordon Bennett, chose to escape just
after the surrender, leaving his remaining men in Japanese
captivity. Allied soldiers and civilians unfortunate enough to
be in Singapore at the time of the surrender were subjected
to hellish years in Japanese prison camps.

People on board the *Vyner Brooke*, the ship on which Vincent
Broom had originally hoped to sail, on February 12, 1942
experienced some of the worst horrors recorded under the
Japanese invasion of South-east Asia. Bombs from Japanese
planes knocked out the ship's engines and holed it enough
that it slowly sank in sight of Bangka Island. Using lifeboats
in various states of seaworthiness, nurses, soldiers, crew and
civilian men and women made their way at night to beaches
on the island, with many finally swimming or walking along
the coast towards fires lit by those who'd already arrived.

When they sought help from local villagers they learned that
the island was under Japanese control. Realising they had no
hope of escape, an officer set off to surrender to the Japanese
in a nearby town. While he was away, a few of the hundred
other survivors decided to also make their way to the town,
leaving twenty-two nurses on the beach to look after the
wounded. When the officer returned to the beach, he was
accompanied by a contingent of Japanese soldiers, whom he
assumed would process the surrender and escort them to the
town. Leaving the nurses under guard, some of the Japanese
soldiers took sixty wounded men around a headland. Soon
afterwards the nurses heard shouts and gunfire. When the
soldiers returned, the nurses were raped, then ordered to

walk into the water up to their waists. They were cut down by repeated bursts of machine-gun fire and left for dead.

Only one nurse, Vivian Bullwinkel, survived: a bullet had passed cleanly through her groin. She stayed silent and motionless until she was sure the Japanese soldiers had left. In pain and with much difficulty she was able to crawl towards shelter under trees by the beach. She later joined the other female survivors of the *Vyner Brooke* in a prisoner-of-war camp and remained there until the end of the war. She kept her knowledge of the massacre from the Japanese, knowing she'd be killed if they knew what she'd witnessed. Her survival and testimony and that of soldiers who had survived the shooting and bayoneting around the point ensured these war crimes were not forgotten although the perpetrators were never identified and punished. Vincent Broom often talked about the stroke of luck that had stopped him sailing on the *Vyner Brooke*.

NEW ZEALAND AT WAR

In 1914, when Britain declared war on Germany and the New Zealand governor-general announced that New Zealand was therefore also at war, Vincent Broom was a ten-year-old living in Gisborne, a small town on the east coast of the North Island. Vincent's father was slightly over the age at which men were called up and had an important role as a veterinarian for the local freezing works, verifying that meat being sent to British civilians and troops was comestible.

Over the next four years, 100,444 of New Zealand's one million inhabitants, around half the men aged eighteen to twenty-five, travelled across the world to fight in Europe.

Over 16,000 would never return, and over 41,000 of those
who came back were wounded.

When Vincent graduated from school, he did national
service with the army and started a marine engineering
apprenticeship. Most of the men with whom he was working
had had first-hand experience from the First World War of
the horrors of rifles, bayonets and trenches; some had seen
comrades drowning in ice-cold seas. Many of his mother's
friends had lived through the loss of a child or the return of
a war-damaged husband.

Twenty-one years later, New Zealand again committed
its soldiers to fight for Britain and its European allies.
In October 1939 the First Echelon began training. Two
months later families farewelled an advance party from
Wellington on the first of a stream of transporters. As the
troops sailed, New Zealand Navy cruiser HMS *Achilles*
was already engaging with German raiders off the coast of
Uruguay. Eventually 140,000 New Zealand men and women
would be sent to North Africa, Britain, Europe and the
Pacific.

But there was also fear at home. Japan was looking expan-
sionist and there were German raiders in the Pacific. In June
1940 one of them, the *Orion*, sank a liner, the *Niagara*, off the
Northland coast. The realisation New Zealand was at risk
led to a home guard being established in August. On August
20 the *Orion* sank a steamer, *Turakina*, in the Tasman Sea.

In late September Japan officially entered into a pact with
Germany and Italy. This was followed in November and
December by more attacks by German raiders on ships in
the seas around New Zealand. They included the sinking of
the New Zealand Shipping Company liner MV *Rangitane* off
the coast between Gisborne, where Vincent had grown up,

and Te Puke where his parents lived. Seven passengers and eight crew members were killed and nearly 300 people taken prisoner.

In the fifteen months before Vincent's visit to his parents in March 1942, blackout restrictions had been gazetted; the New Zealand Army had suffered large casualties in Greece, Crete and North Africa; and Britain, Australia, New Zealand and the United States had frozen whatever Japanese assets they could. As plans were being made for additional rationing of sugar, boots, hosiery and knitting yarns, the Japanese flew reconnaissance flights over Auckland and Wellington. Evacuation plans were prepared.

In New Zealand Vincent was often solicited for his thoughts as one of a steady trickle of men and women from Singapore with first-hand experience of what it had been like to be bombed and shot at by Japanese planes and to have travelled on ships under threat of being torpedoed. What would the Japanese do next?

SUBMARINES IN SYDNEY, AUSTRALIA

Escaping from wartime Singapore was a relief and for those who, like Vincent Broom, made it to Sydney there was a certain sense of safety. But many still felt they were not completely out of harm's way. Broom crossed paths every day with merchant seamen who had returned from coastal runs and deliveries to Pacific islands. He knew more than most about the threat that existed from Japanese submarines.

In late May 1942 the Japanese navy positioned large submarines off the coast of New South Wales. These started to attack merchant shipping. Incredibly, the Japanese even managed to store a floatplane in the hold of one of the submarines and dispatch it to see which Allied battleships were in Sydney Harbour. Although the plane was spotted, the 'impossibility' of such an event led to the report being labelled an error of identification.

Using information collected from the flight, under cover of darkness on the evening of May 31 three Japanese midget submarines, each carrying two crewmen, detached from their host subs and entered Sydney Harbour. The first became entangled in anti-submarine nets and was spotted by harbour patrols. The crew blew up the craft, killing themselves at the same time.

The second passed detection devices without triggering an alarm and followed the Manly ferry through a gap in a partially constructed anti-submarine net. It grazed the bottom of a patrol boat, but again the report of this 'impossible' occurrence was not taken seriously. The submarine was able to make its way close to the USS *Chicago*, which was moored in the harbour. When it was finally spotted and fired upon, the crew managed to submerge. They then took up an excellent position from which to torpedo the *Chicago*.

Sydney authorities were slow to react, but a blackout was finally implemented around the harbour just as the Japanese submarine was readying to fire. The torpedoes missed the *Chicago* but one hit a seawall and exploded, sinking a ferry that was being used as sleeping barracks. Twenty-one sailors on board were killed.

The last of the three midget submarines was spotted and attacked by patrol boats. Enough damage was inflicted that the crew chose to kill themselves by gunshot.

A conflict developed between the press, which wanted to tell the truth, and the authorities, who wanted to reduce the level of panic, but eventually most of the details of the Japanese incursions and the deaths of the sleeping sailors within the harbour became common knowledge. The news shocked Australia's civilian population. Controversy was stirred when the four Japanese submariners who had died in the harbour were accorded an Australian naval funeral.

The submarines that had launched the midget craft remained in the coastal waters of New South Wales and attacked at least seven more merchant ships, resulting in the deaths of about fifty sailors. In the early hours of June 8, 1942 one submarine surfaced just off the coast of Sydney's northern beaches. Ten shells were fired in the direction of the harbour bridge. One landed in the water and the others fell on the suburbs of Woollahra, Rose Bay and Bellevue Hill. Only one exploded but people were injured by falling bricks and rocks from damaged walls.

KUNMING AND THE FLYING TIGERS

In the late 1930s China faced difficulties trying to expand the capabilities of its air force. Compared to the Japanese, the technology and training were amateurish. In search of a solution, Chiang Kai-shek sent men to the United States to recruit an experienced air-combat leader, who would be given the task of recruiting foreign mercenaries and acquiring planes. This was urgent: the Japanese were making their way steadily south from Manchuria towards Shanghai and Nanking.

The man chosen proved popular if controversial. Claire Chennault was a talented pilot and group chief who had been on the point of retiring from the air force because of failing health and lack of career advancement opportunities. Working for the Chinese, he initially got mercenaries and planes from wherever he could find them, and although he had some successes it was clear to both him and his direct contact in the Chinese armed forces, Soong Mei-Ling, Chiang Kai-shek's wife, that a better supply of modern planes was needed, along with pilots and technicians with the specific training and experience needed to operate and maintain them.

With banker T.V. Soong – Chiang Kai-shek's represent-ative to Washington and Madame Chiang's brother – acting as intermediary, negotiations were held with President Roosevelt. One hundred of America's recent crop of P-40B Tomahawk aircraft were earmarked for use in China. Almost as importantly, Chennault was permitted to recruit merce-naries from pilots and engineers in the US Air Force.

When the Japanese attacked Pearl Harbour in December 1941 the men and Tomahawks had already arrived in Burma and been transported to Kunming, from where they had begun to launch attacks on the Japanese. With the entry of the United States into the war, Chennault's operation was absorbed into the American hierarchy and Chennault eventually rose to the rank of general. His famous Flying Tigers were much loved, and their bomber jackets with Chinese characters printed on them to help downed pilots find assistance from local peasants have become iconic.

Located in the south of China, Kunming was the largest Chinese city close to the border with Burma, Vietnam and Laos, and the easiest point into which to fly people and supplies from India, making it vital to Chennault's operations. By the time Vincent Broom arrived on his rescue mission, it had become one of the most important locations for coordinating and supporting the Allied and Chinese Nationalist forces in their activities of defending against and attacking the Japanese invaders.

After Japan took over Singapore in early 1942, many Japanese units that were no longer required were sent to Burma. Here they successfully cut off vital supply routes between China and the port of Rangoon. With these reinforcements, the Japanese progressively took control of parts of China to the north. This led Kunming and the smaller Chinese towns just across the border from Burma to be swamped with refugees.

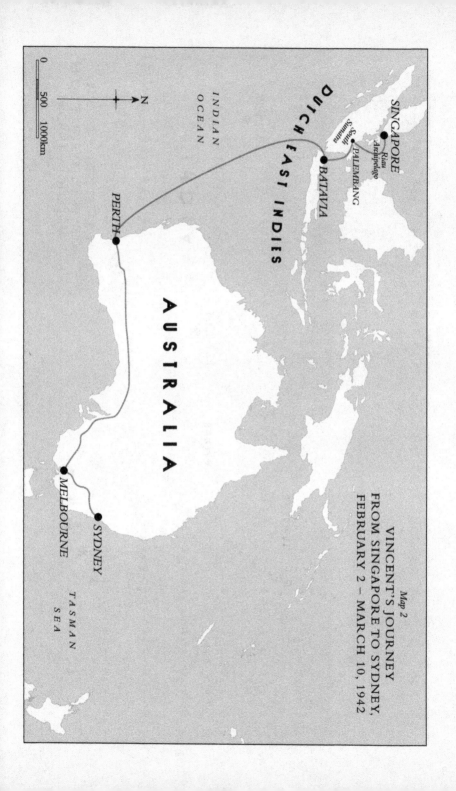

Map 2
VINCENT'S JOURNEY
FROM SINGAPORE TO SYDNEY,
FEBRUARY 2 – MARCH 10, 1942

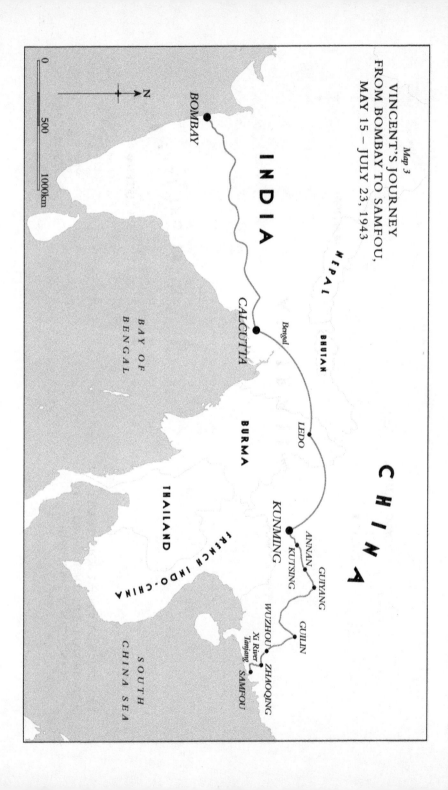

Map 3
VINCENT'S JOURNEY
FROM BOMBAY TO SAMFOU,
MAY 15 – JULY 23, 1943

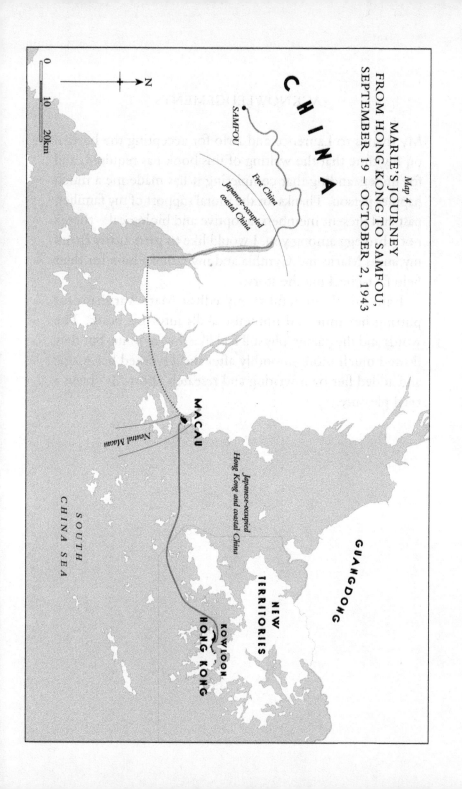

Map 4
MARIE'S JOURNEY
FROM HONG KONG TO SAMFOU,
SEPTEMBER 19 – OCTOBER 2, 1943

CHINA

SAMFOU

Free China

*Japanese-occupied
coastal China*

MACAU

Neutral Macau

*Japanese-occupied
Hong Kong and coastal China*

GUANGDONG

NEW
TERRITORIES

KOWLOON

HONG KONG

SOUTH
CHINA SEA

N

0   10   20km

ACKNOWLEDGEMENTS

My thanks to Laurence and Arlo for accepting the burden on my time that the writing of this book has required, and for understanding that completing it has made me a much happier person. Thanks for the moral support of my families, past and present members, adoptive and biological – there's not a bad egg among you. I would like to particularly thank my aunts Marie and Cynthia and my father Philip for their help fact-checking the story.

I am hugely grateful to my editor Mary Varnham for putting her time and immense skills into this book. The words and the paragraphs still feel like they're mine, but they flowed much more smoothly after she'd worked her magic and added her own writing and research efforts. It's been a total pleasure.